COUNTDOWN

by

JASON WOODS
&
SIAN M. WILLIAMS

Countdown

This is a work of fiction. The story, names and characters are fictitious. Very real incidents and real places are mentioned, but they are presented fictitiously and any resemblance to actual persons living or dead, is coincidental.

Cover design Billy Allinson www.billyallinson.com

Published by CR&SI

2022

Copyright © 2022 Sian M. Williams & Jason Woods

sharn778@gmail.com/jw@jasonwoods-author.com

All rights reserved

The moral right of the authors has been asserted

Countdown

When power is gained and maintained through fear, greed and lies, a legacy of despair and chaos will follow.

Countdown

PROLOGUE

Sunday, September 9th, 2001
Afghanistan

Ahmed Shah Massoud, leader of the Northern Alliance sat back in his chair with his fingers intertwined across his soft robes. Greying black curls peeped out beneath an earthy brown pakol adorning his head as he welcomed in the two journalists from Belgium with a broad smile; the deep lines around the edges of his wise, deep-set eyes crinkled. One of the journalists set up a camera. At forty-eight, Massoud was still a handsome man with strong features and an intelligent, expressive face, but the kindness in his eyes belied the many hard battles he had fought as a powerful guerrilla commander. He was hopeful of getting his message across to a Western audience; for months he had been warning the European Parliament of a terrible act of terrorism if they did not pay attention to what was happening in his homeland.

The man behind the camera nodded at his partner and pressed a button. The loud explosion sent the fake journalists flying, killing one instantly. The air pressure from the blast blew Massoud and his men backwards, traumatizing their internal organs. Fragments from the bomb, and shards of glass from the windows lacerated their skin. Pandemonium followed as the bleeding body of Massoud was pulled out of the wreckage and rushed to hospital by helicopter, but his wounds were too terrible, and he died en route. His death provided the green light

Countdown

for the Al Qaeda attack and two days later, planes crashed into the Twin Towers of New York city.

***

Rhett Millard and his team of twelve SAS operators along with members of the Northern Alliance, moved up the White Mountains in Eastern Afghanistan. Icy cold rain blurred Rhett's vision as he clambered over boulders and muddy earth with the Afghan warriors leading the way. The bleak mountain towered above them, leaving the soldiers susceptible to attack from the higher reaches.

The sun was going down behind the mountaintop; trees, rocks and men became indistinguishable in the growing shadows of twilight and the Northern Alliance guides would go no further as darkness fell. Rhett sat down next to his best friend and wingman, Dan Taylor as they all hunkered down in a rough bunker vacated by their targets who had moved higher up to hide in the caves of Tora Bora. They had a long wait before they could move again.

Dan radioed in their position to the forward base, and they continued to observe the mountainside above them. They spotted the light from small fires dotted across the slopes where the Taliban had made camp and using their state-of-the-art night vision aids and laser designators, they called in the Air Force bombers who were circling above at high altitude waiting to take out the targets.

The steady rain stopped, and silence fell over the camp. Rhett took off his hat, a soft, grey, round-topped pakol and lit a carefully concealed cigarette underneath the thick, woollen blanket wrapped around his shoulders.

'Here we go,' whispered Dan. Rhett nodded.

Within minutes, the black night was illuminated as the booming blast of daisy cutter bombs split the mountain apart in the distance. Changing the geography of the landscape forever, massive clouds of red and orange fire and mushrooms of black smoke filled the sky as AC-130 gunships dropped their fifteen-thousand-pound bombs on the target areas.

Countdown

Eyes on the rocky ledges above them, Rhett and his team moved up and across to where the bombs, striking non-stop for the last seventy-two hours, had devastated the majestic terrain. Wearing the natural-coloured, loose-fitting clothes of the locals over their body armour they crawled and crouched their way up the steep inclines. The morning sun briefly appeared through the dark, grimy clouds, its weak rays doing little to warm the sharp, cold air. The pungent smell of fire and smoke lingered as they reached the edge of the bombing grounds.

Rhett and Dan came up onto the ridge and looked around; if there had been caves, there was no remnant of their existence. Twisted bodies and separated limbs lay scattered across the now barren swathe of land covered in a powdery sprinkling of snow; the smell of burning flesh and cordite hit the back of their throats. Suddenly the crackle of gunfire sent them all diving for cover against the edge of the mountain. The team returned fire and crawled upwards; the dark forms of the Taliban shifted across the slopes above them like shadows. A body tumbled down the mountainside with a bullet hole in his head; sniper support behind them doing its job. Rhett scrambled forward and opened fire on a target up to his left. The body crumpled and the loud exchange of fire erupted all around him as he estimated that there were at least fifty Taliban fighters shooting down at them.

A young Afghani fighter with a short, black beard moved silently past him and then fell back with a scream, his face blown apart by machine gun fire. Rhett sighted the gunman and took him out with a single head shot. For two hours the battle went on as the resolute Taliban fired from their advantageous positions above. Bodies began to litter the slopes as Rhett fired and moved; slowly they gained ground and pushed the enemy upwards.

All went quiet as the attack from above stopped and the Taliban disappeared. The air lay heavy with the stench of blood and metal while groans and cries came from the injured. Reaching the upper level, they discovered that the area had been deserted.

Countdown

The Northern Alliance set up their radio system and over the crackling airwaves they could hear voices, one of which they all recognised as that of Osama bin Laden. He had escaped into the complex system of caves further up the mountain.

Rhett gave the order to make their way back down to the Final Rendezvous Point (FRV) picking up the injured and dead Northern Alliance members on their way; all the SAS members of his team were uninjured. They spread out and began the slog of moving down the mountain, slipping and sliding on rubble and slimy mud trails. Rhett moved easily down the slopes with the grace of a mountain lion and sprang down below an outcrop of rock; the muscles in his legs were aching, but his senses were on high alert. He felt rather than heard a swishing movement, a subtle change in the air, and twirled around with his weapon raised as a turbaned Taliban fighter leapt from above. Like a massive, black bird with his arms and legs outstretched, the man fell upon Rhett as he opened fire. Red filled his vision as the body, spurting blood, hit him, and knocked him backwards to the ground. Rhett's pakol flew off and his skull crashed against a boulder. He saw the dark eyes of the attacker between the swathes of black material wrapped around his head and the glint of steel as he raised his knife. Rhett kicked the man back and rolled out of the way, but the razor-sharp edge slashed under his right arm. The relentless assailant was like The Terminator as he raised his head and crawled towards Rhett. Ignoring the agonizing pain, his head throbbing and dizzy, Rhett reached for his own knife, but his arm wouldn't respond to his brain's instructions. He saw the fighter raise the knife again and he pushed with his feet to scrabble backwards. A single shot rang out from Dan's weapon above and the black head turned red as it expanded and then exploded. Brains and blood smacked into Rhett's face as he lost consciousness.

Countdown

1

Saturday, June 18th, 2005
Republican Palace, Baghdad

Rhett climbed up onto the diving board, took two long strides and dived down into the clear blue water of the pool creating barely a ripple. He swam a length underwater using slow, powerful strokes and with his eyes open he could see the bodies of those swimming above him and circles of sunlight bobbing on the walls and on the bottom of the pool. The sounds of the world disappeared, and he enjoyed a brief respite from the constant noise and tension that had become the norm. Dodging the legs of someone standing in the shallows, he reached the wall at the end of the pool, rose to the surface, and breathed easy. He pushed off, swam a few lazy strokes to the middle of the pool, and turned onto his back. He lay on the top of the water moving his hands and feet gently to keep afloat and stared up at the expanse of clear sky above him; the hot sun beat down on his exposed face, while the rest of his body stayed cool. He heard a loud, regular whirring getting louder and two Apache helicopters came into view like giant insects flying overhead. A tremendous roar of power filled the air as they swooped past and headed across the city.

Suddenly, the water next to him erupted with a sharp crack and a wave of water swept over his face and up his nose, rocking his body over. He regained his balance and coughing and spluttering, he made it back to where he could put his feet on the bottom. Beside him, a glistening bald head emerged, and Rhett swept his hand swiftly across the water to send a slicing splash into a grinning face.

'You idiot!' he said, and then laughed. He pushed a dark mop of dripping, black hair out of his eyes and wiped his hands across his nose and mouth. He held one hand out to clasp that of the man facing him, 'Desperate Dan! Bloody hell, how are you doing, mate?'

They clenched each other in a firm embrace and Dan laughed, 'Caught you napping there, Lardy boy. Thought it was you when I saw the terrible belly flop. Still swimming underwater 'cos you don't want the girls seeing you do your normal doggy-paddle?'

'Get out of here!' laughed Rhett. He hadn't been called Lardy for a very long time. Desperate Dan had not got his name for any resemblance to the cow pie eating giant but rather the opposite; as a slim, wiry guy reaching five feet eight in his boots, he was like a terrier always out to prove that he was as strong and tough as the bigger lads. Similarly, Rhett, tall, strong, and muscular, had never been 'lardy' in the sense of fat. As Rhett Millard, he had always felt they could have found a more flattering nickname but in his young training days at Aldershot, Lardy had stuck. Still, they could have called him Windy.

'What are you doing here? I thought you might still be living in a cave in the Tora Bora looking for Osama,' said Rhett. He hadn't been in touch with Dan since leaving the army after his injuries in Afghanistan.

'Working security for Whiteriver, American corporate big boys,' said Dan. 'Been in and out since the fall of the regime, man. You?'

'I came over a few months after you. I am with a small outfit, security for a telecommunications company,' Rhett replied.
Dan glanced at the scar running across the side of Rhett's chest and up to his armpit and Rhett looked down at it and back up to meet Dan's eyes.

'Cool scar, eh?' said Rhett. 'I tell all the girls I was attacked by a shark.'

Countdown

Dan gave a short laugh and said, 'Glad you are doing alright, mate.'

They both knew that it had been touch and go for a while after Rhett was flown out of Afghanistan. Micro-surgery and six months of physio had saved the use of his arm but even though he had been passed fit, he had decided it was time to get out of the army. Dan had followed him onto the security circuit a few months later. They went back a long way and had been friends since their training days.

'Doing Route Irish?' asked Dan.

Rhett nodded and raised his eyebrows, 'We were running the gauntlet every day last year with clients working at the airport. Now I do the run once or maybe twice a week.'

Dan shook his head, 'Christ, that road at the moment! Insurgents popping up all over the place with their sneaky, dirty tricks. We are okay in our 'Iron Chariot' as we call her; got enough guns to wipe out an army, but it's still fucking scary. Some of the guys they've employed to work with me are just out of kindergarten. Personally, I wouldn't trust them with a peashooter.'

Rhett laughed in agreement but didn't say anything. The situation in Baghdad and the whole of Iraq was out of control. The demand for security workers had surged and a lot of wild, inexperienced guys looking for a quick buck had been taken on by companies desperate for the contracts. He didn't like the big, souped up, armoured carriers that some of the companies were using. They might have the weapons, but they stood out like bikini clad beach volleyball players in a mosque.

They made their way over to the edge of the pool and putting their hands on the edge, flipped themselves out and round to sit on the edge with their feet dangling in the water. The water glistened as it ran off their smooth bodies both sporting tattoos of the distinctive Para Reg cap badge. A beautifully detailed image of a mountain lion ran across Rhett's upper back and the white scar traced its way down the side of his otherwise tanned body. Two athletic looking women distracted them for a moment as they walked past a fountain and along the opposite side of the pool in micro-bikinis and began to settle themselves on two sun loungers. The women glanced across at Rhett and Dan and then took a second look before one said something to her friend and the other slapped her on the arm.

'Guess I've still got it,' said Dan with a broad smile. They both knew that it was Rhett who had caused the reaction. There were plenty of men around them with the same strong physique but not so many with his facial features. Well-defined cheekbones, naturally tanned skin with dark stubble lining his chin and mouth, and golden-brown eyes with black lashes that would make any girl jealous; he had a beautiful face that would melt the heart of the Snow Queen.

'You most definitely have, mate,' said Rhett.

The imperious facade of Saddam Hussein's Republican Palace rose behind them, and numerous people walked across the verandah above. Some were in military fatigues others were office workers in trousers or skirts and shirts and a few of the women wore headscarves and long dresses.

'Unbelievable, isn't it?' said Rhett.

'It's surreal, man. Totally fucking surreal,' replied Dan. I bet Saddam never envisaged his beautiful palace being taken over by the Yanks.'

The splendid Republican Palace sat in the middle of what was referred to as the Green Zone. A ten square mile area in the centre of Baghdad, which the US had sectioned off from the rest of the city with high walls and heavily guarded entry check points. Paul Bremer, the leader of the interim Coalition Provisional Authority (CPA) who was put in charge of Iraq after the invasion and the toppling of Saddam Hussein's regime in 2003, had been based there until 2004 when some control was given to an interim Iraqi government. Rhett remembered visiting the embassy not long after he arrived in Baghdad two years previously; he had spotted Bremer wearing his trademark blue suit and tan, desert boots making his way down a corridor surrounded by large, typically high-profile US bodyguards.

Rhett and Dan sat with the scorching sun of late June beating down on their backs and reminisced about their times together in the forces. They talked about Belfast, the street riots, drinking in the bars, pulling the feisty Irish girls and getting into scraps with the local lads.

'I remember the night you got arrested by the RUC; jeez you cracked that guy. Bang! He collapsed like an old deckchair on the beach,' said Dan punching his fist into the palm of his other hand.

Rhett grimaced and laughed uneasily. He didn't like to think about his reckless drinking and where it had led him in the past. Dan didn't notice his discomfort, 'You still with that lass from Bristol? The one you brought to my wedding.'

Rhett thought about Lorraine. The love of his life for the last few years. He had just met her when he invited her to be his plus one at Dan's wedding. The memory of her looking fabulous in a simple, pale green dress flashed through his head. He had been proud to have her with him as she chatted and joked easily with the mostly military guests and their partners. This memory was abruptly replaced by the image of her face full of pain as she told him it was over for good. The tears and the shouting. The drinking binges that had preceded the break and the ones that followed. It was months ago but he still missed her.

'God, no,' he replied casually. 'Didn't work out. She couldn't deal with this life. I am officially footloose, fancy free, and loving it. What about you? How's Gemma?'

Dan jumped up and went over to where he had folded his clothes neatly on a bed and Rhett stood up and followed him. Dan retrieved his wallet, took out a photograph, and passed it over with a look of pride and joy. Rhett looked down at the face of Dan's pretty, young wife smiling and holding a baby in her arms.

'Nice,' said Rhett.

'Gemma with our son, Kyle. He's three months old now. I was back for the birth, thank God. It was amazing.'

'You always were a soft git,' said Rhett. 'Good to know your tackle's working.'

'This is my last rotation,' said Dan taking one more loving look at his family before replacing the picture inside his wallet.

Countdown

'Ten days and I am out of this hellish sand pit. I've stashed a load of money from the work, can't knock that, but enough is enough. I want to see my son grow up.'

Rhett felt an ache deep inside, a sense of rejection and loss. He and Lorraine had talked about getting married and having children. He knew she wanted a family, but he had never felt quite ready to commit because of the dangerous nature of his work and the many months spent away from her. Deep down he'd always thought it would happen, one day.

'Good for you, mate. Listen, I've got to make a move,' he said, nodding at another man coming towards them. 'Got a load of admin to sort out at the office.'

Dan turned to see a man mountain walking up to them wearing khaki trousers and a blue T-shirt. Rhett was a solid six feet tall, but this guy was at least three inches taller, and his chest was almost as wide.

Rhett introduced Dan to his number two on the team, Marcus, another regiment guy and former G Squadron Blade, and they shook hands. Dan looked up at Marcus noting the short, brown hair and dark stubble lining his strong chin line.

'Jesus, you look like the real Desperate Dan!' said Dan grinning.

'He's not real,' said Marcus in a droll voice, 'He's a comic character. I am for real.' He sounded as though the comparison had been made before.

Dan laughed, 'Listen, I'm having a few drinks at the company bar in a couple of weeks. Bit of a leaving party. It would be great if you could come along. There'll be plenty of cold beers.'

They exchanged numbers and Dan said he would send the details.

'Really good to see you, mate,' said Rhett. 'We'll definitely catch up before you go.'

Two weeks was a long way away.

Rhett threw on his clothes, then he and Marcus made their way into the main building of the extremely grand, temporary US embassy. They made their way along the marbled corridors with huge domed ceilings and sweeping staircases. It had been good to see Dan; they had been thick as thieves whilst serving with 1Para in Belfast – best friends. They both went to Hereford for selection into the SAS, and finally fought alongside each other in Afghanistan. You never lose the bond of friendship formed while serving together in the Paras and the Special Forces.

The halls and corridors of the Palace were now filled with makeshift offices; desks and tables were covered with files and efficient looking people spoke on telephones or tapped on computer keyboards. They walked through the huge dining hall, previously a conference room with chandeliers still hanging overhead and spotted Dennis and Stewart. Two former members of The Det, a Special Forces surveillance team who Rhett had been seconded to in Northern Ireland, they were now working security for an American news team. They were stuffing their faces with burger and chips when Rhett and Marcus joined them at the table having already indulged in generous portions of the free, typical American food earlier. Stewart told them that their clients were talking to some of the top guys about the battle that had gone on a few days earlier. US and Iraqi Forces had engaged with a group of insurgents in the outskirts of the city; an Apache helicopter had been brought down, and there had been a fair few casualties on both sides.

'We were up close and personal to view what went on,' said Stewart. 'They got a lot of footage and now they are getting some quotes to add to their story.'

Rhett and Marcus got some more updates on the situation in and around Baghdad as Dennis and Stewart filled them in with the information they got from the journalists. Street battles raged continuously, a kidnapping had ended with the beheading of an American hostage in Fallujah, a noted hotspot for insurgents. Rhett and Marcus had seen the horrific recordings of previous kidnappings and the tragic results when governments rightly refused to give in to demands. Rhett paid attention to the news, but it wasn't his purpose to wonder about the politics or the dreadful situation getting worse by the day. He had a job to do, and he got on with it.

They drove out of the Green Zone in their battered old Mercedes, along the dusty streets thronged with ancient looking cars and ordinary people trying to go about their daily business in streets strewn with uncollected rubbish, burnt out cars and decimated buildings. Young men wearing fake football shirts, tracksuits or ill-fitting jeans and trainers mixed with older men wearing shabby suit trousers and checked cotton shirts with sandals on their feet. They all looked slightly unkempt as though they had picked up their outfits in a jumble sale. Some wore *shalwar kameez*, tunics over baggy trousers, while others were in traditional dishdasha with skull caps or the ghutra and agal – scarves covering their heads and shoulders with black bands holding them in place. All of the men above a certain age seemed to sport thick moustaches. The women were dressed modestly in long dresses, with hijabs covering their hair. A few wandered along the sides of the streets covered from head to toe in black burkas.

Rhett and Marcus heard a loud boom as a bomb exploded in a street a few blocks away. Plumes of smoke rose into the air but neither of them even flinched; it was as normal as the sound of cows lowing in the fields behind Rhett's house in Canon Bridge, just outside Hereford. There was the brief chatter of semi-automatic weapons and more smoke billowed into the sky from numerous locations across the city. Rhett had his MP5 in his day sack and two AK 47s lay on the back seat covered by a blanket. Both men watched their surroundings with eagle eyes; constantly on the lookout for any strange behaviour or hostile looking cars following them.

2

Saturday June 18th, 2005
Company villa, Baghdad

Without incident, they reached their villa compound in Mansour; a relatively wealthy location in the unprotected area of the city known as the Red Zone. It consisted of a large house with several outbuildings and a guardhouse surrounded by a high wall. A huge yard at the front included a carport where they kept numerous vehicles; unsupported by government forces or by a big contractor they had few resources in the country and had to source weapons, vehicles, and manpower for themselves. Cash flow from the company in the UK was slow and Rhett and his team often had to source and finance supplies and requirements themselves. Necessity being the mother of invention, Rhett had discovered that a good source of income was buying old, low profile, B6 armoured saloon cars and renting them out to other security teams who had begun to realise that going low profile was actually safer than the big convoys with obvious, high profile, armoured vehicles. He had a profitable little business going with other security teams as his clients and also provided body armour and weapons for his customers. There was an exercise area in which they had concreted in steel poles and connected bars for pull ups and dips, along with a punch bag; every day, they followed an intense routine to keep up their fitness levels and to practise drills.

Countdown

They drove in through gates that were opened and closed behind them by two of the local Iraqis they had employed as guards, Nizam and Jibril. Rhett nodded at them and noticed that they were looking worried as they rushed to close the high solid gates. They parked up and Rhett got out of the car and called to Nizam, who ran over to them. A young man in his early twenties, he had a clean shaven, light brown face with large brown eyes and a shock of thick, black hair. He was wearing a dark blue, baggy T-shirt and a clean pair of jeans that looked surprisingly new. A rifle hung over his shoulder.

'Big trouble, Mister Rhett,' he said. His forehead creased with worry as he explained that one of the militia groups from the next neighbourhood had been causing trouble with the group that Rhett employed. There had been a squabble over some money and jealousy about how much the guys working for Rhett were earning.

Rhett raised his eyebrows at Marcus, and they went inside the villa. Walid, or The General as he was usually referred to, was at his desk in the large reception hall talking loudly and rapidly in Arabic. Previously in the Iraqi army, he was now employed by Rhett to oversee the hiring of locals as guards for the house, or members of the mobile teams going out and about in the country. He slammed the phone down and looked up at Rhett and Marcus.

'We have a big problem,' he said standing up. He was a tall man with short, curly hair, greying at the temples and a thick silver moustache. He stood with a straight back in a grey shirt unbuttoned at the top and black trousers.

Before he could begin his explanation, they heard shouting coming from the street outside the walls of the compound. Rhett ran up the stairs three at a time and looked carefully out of a window on the landing. A crowd of men was gathering outside the front walls, and more were joining them; the mob of angry looking Iraqis were shouting and waving weapons in the air. Most of them were dressed in varying western attire and a few were wearing beige or light blue shalwar kameez, but all had *shemaghs*, checked scarves wrapped around their faces.

Countdown

Suddenly, shots were fired up at the top floor of the villa. Glass shattered and Rhett ducked down and shouted for everyone upstairs to get down to the ground floor and to move into the improvised safe room they had built at the back. Two guys and three women hired for clerical work crawled out of one of the rooms converted into an office. Their eyes full of fear, they bent down low, and Rhett hurried them to the stairs. The guards took up their places at the downstairs windows and doors, Nizam and Jibril ran back to guard the gate, and Marcus collected weapons and ammunition from the storeroom they had converted into an armoury before joining Rhett on the landing upstairs.

The wall surrounding the compound prevented the mob from shooting straight at the villa, but Rhett saw the hands and then the head of one of them appear at the top of the wall. He pulled his MP5 out, aimed and fired, and the figure dropped away with a shout. The bullet ricocheted off the top of the wall, leaving a deep crevice in the brickwork just to the side of where the man had been. Exactly where Rhett had aimed.

Edging along the upper floor, Rhett took another look out of the window to see what they were up against and to assess the situation. There must have been about thirty guys now gathered in the street below. The shouting, pushing crowd began aiming their guns up at the top part of the villa. Rhett quickly realised that they were not organised; it was not a well-planned attack on the villa. Tensions had been building over the past few weeks; a petty argument over some money between the two neighbouring militias had got out of hand. The difference between neighbours squabbling in the UK and in Baghdad was that not everyone in the UK owned an assault rifle. The glass fragmented as a bullet sliced past Rhett's head and he pulled back. He nodded at Marcus who was below the window further along the corridor and Marcus stood up and blasted a few rounds in the direction of the mob but aiming above their heads; the last thing they needed was a pile of dead bodies outside their front door. Rhett sat down with his back to the wall below the window and called the US army Quick Response Unit. He then called Stewart and

Dennis in the hope that they were now back at their base which was only a couple of blocks away; they always promised to cover each other's backs. It wouldn't be long before more of the horde below decided to breach the walls and a messy battle would ensue. They had drilled their team of Iraqis well but there were only a handful of them.

After a brief lull following Marcus' rounds, another chatter of shots slammed into the upper story walls and more windows shattered. Rhett and Marcus took it in turns to fire, constantly moving positions along the landing and Rhett saw five or six militia reach the top of the corner of the wall. Suddenly, Nizam rushed out from his guardhouse shooting up at the intruders as he ran across the compound towards the main villa. Most dropped back but one stayed and fired at Nizam. Rhett couldn't see where Nizam was, but he aimed his weapon at the attacker and pulled the trigger. Blood spurted from the man's shoulder, and he screamed before falling back and leaving a trail of blood across the top of the wall. More men began climbing over the opposite walls and they heard the smash of breaking glass coming from the office at the end of the corridor.

'Fuck!' said Rhett.

He signalled Marcus to get behind him as he crouched down against the wall and they both edged towards the open door. Rhett stood up, pointed his MP5 around the edge of the doorframe and began firing as he burst in and dived down to the left. Marcus charged in after him, bullets pumping out of the nozzle of an AK47 with folding stock and a special shortened barrel as he went to the right. Three guys with their faces wrapped in red and white scarves had climbed up onto a balcony and broken in through a window. One man, perched on the window ledge, screamed as bullets ripped into the window frame beside him and he jumped back out of the window. Another one lay slumped across a desk, his blood messing up a mass of paperwork and the other was huddled behind the photocopying machine. Marcus and Rhett circled in opposite directions moving in on him. Suddenly, he stood up and began firing an ancient looking Kalashnikov in the direction of Marcus who dived across the room to land and roll behind a desk as wood splintered and cracked around him. Rhett charged, knocked the barrel of the rifle upwards and out of his hands, then he smashed his own weapon into the face of the attacker. He heard the satisfying crunch of broken bone and blood soaked into the scarf covering the nose. A quick swivel and with a sharp, heavy jerk he brought the heavy butt of his MP5 down on the man's skull and he dropped to the floor with a heavy gash opening up on the side of his head. Marcus ran to the window and saw a few more of the assailants scrambling back over the wall dragging a blood-streaked comrade with them.

Another massive burst of fire slammed into the upper walls and windows of the villa. They could hear shouting and gunfire coming from their guards below and leaving Marcus to watch the upper floor of the villa, Rhett ran to the top of the stairs and using a pillar for protection he glanced down. Their own guards had done a good job of keeping the attackers from reaching the entrance. He moved across the landing and looked out of the window to see more guys climbing back over the walls at the front dragging their injured friends. They hadn't managed to get to open the gates. Rhett's phone rang and sliding down below the window, he pulled his local Nokia cell phone out and put it to his ear. The voice of Rynold came over the line. Ex member of the Recces, the South African Special Forces, he was mainly in charge of doing border runs to take people into neighbouring Jordan or picking people up to bring them to the city.

'I have this, boykie,' was all he said, and the line went dead. Rhett looked over at Marcus who asked him what the hell was going on. Before Rhett could answer, they heard shots being fired and the blast of a grenade going off at the end of the street followed by shouts and yells. They both looked out to see smoke filling the road and the frightened militia running in the opposite direction. Some were spattered in blood, but still able to move. Stewart and Dennis arrived in a small, armoured jeep and their presence increased the speed at which the chaotic rabble departed.

Countdown

Rhett and Marcus ran down the stairs to check on the welfare of everybody and saw Jibril muttering prayers as he crouched down next to Nizam who was sitting with his back up against the wall with a large, red stain spreading across the leg of his jeans. The other guards stood around looking helpless and The General emerged from the back of the house with the staff he had been guarding in case the attackers made it inside. Rhett told The General to organise the clearing of the rooms upstairs and the courtyard.

Nizam was whimpering with pain, his face ashen as he looked up at Rhett. Rhett grabbed his med-kit and Nizam cried out, 'No cut, no cut!'

'What are you on about mate?' asked Rhett as he held a pair of scissors up.

'No cut my jeans. Expensive,' said Nizam through clenched teeth.

'I'll buy you a new pair,' said Rhett as he cut through the bloody, soaking material and revealed the small hole pulsating blood on the outside edge of Nizam's thigh. The bullet had gone clean through the side of his leg contacting with soft tissue only. There would be a huge amount of bruising but otherwise he was going to be okay.

Rhett's phone rang and he handed it to Marcus who answered it and put it on speaker as Rhett got Jibril to put pressure on the wound while he got ready to dress it and if necessary, put on a tourniquet.

Rynold's voice boomed out from the phone, 'Where is Nizam? I am waiting outside the gates, and no one is opening!' Nizam called out, 'I am dying, Mr. Rynold,'

'What the hell!' said Rynold, 'I will kill them for you! But someone open these damn gates.'

Rhett nodded at Jibril who ran outside and across to the gates to let Rynold drive in. They put Nizam into one of the other cars and told one of the drivers, Karim to take him to the local hospital to get checked out by a doctor.

Rynold climbed out of his soft-skinned BMW; his bushy, brown hair stood out around his tanned face as he walked with a cocky gait over to them grinning, 'What the fok was that? Children's play time?'

Rhett, Marcus and Rynold walked out of the gates and into the street. A few women and children huddled at the corner of the road watching them with wary eyes, and a dog sniffed and licked at a pool of fresh blood drying on the tarmac. Rhett saluted Stewart and Dennis in their armoured jeep, pleased to see that they hadn't brought their news team with them. They raised their hands in acknowledgement and drove away just as two beige, armoured Humvees rumbled into the other end of the road. US troops jumped out and began cordoning off the area in a slightly belated arrival of the cavalry.

Rhett was glad that they were late; their handling of the situation may not have been so gentle. Since the 2003 'shock and awe' invasion, the Sunni supporters of the regime had set about a reign of terror and destruction. Al Qaeda cells had been growing in number and were causing mayhem. Even the Shi'ites who had welcomed the removal of a leader who had oppressed them for decades had lost faith in their so-called liberators. In short, there were many different factions fighting against each other for power, but all resented the Americans and their coalition allies who were at a disadvantage with no knowledge of the language and cultures of the people. The average soldier could not tell the difference between any of them and had come to live in fear and suspicion of the people they had come to liberate and protect. Saddam Hussein had imprisoned and murdered thousands of his own people and now the Americans were not doing themselves any favours in terms of winning the hearts and minds of the population.

After the honeymoon period following the 'winning' of the war when the troops had arrived with smiles and sweets and had been greeted as heroes by the population, things had gone steadily downhill. The disbanding of the army and the police and no policy in place for what to do with the country next, the people had become desperate. Unchecked looting had sent the people wild; militias and insurgencies began to grow. The soldiers were suddenly having to face and deal with suicide

Countdown

bombers, improvised explosive devices plus random attacks from rocket launchers and small arms fire whilst out on patrol in the city. They didn't know who the perpetrators were, and fear kicked in. To many of them, all Iraqis were hostile and dangerous, and some had begun to treat them all with aggression and brutal force. Creating a catch 22 situation for themselves, their rough treatment of innocent people caused many to become sympathetic to the insurgents or even to join them.

After giving the soldiers a brief run down on the situation, the three men returned to the villa noting the upper stories, which now looked like a shooting gallery.

'Guess we need to make some home improvements,' said Rhett.

***

Rhett, Marcus and Rynold sat in the kitchen with the other two members of the team Glen and Steve. Glen, a short, burly Welsh-man with light ginger hair was an ex-Para. He was a good guy, but he did have a very strange high-pitched laugh. Steve was ex SBS; he was medium height and lean with mousy, almost permanently greasy, lank hair which, along with the wispy facial hair on his chin and upper lip, gave him the look of an adolescent teenager. They were both solid and reliable members of the team who had arrived to see the villa riddled with bullet holes and the area swarming with US soldiers after taking a client back from site to his hotel. They were disappointed that they hadn't been there. The house and grounds had been cleared as far as possible with the help of the US military. Guards remained at all the broken windows and outside in the street.

The remains of a take-away meal lay scattered across the table. Rhett topped up his glass of whisky and passed the bottle round. A saucer in the middle of the table spilled over with ash and stubbed out dog ends. The General had made some more phone calls and it seemed that for the time being the situation was calm.

They debriefed on the incident, discussed how to increase their defences and Rynold took great pleasure in describing how

Countdown

he had come up behind the frenzied group. Taking them by surprise, he had shot a few rounds into the crowd and those nearest to him had quickly dispersed dragging their injured friends with them. He followed this with a stun grenade, causing a little bit more carnage, and the whole lot had decided to flee. He described the incident with embellishments to add to his bravado.

'Should have seen the face on this *chop* when I shoved my AKM up his fat arse!' he said laughing.

Glen's high-pitched laugh rang out and they all looked at him. He sniffed, and they all raised their glasses to Rynold, their saviour of the day.

Rynold nodded his head and raised his own glass to his lips. 'Pleasure in the job puts perfection in the work,' he said before knocking back the glassful.

'Don't tell me, Bob Dylan,' said Rhett with a smirk.

'That is Aristotle, you philistine,' said Rynold with a wave of his hand.

'Who does he play for?' replied Rhett with a straight face.

They all laughed and felt the tension that none of them would admit to, move down a notch and the adrenalin that had been pumping through their bodies lowered but didn't disappear. They lived in a constant state of alert, never knowing what was going to happen, who they would next come into contact with, where a bomber or an IED might be lurking, or where a stray rocket might land.

3

Saturday, June 18th, 2005
Company villa, Baghdad

Leaving guards on the top floor and downstairs, Rhett went to bed. He placed his pistol under his pillow and lay for a while staring up at the ceiling in the dark. He felt the whisky swirl around his brain, soothing and distracting the taut nerves in his arms and legs. They'd only had a couple of glasses each; they normally worked with a dry (no alcohol) rule, apart from Thursday nights at the end of the working week. They had allowed themselves a treat after all the excitement, but Rhett had stopped after two before the taste got a hold and he couldn't stop.

Things were steadily changing in the city, the underlying anger and frustration felt by many that life had not improved with the removal of Saddam was growing exponentially. Without the dangers, Rhett wouldn't have a job, but the recent increase in attacks and kidnappings had meant a huge growth in the demand for security companies and a lot of them were not properly trained. They were all a bit trigger happy and becoming a danger in themselves to Rhett and his team, as well as innocent Iraqis. Rhett was good with people and didn't prejudge them. If anyone threatened him or presented a problem, he would deal with it as and when necessary, but until then, he treated everyone with respect. He worked hard at getting to know the Iraqis around him; he trusted the guys working for him, looked after them and had met some of their families. They were ordinary people struggling to get by and live their lives as normally as possible.

The random attack from the militia bothered him; something wasn't right. Luckily, it had not been well planned. If it had been well-organised, it could have been very messy, but as it was, nobody had died. They now had to put far more protection in place even though The General, Walid had told him it was nothing and that he had it under control. It didn't help that weapons of all kinds were readily available to anybody.

However, it wasn't the attack that was keeping him awake. Seeing his old mate, Dan had really disconcerted him. He didn't like to dwell on the past; he could section off everything but the immediate present, focus on the job in hand and function as a security operative at the highest level. This was essential for survival in this lawless land; nothing else could intrude on self-preservation and protection of the client or you became careless, distracted. Now memories were invading his mind from all angles.

Dan had made him think about Lorraine; he couldn't help but see her face, remember how her thick, shiny hair fell over her face as she leaned in to kiss him. Her flashing, dark blue eyes when she laughed and her long, shapely body dancing. How she loved to dance. He loved her with all his heart, but he had destroyed what they had, and he didn't know how to change it.

It had been about five months since he had last seen her. Since she had walked out two days before he had to head back to Iraq after a month's leave. He had left her to cool off, but she hadn't called and then he had to switch back into work mode and headed back to Iraq without hearing from her at the end of December. That had been one miserable new year in more ways than one.

He'd been back on leave since then, but she had changed her number and moved to a new house. He'd gone to the house that she rented but there had been no answer when he rang the bell. Looking in the window, he realised that the furniture had changed and that she wasn't living there anymore. Neighbours

Countdown

said they didn't know where she had gone. He called the school where she taught, and they told him that she no longer worked there. He didn't believe them; he knew she would never leave her class in the middle of a school year, and he had waited outside the school until the last person left. He had watched as boys and girls in neat uniforms came rushing out of the doors carrying backpacks that were almost as big as they were. They ran towards their mums, nannies and a few dads smiling and clutching paintings, works of art that would adorn fridges with pride. He'd felt a pang, an overwhelming desire for a normal life with Lorraine and their own kids. The playground had finally emptied, and the janitor had come towards him. A short, stocky man with wisps of grey hair smoothed across his head and deep crows' feet spreading from the corners of his grey eyes, he shoved his hands into the pockets of blue overalls and standing back from the iron railings he gave Rhett a look of concern.

'You all right, mate?' he asked, looking at the handsome young man dressed in jeans and a smart polo shirt with a look of sadness around his golden eyes.

Rhett suddenly realised that he was behaving like a stalker and could easily be taken for some kind of paedophile hanging around outside the school. He told the janitor that he was looking for Miss Carter and the janitor shook his head and said that he was new there, didn't know a Miss Carter.

Rhett knew that the old man was lying. He also knew that he could easily persuade him to tell the truth, but it suddenly hit him like a ten-pound mallet smashing into his guts that she didn't want him to find her. He had walked away.

Lying in his small bed in Baghdad, he listened to the familiar background sounds of explosions, helicopters flying overhead and sirens. There was a battle going on somewhere in the city that night.

Now he wondered if he should have tried harder. He could have phoned her parents in Bristol, they loved him, but he had been too proud. Called her friends? He had only met a couple of them. She often talked about doing things with someone called Sal that she had met since he'd been in Iraq, but he had never met her. There were a few teachers that she called friends and with whom he had spent a couple of very boring evenings, but he realised that he didn't have any of their numbers or know anything more than their first names. When he was back, she moved into his cottage overlooking fields and a river and drove the twenty miles or so to work in Ross. They spent time alone together or met up with his friends. Or, as he realised with a jolt, more often than not towards the end, he went out on his own with his mates and came home late and drunk.

'*If you love someone, set them free,*' came into his head. He had no idea who originally said it. A song by Sting? The trouble was that he hadn't set her free, she had dumped him and disappeared from his life. In his heart, he still hadn't let her go, but what did he have to offer her?

This was his life; this was what he was trained for and what he was good at doing. He felt comfortable in discomfort and going back home was when the demons started to play out in his head. The only way he could block them out was by meeting up with his mates who worked in the same business, talking with bravado, making jokes and most importantly obliterating everything with alcohol.

He tried his best not to let his mind continue to wander, but the familiar beating pulse in his temple began and he fell into a restless sleep.

A giant bird flapped its wings across a desolate plain and swooped down from the white sky towards him. He couldn't move, his arms were pinned to his sides and his legs were stuck. He screamed at himself to move but the black wings beat the air in front of his face and then he saw the face of a young man with wild, dark, staring eyes.

Rhett jerked awake with sweat pouring down his face and reached for the bottle of water by the side of his bed. He swung his legs round to sit up on the edge of his bed and ran his fingers through his hair. The dream had gone; he tried desperately to cling onto the images and remember, but they dissolved into fragments at the edge of his consciousness. The nightmares had

Countdown

started nearly two years ago, not long after he arrived in Iraq, and he couldn't work out what had triggered them.

4

Thursday, June 23rd, 2005
Hereford, UK

Stepping out of the shower after her morning run, Lorraine felt a tiny swirling movement inside her, like the flutter of a butterfly. It was exquisite and she filled with a strange excitement. She dried off and walked through to her bedroom naked. She smoothed body cream over her legs, arms and body and stared at herself in the full-length mirror. Her wavy, auburn hair hung over her shoulders dripping water down over her large breasts, which had definitely grown. She still looked her normal tall, slim self from the front and even standing to the side only she would know that the curved belly was not as flat as normal. Time to get you checked out, she decided.

She had known for months that she must be pregnant but hadn't been brave enough to even check. It was too much to face after the break-up. Her periods had stopped but they were never regular, and she'd put it down to stress. Then when she'd had a bit of bleeding about a month earlier, she convinced herself that she couldn't possibly be pregnant and the reason she was putting on a bit of weight was because of all the comfort eating she had been doing. *'Oh, the ways in which you try to deceive yourself,'* she thought. She also knew that the reason that she hadn't checked earlier was so that she wouldn't have had to face the option of keeping it or not. She had no strong feelings on the topic; getting rid of it just wasn't something she felt that she could do – it was a part of her and Rhett. She still loved him and wondered now if she had been too rash when she had walked out saying that she never wanted to see him again.

She had tried to understand his moods, his drinking, but it had become too much. She loved the kind, funny, laid-back man she had first met, but over time, she had seen a darker side to him. He was never violent towards her; he just sank into deep silences and wouldn't communicate. She had tried to work out what had caused the change. Recovering after his injuries in Afghanistan he had been light-hearted and pragmatic. He was determined to get full movement back in his arm and had followed the doctors' advice at all stages. He accepted that there would always be some damage and had worked hard to strengthen his left arm to compensate for any weakness in the right. His decision to leave the army had been made together and he was excited about moving into private security work.

He always told her that the first job working for some rich businessman was a doddle and he was certainly great to be around on his leave during that time. She thought about the fun times they had, eating, drinking, dancing, his concern about leaving her on her own and insistence on teaching her survival tactics and self-defence. Sessions that generally ended up with them both collapsing in giggles and making love on the carpet. Then he had left that job, quite suddenly, saying he was bored and wanted to be where the action was in Iraq. That was when he had begun to change.

When she walked out after a miserable Christmas with him, she had spent the next few days waiting for him to call but he had gone back to Iraq without contacting her. She had been furious and determined never to see him again. She worked at a small primary school and had broken down in tears one day with her friend Mary, who was the receptionist.

She still loved Rhett and was afraid that if she saw him again, she would weaken and fall into his arms, hopeful that it would be better, that they could work it out but knowing that it would just be the same spiral of anger and frustration.

Countdown

Mary advised her to break all ties and so she changed her phone number, found a new place to rent before his next leave was due, and Mary promised to tell Rhett that she didn't work there anymore if he called. She was pretty sure he wouldn't call her parents out of pride, and he didn't know any of her friends well enough.

She had seen him outside the school that day and had dodged back inside and hidden in one of the classrooms. When he was still there after all the children and the other teachers had left, the janitor, Barry found her sitting in the classroom in the growing dark. He was a tough character who had been around the block, but he had a gentle and compassionate soul. He didn't take any nonsense from anybody, but he was also realistic; he wasn't going to take on an ex-SAS soldier. He told Lorraine that he would see what he could do when she explained the situation. Her heart had been in her mouth as she watched from the shadows of the old classroom; she wasn't worried for Barry, she knew Rhett wouldn't hurt him, but she knew he would be able to tell if he was lying. That had been well over a month ago, he would be back in Iraq now.

She felt embarrassed when the mid-wife asked her about her last period. She had no idea. The urine sample had, of course, proved positive.

'It's crazy, I know. Me an educated woman in charge of educating the future generation of leaders,' she said with a nervous laugh.

She looked up at the mid-wife standing over her as she lay back on the examining bed. Nurse Wendy was a large buxom lady in her forties. She smiled and said, 'It happens, don't worry. You'll be in good hands now. But it would be useful if you could educate some decent future leaders.' They both laughed.

'Any sickness?' she asked as she palpated Lorraine's stomach with gentle hands.

'No, no sickness. A little dizzy sometimes and a strange desire for strawberry milkshakes at the oddest times,' she said with a shrug.

Countdown

'Do you know who the father is?' asked Wendy sensing that there was a reason why her patient had waited so long before confirming the pregnancy.

Tears pricked at Lorraine's eyes, and she nodded, 'Yes, I know who the father is, but we, we broke up.' She breathed deeply, willing the tears not to fall. 'He's in Iraq,' she stated, looking up at the nurse.

Wendy drew in her breath sharply and paused before speaking. 'You are five or maybe six months along, but I will send you for a scan to confirm,' she said, removing the stethoscope she had used to listen for the baby's heartbeat from her ears.

She pulled Lorraine's shirt back down over her bare stomach and patted her on the shoulder. Lorraine sat up, swung her legs around and pulled up her trousers.

'My husband is there,' said Wendy.

It wasn't unusual in Hereford, many of the women living and working in the city were related to the military.

Wendy said that she only had the news to watch for any information. Her husband was in Basra, in the south of Iraq; he called every week, but he always joked and laughed and told her and the kids that it was all under control. She sighed.

Rhett rarely if ever called Lorraine. He sent the odd message but always told her that it was too distracting to be in contact with people he loved. He liked to keep the two worlds separate and she knew very little about what his job entailed.

Two hours later, Lorraine lay back on another hospital bed as the sonographer, a thin, middle-aged lady with bleached blonde hair pulled back into a ponytail introduced herself as Janet and had a badge to confirm it. Janet tucked paper towels into the top of Lorraine's pants, spread gel across her lower belly apologizing for the coldness of the slimy substance, and began moving a probe across the tight skin. Lorraine winced slightly as the probe pressed down on her swollen bladder but otherwise it was painless. Janet smiled and turned the screen so that Lorraine could see the image. There, curled up in the cave of her womb, were the black shadows forming into the shape of a baby. She

Countdown

smiled weakly at Janet as tears fell down her cheeks. Now it was real.

Janet had seen most scenarios in her job and did not question her patient's reaction. She handed her some tissues and told her in a cheerful voice that the baby was healthy, certainly around twenty-four weeks and that she could tell her the sex if she wanted to know. Lorraine blew her nose and shook her head. Chatting away, Janet told Lorraine that the foetus was about the size of a large pomegranate and that its ears should be fully formed and able to hear. She gently wiped the gel off Lorraine's tummy and drew her loose top down to cover the barely discernible bump.

In a daze, Lorraine left the hospital clutching the image and wondering how large a large pomegranate was. She walked across the parking lot with the summer sun glinting red and gold on her hair, got into her car, put her bag and the image on the passenger seat and sat staring straight ahead without seeing. She moved her hands onto her stomach and looked down.

'Can you hear me?' she said to the bump. 'We're going to be okay. I love you, my large pomegranate.'

She thought about making love to Rhett and knew in her heart when she must have got pregnant. She'd had a bad stomach for a few days before he came back on leave. It had been more than the usual nervous tension she always felt in anticipation of his arrival. She was on the pill, but the sickness must have upset its effectiveness.

As usual when he came back, he was still high on adrenalin, full of energy and couldn't seem to get enough of her. She went over to his cottage after school and stocked up on provisions in the local supermarket on the way. In the middle of preparing a special dinner for him, he had arrived earlier than she expected. He walked in the door grinning, threw his bag down in the hallway and said, 'Something smells good,' before picking her up in his arms and kissing her until she felt she could barely breathe. Tugging her top over her head, his hands deftly undid her bra and he fell on her breasts caressing and licking and fondling as her excitement grew. Tearing at each other's clothes, they stumbled into the lounge kissing and touching and fell onto the sumptuous settee naked. He pulled her legs up around his waist and entered her with an ardent thrust and their bodies joined.

He paused and looked down at her with his golden eyes dark with desire, 'God, I've missed you,' he whispered, and then his thick lashes fell upon his cheeks as he closed his eyes and they moved in perfect unison, swapping 'I love yous' as their passion rose to a climax.

Lorraine smiled remembering the dinner that had been ruined and the love making that went on all night. Then she sighed as the less pleasant thoughts intruded. After a few days, once the adrenalin withdrew, the tiredness came upon him. He had no energy to do anything, he was snappy and irritable and then the drinking started.

Another ruined dinner came into her mind and a dull, sickness hit the pit of her stomach. It was her mother's birthday and her father had booked dinner for friends and family in an expensive restaurant in The Cotswolds the weekend before Christmas. Lorraine had booked a room in a hotel nearby and they planned to go down in the afternoon. Rhett had gone out at lunchtime to meet some mates and promised to be back on time. He hadn't got back and unable to contact him, she had eventually gone without him. She was furious and hurt that he'd let her down. In the middle of the meal, he had turned up in the restaurant completely drunk, barely able to walk straight. Everyone had shifted uncomfortably in their seats as Lorraine tried to persuade him to leave, but he had staggered over to her mum singing happy birthday in a loud, slurred voice and picking up a glass of red wine from the table. Lorraine touched him on the arm; he swung round with lightning reflexes and threw red wine over his left hand and all over her cream outfit. He dropped the glass and it fell to the tiled floor with a smash. Waiters rushed around but he just stood there swaying and staring at the red liquid dripping down his fingers, and then she heard him mumble, 'Blood on my hands.'

Countdown

Lorraine had managed to lead him outside and into a taxi; she got him to the hotel room where he collapsed comatose on the floor and, unable to move him, she left him there. The next day he barely remembered any of it and apologised profusely; he'd even rung her parents and charmed them into forgiving him, but for Lorraine it had been the beginning of the end. They had struggled through Christmas with Rhett on best behaviour but on the day after Boxing Day he had come home from the pub late and drunk and they'd had the huge row that resulted in her walking out. Now she regretted not trying harder to help him, to understand what had made him change.

She breathed in deeply, tears once again threatening to fall and told herself to get a grip. She turned the ignition, reversed out of the parking space without looking, and nearly crashed into a passing car. The driver raised his fist at her, and she pulled back in and burst into tears. She wanted Rhett. She wanted him there to put his big, strong arms around her, to stroke her hair and to tell her that it was going to be all right. More than that, she wanted him to grin with joy at the prospect of being a father.

5

Thursday, June 23rd, 2005
Company Villa, Baghdad

Rhett stepped out of the shower on Thursday morning; it was the end of the week at last. The water had been cold, but he was relieved that it had lasted long enough to wash off the soap. He rubbed his head with a towel, leaving tufts of hair sticking up in all directions, then moved the towel briskly back and forth across his back and over his body before getting dressed. He had been awake since the call to dawn prayer had echoed across the city from every minaret. At sunrise, he had gone out into the yard to do an intensive workout and had then put his Iraqi guys through some drills.

After some breakfast and a couple of strong coffees, he went over the day's plans with his team. Walid was in charge of the workforce installing steel reinforcements in and around the villa and he got an update on their progress. He and Marcus were heading over to have a meeting with one of the clients and then bringing him back to the villa to work in their offices.

Rhett and Marcus arrived with their two-car security deployment outside the ironically named Paradise Hotel. A small hotel in the Al Wahda area, it was used by a number of foreign journalists and contractors. He carefully checked the street. It was quiet, a few men in ill-fitting western clothes, an old man in a full kandura with a skull cap and a couple of women in long drab dresses with hijabs covering their hair made

Countdown

their way along the sidewalk. Battered cars that looked like they had been made fifty years previously were parked on the kerb. A truck carrying pieces of old furniture that had been heaped haphazardly onto the back came down the street towards them and Rhett sat quietly watching the eyes of the driver. He was an old man with a drawn, sallow face and a thick, grey moustache. Leaning his arm on the open window, he drew on a cigarette as he drove slowly along, looking only at the road ahead. Rhett let him pass, got out and went towards the hotel to meet the client while Marcus and the team kept an eye on things outside.

Wearing his body armour under a scruffy, baggy shirt that hung down over his jeans, his weapon was concealed and with a shemagh tied loosely around his neck, he didn't stand out from the journalists and engineers who frequented the hotel. He walked past the bollards offering some protection to the frontage and in through the glass doors where he nodded at the doorman, a tall, thin man with dark skin and short black hair who was always smiling. He was a simple man who loved his smart uniform and took his job very seriously; his name was Samir, but everybody called him Sam.

'Hi Sam, how are things?' asked Rhett as he walked past him. 'All in order?'

'Very good, sir. All in order,' he said grinning and revealing brown stained teeth.

Rhett found the client, Malcolm Johnston sitting in the open bar area drinking coffee and went over to join him at the small round table next to the bar. A few people were at the other tables talking in low voices and eating breakfast or drinking strong coffees. A strange silence fell across the room as a journalist came in rubbing his face with his hand. He looked like he hadn't slept, and his frizzy hair was flecked with grime. He was wearing grubby jeans and a flak jacket over an old polo shirt. He ordered two strong Arabic coffees, went over to sit at an empty table with his laptop, and began banging away on the keyboard.

A photographer soon followed him in; a camera with an impressive looking lens hung from her neck. She was also looking extremely tired; her plain face was worn with stress.

Countdown

Bedraggled, dull curls fell around her shoulders, and it looked as though she was wearing a veil of dust. Bulked out by a flak jacket and wearing baggy khaki pants over monkey boots, her body was shapeless. A battle had been raging all night in a street just ten minutes' drive away between American troops and Sunni insurgents. As she passed by Rhett's table, she smiled thinly and said a polite good morning to Malcolm.

A few other guests, mostly men, of varying nationalities wandered in and out of the bar. Malcolm was a large, stocky man in his early fifties with a substantial beer belly and a round chubby face that he mopped with a handkerchief, despite the early hour and the relatively cool temperature. The air was warm, but the June temperatures would soon rise into the forties as the day went on. Malcolm got up with more agility than he looked capable of as he smiled at the young woman.

'Good morning, Michele. Can I get you a coffee?'

'I'm fine thanks, Malcolm,' she said. 'See you later.' She nodded briefly in Rhett's direction without paying him much attention and went over to join her partner at a larger, square table on the other side of the room by the window looking out onto the street.

'What a job,' said Malcolm, indicating with his head towards Michele and her partner. 'Lot of noise last night, thought it was right outside my door.' He spoke in a calm, resigned voice; he'd been in Iraq before.

Rhett discussed the new engineer who was flying in on the following Monday to join Malcolm. Rhett and his team would head to the airport to pick him up and then on Tuesday, he would pick them both up from the hotel and take them over to the site they would be working on north of the city.

'How are you finding the hotel?' asked Rhett looking around the clean, but slightly shabby surroundings.

'The bed is comfortable enough,' said Malcolm raising his eyebrows, 'or it seems to be serving its purpose with the help of a few whiskies.'

Countdown

'Looks like you've got good company for the weekend,' said Rhett. He glanced over at the young woman talking animatedly to the journalist and winked at Malcolm.

Malcolm chuckled, 'Young enough to be my daughter, but an exceptionally good drinking partner.'

Rhett liked Malcolm; he was an affable, intelligent man who listened carefully to Rhett's instructions and advice. He was under no illusions about how dangerous life in Baghdad had become. He was a strong family man and often talked about his wife and his boys, who were everything to him.

Rhett called Marcus to say that they were on their way outside and led Malcolm to the door as the soft-skinned BMW driven by Said with Marcus and Faris inside drew up followed by the armoured old Mercedes 500. Malcolm got in the back of the Mercedes behind Abdullah, who was in the passenger seat next to their driver, Karim. Rhett took a quick look around before getting in next to Malcolm. The hotel was in a back street. A few dented cars and trucks went past, and various people made their way along the pavement, going in and out of apartment blocks and the few shops. As the sun rose higher in the sky promising more heat, only the sound of intermittent traffic filled the air. It wouldn't be long before the clatter of automatic weapons and explosions began again.

Rhett bent to climb in, and his eye caught a movement on the corner of the street. He wasn't sure what drew him to glance up, but he saw a slim, young guy with thick, black hair, wearing the faded blue and red stripes of a Barcelona football shirt, staring at him. Their eyes locked for a fraction of a second before the boy looked away and pretended to be looking in a shop window. Rhett also moved his eyes away and looked up and down the street as if he hadn't noticed the teenager. He got into the car and looked out of the back window as they drove away. He saw the young man, who he guessed to be about seventeen or eighteen, look round and watch the car moving away before taking a phone out of his pocket and making a call.

Rhett wasn't sure what he had seen but something didn't feel quite right. He logged it in his mind and focussed on checking their surroundings as they made their way back across the Tigris and towards Mansour avoiding the Green Zone and sticking to the back streets.

Checking all around as they moved along the streets, Rhett spotted a dull red, saloon car not far behind them, that he had noticed earlier. He thought about the young boy outside the hotel. Had they been targeted?

He kept his eye on it for a while as they made their way steadily down a busy street. There were stalls on either side between the columns supporting a walkway with apartments above. As Karim took a left into a smaller street, the red car followed.

'Possible hostile behind,' said Rhett pulling his MP5 out of his day sack and laying it across his lap. 'See if you can lose it,' he said to Karim. He called Marcus in the car ahead and told him to get behind them; they were taking a right turn.

Karim looked in his mirror and putting his foot down he made a sharp right into another street. The car followed, also increasing in speed. Karim knew the streets well; he swerved to avoid a donkey pulling a cart and caught the edge of a stall selling cassettes and DVDs. Plastic cases cascaded into the street and people jumped out of the way as they careered on down the road with the red car staying not far behind. Rhett put his hand on the back of Malcolm's head and pushed him down. As they screeched round to the left, a car swerved across in front of them and in panic Karim took a sharp right into a quiet residential street.

'Shit!' exclaimed Rhett as he saw that the street ended in a small square with three-storey, concrete apartment blocks staring down at them on all sides. He messaged through their position to Marcus as Karim pulled on the handbrake and the tyres screamed as the car leapt around to face back the way they had come. The red car came to a halt fifty metres away and the doors opened. Four men with shemaghs covering all of their faces apart from the eyes emerged with assault rifles and started walking towards the car with their weapons raised. The man in the lead suddenly opened fire and bullets tore into the front of the car and ricocheted off the bulletproof windscreen.

At that moment, the BMW with Marcus and Faris on board screamed down the alley towards the red car and screeched to a halt diagonally on to the assailants. Marcus and Faris leapt out and opened fire on the four men who had barely begun to turn around. Bullets ripped through the bodies of two of them and they died with looks of surprise still etched into their eyes.

'Drive!' yelled Rhett, and Karim put his foot to the floor. Marcus kept up a stream of fire aimed at the other two men as Rhett's car raced back down the street and out of the cul-de-sac.

The other insurgents reached their car but as Marcus and Faris strode forward firing and covering each other, they made it no further. One slumped by the front wheel and the other lay by the door reaching feebly for his automatic weapon as Marcus fired one more round.

Back at the villa, Rhett took Malcolm inside and asked him if he was okay.

'Well, I wouldn't say no to a stiff drink,' Malcolm said, wiping his head with his hanky. He made a small cough as though to clear his throat and leant in closer to Rhett. Looking around to make sure that nobody could hear, he said, 'And I think I might need a fresh pair of pants.'

Rhett patted him on the shoulder suddenly recognizing the unpleasant odour that had filled his nostrils. 'Good as done. Don't worry about it,' he said.

***

Malcolm was safely back at his hotel in clean undies, the banging and hammering of the new steel walls and stairwells being installed had finally stopped and the team were sitting around the table in the kitchen opening cans of beer as they had a quick debriefing before the weekend could truly start. Rhett had heard from Dan and he and the rest of the team were on the guest list for the party at his company villa.

6

Thursday, June 23rd, 2005
Hereford, UK

Lorraine sat in a small café sipping jasmine tea. She had driven away from the hospital in a daze and when she nearly hit a moped pulling out at a junction, she had decided she wasn't in a fit state to drive home until she had calmed down. She called her friend, Sal who had immediately said that she would come to meet her. The bell on the door tinkled as it opened and a striking woman in her mid-twenties stepped inside and looked around. Lorraine waved at her, and she smiled and hurried across the room to join Lorraine in the corner.

She had met Salma completely by chance the previous summer. Rhett had been over in Iraq for nearly a year by then and he had just gone back after a difficult leave. She had been wandering aimlessly down the aisle in the local supermarket when someone had crashed into her, knocking her basket out of her hands and dropping their own shopping. Products went flying across the floor as they both apologised at the same time and then laughed. After picking up all their stuff and trying to decide which bags of vegetables and fruit belonged to whom, Salma suggested they get a coffee in the café next door.

Over cups of cappuccino, they discovered that they had lots in common and most importantly for Lorraine, she discovered that Salma was from Iraq.

Countdown

'He's not a soldier,' she had explained to Salma when she told her that her boyfriend was in Iraq. 'Well, he was – ex Special Forces. Now he works security, providing protection for engineers going over to try to improve telecommunications and rebuild the country. He talks fondly of the Iraqis he has met,' continued Lorraine. She knew she was defending him.

'How is it in Iraq?' Lorraine had dared to ask. She watched the news, masochistically wanting to be in contact with where Rhett was. Bush and Blair made broad statements about making great progress and freeing the Iraqi people while the stories of kidnappings, beheadings and suicide attacks from insurgents increased.

Salma told her that her mother had brought her and her sister and brother to Britain in the early nineties. They still had many family members in Baghdad. At first, they had been overjoyed that Saddam was gone, they had hoped for and expected a better future for the whole country, but it had all gone wrong. There was no clear path forwards. Once again, her family lived in fear every day. She told Lorraine how lucky she had been to come to England and how much she loved living there.

Lorraine had no idea what it must be like to live in Iraq, but she understood the continual fear of wondering what was happening there, worrying every time she heard about a bomb or an attack. Praying every night that Rhett was safe.
Salma had nodded. 'It is very hard loving someone who is going through a hell you can't share,' she had said.

They moved onto lighter topics and discovered that they liked the same things. Salma asked her if she wanted to go to the cinema one night and they began meeting in Hereford on a regular basis. Lorraine now considered Salma to be one of her best friends; she was a good listener and didn't seem to mind that Lorraine constantly talked about Rhett.

Now, Salma sat down opposite Lorraine and reached over the table to take her hand. Her glossy, black hair, cut in a shoulder length bob, swung around her face as she looked at Lorraine with almond shaped, dark brown eyes framed by dark, neatly shaped brows. Her skin was smooth and pale, the nose small and rounded above full lips.

'What is it? What's happened?' she asked with concern in her face.

Lorraine took a deep breath but couldn't stop tears from falling as she said, 'Oh Sal, I'm pregnant.'

A dark look of shock and surprise passed across Salma's face, but she covered it quickly with a beaming smile and said, 'Mabrouk, congratulations!'

Lorraine smiled weakly and reached into her bag for a tissue. She wiped her eyes and blew her nose as Salma fired questions at her.

'Six months! Wow, how did you not know? How did I not notice? Have you told Rhett?'

'I've only just had it confirmed. I guess I did know, I just didn't want to face up to it. I can't tell Rhett. We are over, finished. He'll think that I've trapped him.'

Salma frowned and looked at Lorraine with her face full of sympathy.

7

Thursday, June 23rd, 2005
Walid's apartment, Baghdad

Marcus and Rhett had promised to stop by at Walid's home on the way to Dan's leaving party. It was the birthday of one of Walid's nieces so Steve, Glen and Rynold went straight to the Green Zone with another driver.

They arrived at the apartment block where Walid now lived. Before the war, he had lived in a large villa compound but losing their jobs in the army, both he and his much younger brother, Farouq had been forced to move their families into two small apartments in the same block. Rhett and Marcus made their way up the stairwell, the smell of urine and rancid cooking filled their nostrils.

Walid greeted them at the door and welcomed them in apologizing for the humble home. A small girl dressed in a fancy, frilly, pink dress hid behind his legs and her huge dark eyes stared up at the big men. Walid picked her up and introduced her as his niece, Rania.
Rhett had learnt Arabic courtesy of the SAS a few years previously and he said hello, wished her a happy birthday and asked her how old she was in perfect Arabic as she hid her face in her uncle's chest. Rhett held out a bag of sweets as a present and she took it with a shy smile and whispered, *'Shukran'*.

Countdown

'She is not usually so quiet,' laughed Walid. 'Come through. I didn't realise that you spoke such good Arabic,' added Walid as he closed the door.

'That's about it, I'm afraid,' lied Rhett. 'Just the basics before I came out here.' He didn't want him to know how good his Arabic actually was.

Rhett and Marcus walked a short way along a dark hallway and into a lounge area. There was virtually no furniture, Walid's mother-in-law, an old lady all in black with a veil wrapped around her head, sat in the corner of a battered settee and looked at the visitors with wary eyes. Next to her were Walid's daughters; two attractive, young teenagers wearing colourful salwa kameez and hijabs covering their hair. A young boy, about four years old sat on the lap of one of them, his sweet face marred by a scar running down the side of his cheek.

A large table that had been pushed against the wall was covered with plates of food. Rania escaped Walid's arms and joined two more young children who were sitting on the bare, tiled floor. Hisham, an older boy who was Walid's eldest son, stood leaning against the doorframe leading into the kitchen; his head was down as he checked his phone. Rhett and Marcus had met Walid and his family before, but it was the first time that they were to meet his brother, Farouq and his family. Despite the number of people, the atmosphere seemed subdued; even the small children sat quietly and stared with large, innocent, black eyes up at the huge men.

Walid's wife, Hadia appeared from the kitchen with another dish. She smiled at Rhett and Marcus and welcomed them in, speaking good English. In Arabic she told one of the older girls to get drinks and Marcus and Rhett were soon handed glasses of fizzy lemonade. At that moment Farouq arrived and the children on the floor shouted 'Baba!' and ran to him. Jamal, the boy sitting on the girl's lap slid off and limped awkwardly over to his father with his arms out wide and his face bright with joy. Farouq cuddled his children and introduced himself to Rhett and Marcus. He had a strong, solid build with broad shoulders and a large bald head that seemed to sit on his shoulders with no neck.

Countdown

His pate was smooth and shiny, but he wore a thick, dark moustache that dominated his lower face. He smiled at Rhett and Marcus with gleaming, almost black eyes.

'Good to meet you at last,' said Farouq. 'Walid has told me a lot about you.'

'Hisham, where is Tariq?' asked Walid addressing the young teenager with the phone. The boy glanced up, shrugged his shoulders and said that he didn't know. 'Call him and tell him he should be here,' ordered Walid.

'Let him be,' said Farouq, 'He is a young man now. He doesn't need to be at a children's birthday party.'

'He should be with the family when we are all together,' said Walid.

Hisham dialled a number and walked into the kitchen to talk to his cousin.

Farouq's wife, Amina came out of the kitchen with another plate of food and made space on the table for it. Hadia removed the covers from all the dishes and Walid invited Rhett and Marcus to eat. They had been before and knew that it would be no good protesting about going first. The delicious aroma of Arabic herbs and spices made their mouths water, and they happily began putting food on their plates. Rhett wanted to give his belly a good lining before the drinking that would follow later and piled on helpings of the simple but tasty choices of *kibba*, small patties of fried mince, *kheema*, meat paste with chickpeas, *dolma milisi*, stuffed onions, and a small amount of salad made from fresh tomatoes with olive oil, lime and mint. He added a piece of *samoon*, the Iraqi flatbread and went to sit on one of two small chairs opposite the settee; Marcus sat next to him, and they tucked into the delicious food.

Walid and Farouq filled their plates once the rest of the family had had some food and stood at the side of the room eating. Once the food was served, the atmosphere lightened; the children seemed to start making a lot more noise and the women and girls chattered loudly on the other side of the room.

'How is the ambulance driving going?' Rhett asked Farouq as he stood up and joined the two brothers.

Countdown

Farouq swallowed a mouthful of meat and rice biryani and nodded. 'At least I am earning again,' he said. 'And busy,' he added with a rue smile. 'I am lucky to get a little time off for Rania's party.'

Marcus joined them and the four men talked about the attack on the villa in hushed voices. Walid shook his head and assured Rhett that it was over nothing. 'They are all big and brave with their guns,' he said. 'I have sorted it with the ringleader, no problem.'

Rhett knew that sorting it had cost a large amount of money that he had supplied to keep the peace and hoped that didn't mean that they would be back for more.

Hadia came out of the kitchen carrying a simple birthday cake and everyone sang *Sana Helwa*, happy birthday to Rania.

Everyone clapped and after politely eating a piece of cake, Rhett said that he and Marcus had to leave. Thanking the women and saying goodbye to the others they left the room, followed by Walid. As they stepped into the dark hallway, they heard the front door open and a tall, skinny teenager wearing a Barcelona football shirt walked into the flat. Rhett immediately knew that it was the young lad he had seen near the Paradise Hotel but gave no sign of his recognition. Walid stepped forward and introduced them.

'This is Tariq, he is the son of my older brother, Yusef, God rest his soul, but he is our son now,' he said, smiling at the young man.

Tariq looked like a rabbit caught in the headlights when he saw Rhett and nervously said hello.

Farouq suddenly appeared behind them, 'Tariq said that he saw you a few days ago. He was going to the market in al Wahda area. They have the best fresh fruit and vegetables: tomatoes, sweet peppers, watermelon. Hadia is always sending him on missions to find the best food at the best prices. Isn't that right, Tariq?'

Tariq glared at his uncle. 'Yes, she is always making me do the shopping when the girls could go,' he complained. He moved past Rhett and Marcus with a quick nod and went into the living room to shouts of joy from the little ones. Farouq said goodnight to Rhett and Marcus and turned to follow Tariq.

'Tariq is a good boy,' said Walid. 'He has a difficult life – like us all – but his mother took his two older sisters and his brother to England when he was four years old. We took care of him. His father is my, and Farouq's, older brother, Yusuf. He was a professor in the university, and he was always in danger under Saddam's rule; he did not like the government, but he tried to be careful. Then he was arrested when he refused to bring his teenage girls to a party for Saddam's son, Uday. Everyone knows that he took any girls he wanted and did unspeakable things to them. Yusuf arranged for them to leave before his men came for the girls. His wife, Reem she had to make an extremely dangerous journey to escape and a four-year-old would have made it impossible, so our mother looked after Tariq. When they found out that the girls had gone, they took Yusuf and, weeks later, they dumped his beaten body outside our mother's home. She never recovered from the shock and died soon afterwards. We took Tariq in, to live with us. He speaks to his mother and his sisters regularly, but his home is here with us.'

Rhett nodded and then asked, 'What about his brother? You said he speaks to his mother and sisters but not his brother?'

'Walid looked at the floor and then back up with great sadness, 'His brother died two years ago.'

'Poor kid,' said Marcus, and Rhett nodded in agreement.

Suddenly they heard the haunting, flowing strains of a stringed instrument coming from the living room. Walid smiled and said, 'Ah Tariq is playing his oud. He is a very skilled player; such a gentle, artistic soul.'

'We'll let you get back to the party,' said Rhett. He shook Walid's hand and said, 'You are a good man, Walid. Thanks for a great party and have a good weekend with your family.'

Rhett had heard the stories about Uday Hussein, Saddam's eldest son, a cruel sadist who brutally raped young girls and women before killing them or leaving them with their lives

Countdown

ruined for ever. He and Marcus got into their car with Karim driving and headed off for a few well-earned beers.

8

Thursday, June 23rd, 2005
Green Zone, Baghdad

The testosterone in the room was almost tangible, a bubble of male energy. Groups of men, displaying an array of weapons, downed cans of beer, and spoke in loud voices as they joked and exchanged stories. Americans distinguishable by their short crew cuts or bald heads with little goatee beards flexed their bulging muscles. In their tight T-shirts and khaki combat trousers they flirted with the relatively small number of women. Rhett acknowledged Glen, Steve and Rynold who were drinking shots up at the bar. A few, mainly British security operators with longer, scruffier hair, baggy T-shirts and jeans sat around a table listening to Dan who was holding court telling a lewd joke. His face deadpan, he embellished the story and carefully built up to the corny punch line which resulted in the guys around the table bursting into a mixture of groans and laughter. The guy next to Dan shook a can of beer vigorously and snapped the ring pull holding it next to Dan's face. Beer exploded out of the opening and hit Dan on the shoulder as he dodged away, laughing. He saw Rhett and Marcus coming in and called them over.

Rhett took in the room. A fully fitted bar extended across one side of the back wall, a small stage had been erected on the other half of the wall with speakers, microphones and a drum kit set up on it. As well as the burly security operators, there were men in chinos and open necked shirts and the women dressed up to the nines in high heels and skimpy clothing. The hubbub of chatter and laughter sounded like a lively bar anywhere in the world.

'Glad you could make it,' said Dan smiling. He waved a hand around the table. 'Meet some of the lads I will be happy never to see again come next Tuesday.'

'Sod you!' said a man with curly, ginger hair, a pale and freckled face and a misshapen nose.

'Thank you, Baz,' said Dan raising his can. He turned to Rhett, 'Meet our eloquent, Scottish representative and the ugliest man on Earth.'

Baz smiled revealing crooked, yellow teeth with a black gap where an incisor should have been.

'Get some beers in and grab a seat,' said Dan sitting back down.

Marcus sat down next to a guy who introduced himself as Molly. He was an Australian with a fresh, young-looking face. He was short but his arms were strong and muscular.

'Can I see some ID?' asked Marcus with a straight face as he pulled in his chair.

Around the table guys spat out their beer in surprise and roared with laughter.

Molly looked at the size of Marcus and said, 'Yeah, yeah very funny. You're all just jealous of my boyish good looks and charm.' He pointed at his crotch and added, 'I may be young, but I've seen more action than you ugly looking bogans.'

'Who's talking about sheep shagging?' asked Rhett putting a bucket of cold beers on the table.

The guys fell about laughing and a series of related jokes ensued. Rhett took a seat, snapped open a beer and took a long, satisfying swig. More people came into the large room. Two women in skimpy shorts with high heels clacking across the tiled floor walked past the table. All the men watched them as they wound their way to the bar between tables and groups of men.

'I'll be rooting one or both of them before the night ends,' announced Molly setting off a new round of insults and jokes.

Countdown

Cliff and Matt, two guys with rippling muscles and hair tied back in ponytails got up on the stage; Cliff plugged in a guitar and Matt went to sit up behind the drum kit. A sudden screech from the sound system set everyone's teeth on edge as a third man, Harry went on and adjusted the levels before picking up a microphone. He introduced the band as *The Grits,* and everyone booed and told them to get off the stage until they started playing *American Pie* and before long everyone was joining in with the chorus – the only lines they knew.

Harry wore a black T-shirt with *Born to Run* splashed across the front. His strong arms were covered in tattoos, and he held the microphone in long artistic fingers. His blonde hair, cropped to half an inch, stuck up in short, gelled spikes above a handsome, young face. The song came to an end, and he spoke to the audience in the clear, posh voice of a public schoolboy.

'Good evening gentlemen, and ladies. Bit of respect please.'

'Get off the stage, Prince Harry,' yelled a drunk American.

Ignoring him, Harry held up his palm and continued, 'Our good friend, Dan Taylor has asked us to play a few songs.'

A loud whoop went up as Dan's name was mentioned and Rhett smiled remembering how Dan always got to know everyone wherever he went and was always the life and soul of the party.

'So, without more ado,' said Harry picking up a beer, 'Thanks for the drinks, Danny, and this one's for you.'

Dan raised his beer and grinned as the band launched into *Don't Look Back in Anger.*

The music continued in the background; the volume was not too loud on the instructions of the company bosses. A few women got up to dance in front of the band, trying to get the attention of the good-looking lead singer who was guaranteed a happy ending to the evening. Several men, including a drunken Dan, soon got up and joined the women.

Rhett sank more beers as the guys exchanged dits; each one trying to outdo the next with their stories. He began to relax, the tense muscles beginning to give a little, the adrenalin that had surged during the attack earlier starting to subside, but he still

Countdown

didn't feel drunk. He glanced up as a group of civvies entered the room. Three older looking men with neat, short hair wearing smart polo shirts tucked into neatly pressed jeans in the hope of looking casual stuck out like sore thumbs amongst the military guys. A lovely looking woman was with them, also a notable sight; she stood out like a poppy in a cornfield.

Rhett watched her as she smoothed her long, wavy blonde hair with one hand and pulled self-consciously at a short fringe as she took in the room with intelligent looking, blue eyes. The group stood for a while looking around until the woman pointed across the room at the table next to his; Rhett already knew that a couple more civvies were sitting there. She modestly adjusted her simple, short-sleeved, red blouse that had slipped off one shoulder and led the way across the room. She squeezed past a group of Americans comparing biceps and Rhett couldn't help noticing the snug fit of the jeans on the petite woman. As she neared, he had a feeling that he had seen her before somewhere.

Her group joined another man and a woman on the table next to the wall and the small woman went to sit down, next to an older, suave looking man who exuded confidence and spoke in a quiet, southern American accent as he welcomed her.

The banter around the table continued and Rhett joined in with the lads but after a while his eyes slid back to the adjoining table, and he looked over at the attractive lady. She glanced up and caught Rhett looking at her; their eyes locked and suddenly the lady smiled. Her full lips parted to reveal a neat row of white teeth and her eyes crinkled at the corners. She waved and excusing herself from the rest of her group, she made her way over to Rhett.

Baz's mouth fell open and Molly banged it shut with the back of his hand as all the guys went silent at her arrival.

'Hi, how are you?' the young woman asked Rhett. 'I'm Michele.

We didn't get properly introduced earlier.' She held out her hand, ignoring the lewd and suggestive remarks that were being muttered around the table.

Rhett did a double take. It was Malcolm's photographer friend from the hotel.

Countdown

'Rhett,' he said shaking her hand and just about managed to stop himself from saying, '*You brush up well.*' He looked around the table. Most of the guys were staring admiringly at Michele's body and he felt strangely protective of her. He needn't have worried.

'Hi guys,' she said looking at them all. 'Cat got your tongues? What does a girl have to do to get a beer around here?' The guys laughed as Molly nearly fell off his chair trying to get up and offer to get her one. Rhett told him to sit back down.

'Come on, I'll get you one,' he said and, standing up, he steered her in front of him with a gentle hand on the back of her upper arm away from the leering men as they shouted rude comments to his back. He felt the firm muscles in her arm and realised that she wasn't as fragile as she looked. He also felt a strange tingle of electricity as he touched her skin.

'Don't mind the lads,' said Rhett handing her the beer she'd asked for up at the bar. 'After a few more drinks they'll think they are Brad Pitt; they will be chatting up everything on offer with bravado, and still go home alone.'

'I see you don't have that trouble,' she said.

He looked at her, confused, and asked her what she meant.

'I've spotted at least four women that you've slept with,' she said with a little grin. She nodded briefly at a woman on the dance floor who was glancing their way. 'There's that one,' she said, and then turned and nodded at another woman across the room. 'And there are two more over there,' she said jerking her thumb in the direction of the tables behind.

He looked quickly at the women she was indicating and then back at her and gave a brief nod. 'Very astute,' he said, briefly raising his eyebrows. She took a swig of beer and the sleeve of her red top slipped down over her shoulder revealing a glimpse of a lacy black bra and the smooth curve of a rounded breast. She adjusted her blouse modestly and looked him straight in the eyes; he noticed how blue they were, a light, bright blue.

'You must be Clarke Gable,' she said with a smile.

He raised his eyebrows, 'You would be surprised how few people say that.'

Countdown

She laughed, 'Rhett Butler from Gone with the Wind. Your mother must have been a fan to give you a name like that in England.'

'Her favourite film,' admitted Rhett. 'Luckily, most of the people I work with don't have a clue where the name comes from. I usually tell them that I have an American mother if they ask.'

'And was she?'

Rhett looked at her, 'Yes, she was. Most of the guys call me Lardy,' he said, keeping things light as her use of the word 'was' made his neck stiffen.

'Ah, yes. A clever play on the name Millard,' she said raising one eyebrow.

Rhett frowned, his radar up; he hadn't told her his last name.

'Malcolm told me your name is Rhett Millard,' she explained. 'He also said he had a bit of a fright this morning.'

'Nothing we couldn't handle,' said Rhett finishing another beer. He got the barman's attention, 'Another one for you?' he asked Michele, and she nodded.

At that moment, Dan leapt up beside them, his head glistening with sweat from dancing.

'Get one in for me, mate,' he said putting an arm around Rhett's shoulder. 'Hello. Michele, isn't it? Having a good time?'

'How do you two know each other?' asked Rhett.

'Michele here is joining us on details. Embedding with our company for a couple of weeks.'

'Is that so?' said Rhett.

Michele said, 'Yes. John is over there with the top guys from Whiteriver now.' She glanced over at the table, 'That's Chuck Elmsworth, the CEO sitting next to John.'

Rhett glanced over to the table of men she had come in with and realised that John was the journalist he had seen that morning. He also brushed up well. Something didn't feel right despite the alcohol seeping into his system, relaxing his nerves and muddling his synapses.

'Trust my luck that I'm leaving just when we get some beautiful company on the job,' said Dan.

Countdown

'Which paper do you work for?' asked Rhett.

'I'm a freelancer. I've known John for years and when his normal cameraman went down with flu, he gave me a call,' she said smoothly.

The band started playing *London Calling* and Dan whooped.

'They're playing my song!' he shouted. 'Coming for a dance?' he asked Michele.

'Maybe later,' said Michele with a sweet smile.

'I take that as a promise. Be gentle with Lardy, he's got a broken heart.'

'I heard,' said Michele looking up at Rhett.

Rhett grinned and mock punched Dan, 'Get out of here. You're the one breaking my heart!'

Dan charged onto the dance floor with his beer and began leaping around and singing along with the band.

'Do you want to get some air?' Rhett asked Michele. He indicated a door behind the bar that led out onto a balcony.

'Sounds good,' replied Michele.

They sneaked out of the door onto the large balcony that wrapped around the villa. The air was still warm but not humid. The lights of the Green Zone and across into the city twinkled all around and stars glittered in a clear sky above. It was a beautiful view spoilt only by the fire and smoke rising into the sky in the distance and the sound of sirens.

Rhett led the way around the corner of the building. Michele followed him and he suddenly turned on her, grabbed both of her wrists and held them up over her head as he pushed her back against the wall.

'Haven't you heard of foreplay?' she gasped.

He leant his head down towards her until his nose was just touching hers.

'Who are you?' he growled in a low voice.

Her knee jerked upwards between his legs, and he just moved back in time to maintain the possibility of having children, but his hands relaxed, and she twisted her hands out, grabbed his right arm and dragged it back into an arm lock as she sprang around behind him and pushed him against the wall. Electric shocks of pain radiated across his arm and chest due to his old injury. He stamped back on her foot, and she yelped but held firm, pushed his wrist higher up his back and began talking.

'Rhett Millard, ex Para and SAS decorated soldier. Active in Northern Ireland, Sierra Leone and Afghanistan. Hospitalised for two months after a knife wound sustained in Tora Bora attack, full recovery after micro-surgery and passed fit for return to duty after six months but quit the army. Security Operator for British billionaire businessman, Hugh Wormsley, until start of Iraq invasion. Took on new position as team Leader for Aztec Security Company two years ago in May 2003. Father, Thomas Millard, butcher; mother, Lindsay nee Nielson deceased. Ex-girlfriend …'

His elbow swung back with considerable force, caught her on the side of the head, and knocked her sideways. He grunted with pain as she released his arm and then span around to face where she stood two yards away rubbing her head and watching him. They both stood staring at each other for what seemed like an hour. Rhett's hand hovered over the gun tucked into the top of his jeans.

Michele finally broke the silence, 'Michele Tring. Father, David Tring QC. Mother, Judge, Right Honourable Marilyn Tring. Attended Trancham Girls' School, graduated Oxford University and recruited to MI6.'

'Enough,' said Rhett. 'I am not interested.'

He flexed the fingers on his right hand and walked away.

***

Rhett strode away from Michele cursing the bloody spooks. He walked around the corner and paused outside the door to the bar, his head filling with memories. He pictured his mother laughing, vivacious and strong-minded. Every Christmas she made him and his father watch *Gone with the Wind;* his father would fall asleep, but she would sit cuddling Rhett and explaining to him why she had named him after the charismatic leading man. 'He's strong and handsome but he's a realist, Rhett, and he doesn't care what anyone thinks about him. He lives by his own moral code and does what needs to be done to survive, but he is kind and most importantly he is capable of great love.' Then she would pull him close and tell him how much she loved him and his father.

He thought about the women that Michele had pointed out in the bar. They were all women he had had a dance and even a kiss with in the past few months at various parties; they had all wanted more but he wasn't interested. The truth was that he loved Lorraine, but he felt disconcerted by Michele; she had caused a reaction that he hadn't felt in a long time, a definite chemical attraction. But she had tried to play him. He didn't like people who played games in relationships, but if they did, he would go all out to win.

He opened the door to the cacophony of the band and people shouting at each other to be heard over the music; everyone was laughing and chatting in the atmosphere of wild revelry induced by living life close to the edge.

'Wanna shot?' yelled Rynold seeing Rhett's angry face. Rhett nodded and went over to join him and Steve at the bar. He downed a tequila shot and held his glass out for another which Rynold duly poured for him. Rhett downed that and grinned.

'Welcome to the party,' said Rynold clinking his glass with Rhett's.

Rhett grabbed two beers and weaved across the room through the tables to the dance floor where Dan was playing air guitar. Rhett handed him a can and they both drank and danced with more beer going down their shirts than in their mouths as Harry sang, *'Going Underground'*

***

Michele leant against the concrete wall of the balcony and looked out at the lights of Baghdad with tears pricking her eyes. She was so angry with herself. She thought she was being so clever, and she had completely blown it. They had told her to get close to him, to find out more about his links with Hugh Wormsley and the connection with Walid and Farouq. She had expected him to be arrogant and coarse; she had seen his photograph and read his files and knew that he was good-looking. She thought that he would be a jumped up, over-confident bore, but he wasn't. She certainly hadn't expected to be so attracted to him. Watching him and listening from the next table she had noticed that although he swore, he wasn't crude like most of the others. When he was talking, he commanded complete attention and had the ability to make a simple story interesting and hilarious with everyone hanging on his every word. There was a vulnerability and a gentleness in his light brown eyes and when he had touched her arm it had sent a delicious tingle right through her body.

She metaphorically kicked herself, how stupid of her to mention his mother in the past tense. She could pretend that Malcolm had told her certain things but definitely not that. She had read all of his files and knew all about the romance between an American student travelling around Europe who'd met Rhett's father, a chatty, young butcher in a quiet Dorset village and stayed. Rhett was their only child and he had been in the car with his mother when a lorry carrying steel poles had braked suddenly in front of them. The badly tethered poles had become dislodged, and Rhett's mother was killed instantly as a pole smashed through the windscreen and impaled her. Rhett had been knocked unconscious when the car careered off the road into a wall but was otherwise unharmed, and apparently, he had no recollection of the accident. He and his father were devastated by her death, but his father was a strong man and he had helped Rhett to cope with his grief. Five years afterwards his dad met and married someone else, but Rhett did not get on with his stepmother and left to join the army after completing his A levels.

When she'd mentioned his mother in the past tense, he had not reacted, but she had seen a flash of steel pass across his gentle, gold-flecked eyes and knew that she had underestimated his intelligence.

This was her first overseas assignment, and she was so determined to make a good impression on her bosses and of course her dad. She had spent her life trying unsuccessfully to make him proud. Despite excelling in sport and every subject at school, getting a first in Philosophy, Politics and Economics from Oxford and going on to complete an MA in International Relations, he always made her feel that she was a disappointment, and now he was right. Sighing loudly, she rubbed a finger along the bottom of each eye to check for smudged mascara, smoothed down her hair and headed back into the bar with a smile fixed on her face. She glanced around the room and saw Rhett on the dance floor and although he carried on laughing and knocking back beer, she knew that he was watching her.

She went back to the table and began chatting animatedly with the suave American who was the CEO for the company that Dan worked for and was in Baghdad to check on a new contract, that would make him a few million dollars richer.

9

Thursday, June 23rd, 2005
Walid's apartment, Baghdad

Walid was pacing up and down the small balcony outside the apartment in agitation. The noise of traffic came from the street below and the familiar sounds of his family rose and fell inside the kitchen behind him: Hadia's sharp voice nagging the children, complaints and shouts, the rattle and clatter of cutlery and plates being cleared away. The sounds of the family rose in volume as Farouq opened the door to come outside to join him and faded as he closed it behind him.

Farouq lit a cigarette and inhaled deeply as he leaned on the balcony wall and stared out across the city.

'Something is bothering you, Walid?'

'What the hell is going on?' asked Walid in a low voice.

Farouq shrugged and blew smoke up into the still, warm air. It lingered and swirled before wafting into the night.

'I am not stupid, Farouq. What was Tariq doing near the hotel where our clients are staying?'

'It is time for you to wake up, Walid. We have to fight back against these invaders who are destroying our country.'

'What are you talking about? You were dancing in the street when they removed Saddam from power. You hated Saddam, look what he and his family did to our brother, our mother. The number of our friends that he arrested, never to be heard of again.'

Countdown

'Saddam was not perfect, but he had control. Our country was rich, thriving. You and I had good positions, money to feed and educate our children and now what do we have? These trespassers took our jobs, threw us out onto the streets, invaded our homes. Look what they did to Jamil, my poor little boy who will never play football or even walk properly ever again because of the invading soldiers.' Farouq stubbed out his cigarette and flicked it over the edge of the wall.

'So, what does the hotel with our clients in have to do with anything? Rhett is in security. He is helping protect people who are rebuilding the country. You told me to go to work for him, for God's sake. He keeps my family fed. He is a good man.'

Farouq patted Walid's shoulder and looked at him. He smoothed down his moustache with his thumb and forefinger and stared deep into Walid's eyes before taking another cigarette out of the packet. He offered the pack to Walid who took one. Farouq lit his own and passed the lighter to Walid as he drew in deeply.

'Rhett killed Ali,' he said watching Walid closely.

Walid's eyes opened wide, and he whispered, 'What? Ali died in a mugging. He was a good boy, earning money delivering pizzas while he studied.'

'Ali worked for us.'

'Who in the hell is *us*?' asked Walid sitting down on one of the two old chairs that stood on the balcony next to a cheap plastic table.

'We call ourselves the Brothers of Truth. We were doing a deal with Rhett's boss and Ali was the messenger, he didn't know what he was involved in, he just took pizzas to the dealer with notes hidden underneath and was given simple messages to pass on to his boss. Ali's body was found in an alley and put down as the victim of a mugging attack. He couldn't be linked to Wormsley or to us. As far as Rhett was concerned, he was protecting a rich businessman who worked in construction and asset management, but Hugh Wormsley is an arms dealer. He took on Rhett, as a washed-out soldier, gravely injured in Afghanistan, who would be looking for a cushy number and not paying attention, but he proved to be good at his job. It took us a while to find out what really happened, but eventually Wormsley told us. Rhett Millard killed Ali in cold blood and made it look like a random attack, but then Allah sent him to us, here in Iraq.'

Walid stared ahead slowly smoking, trying to take it all in. 'You sent me to work for him so that you could find out about his movements? The attack on the villa, the attack on his car, today, Tariq watching the hotel. You were trying to kill him? To take revenge? You could have done it any time in the past year since I have been working for him.'

Farouq smiled; a wicked, sly look appeared on his face. 'It is not time yet; we are just trying to rattle him. The attack on the villa paid us well,' he laughed. 'I amused myself with the idea of Rhett helping to finance our battle, but we have a much better death for him planned and we will make sure that he suffers losses, just as we have, before he dies in humiliation and terror. He is only a small part of a much bigger plan. Every time the West commits more sins, our numbers grow, here and across the world.'

'This is chaos,' said Walid.

'The western governments brought chaos to our land when they decided to blame us for the attacks on America. Now we will show them what chaos is like. Be prepared Walid, we need you to be with us in the coming weeks.'

'I always knew that you were crazy Farouq but how could you involve Tariq in all of this? He is a gentle soul who loves to play his music; he has a chance of becoming something special with his oud playing and his beautiful voice.'

'He will get to play his oud to a very wide audience, Walid. He is not a child anymore and he can see what needs to be done for our future.'

Countdown

10

Monday, June 27th, 2005
Route Irish, Baghdad

As they reached the intersection that would take them onto the airport road, Rhett paid close attention to everything going on around them. This was a favourite spot for insurgents to plan attacks as the traffic slowed and jammed. A few weeks earlier, a convoy transporting clients to the airport had come under fire leaving a client and three security operators dead.

It was the Monday after Dan's leaving party, and they were on their way to the airport to pick up the new member of Malcolm's team. They moved forward slowly and joined the traffic on the treacherous ten-mile stretch between the city and the airport; Route Irish, or 'Death Street' as it was known by the locals. It was busy but flowing with minibuses full of workers, trucks laden with goods, saloon cars in various states of poor repair.

Karim jerked his chin up and Rhett checked in the mirror. A long way back, a grey saloon car with blacked out windows accelerated past a couple of cars and then veered back in behind a truck. A couple of seconds later it repeated the action; it was gradually getting closer to their vehicle. Rhett moved his hand up and down to indicate to Karim to go slow and stay calm.

Keeping an eye out behind them, Rhett saw a convoy of three large, souped up, armoured vehicles thundering along in the outside lane. Holes in the sides of the front vehicle revealed the noses of automatic weapons. They were mean machines but also highly visible.

As the second vehicle came level with them, Rhett looked up and saw Dan sitting in the passenger seat of a B6 armoured Land Cruiser. Dan looked down into the low-profile armoured Mercedes and seeing Rhett, he gave him a two-finger salute, briefly touched the rim of his helmet, and grinned. In the seat behind Dan, the client, a man in his fifties with lanky, grey hair and wearing glasses, stared straight ahead. Next to the client, Rhett could just make out the handsome profile of Harry, the singer in the band. Rhett moved his head backwards trying to indicate for Dan to look behind, but his vehicle had already moved past. It was followed by the third vehicle, a black GMC with the tail gate down revealing a machine gun rigged up in the back. Rhett recognised the fresh, young face of Molly from the party manning the weapon. Rhett's heart went into his throat. Dan was in the grey zone; his mind was already out of Iraq and home with his family. It was a dangerous time for all military and security personnel; a few days before leave when you were dreaming about time with family and friends and a couple of days after your leave when you missed everybody like hell and the post-leave blues had you in their grip. Concentration was lower, focus distracted.

Dan's convoy trundled on, slowed briefly by heavier traffic up ahead, and Rhett told Karim to go even slower. He watched as the grey saloon with the blacked-out windows moved to within two cars behind them and he pulled his shemagh up over his mouth. With his dark hair and olive skin, he could pass for Arabic if not looked at too closely. He had his weapon at the ready but out of sight.

Suddenly the grey saloon shot out from behind a van and raced towards them. Rhett's hands gripped his MP5.

The car came up alongside them, it seemed to slow down and stay level, but they didn't know if the driver was looking at them or not. It could be a car full of insurgents ready to suddenly open their windows and open fire or a VBIED. To be more precise, a lone suicide bomber with a car as the bomb. Karim continued driving at the same steady speed, looking straight ahead.

They heard the growl of the accelerator as the saloon car surged forward with greater power than seemed possible from all outer appearances. It sped forward, its chassis low to the ground, and veered back in behind a minivan. Rhett watched as it got closer and closer to the armoured GMC, which was about one hundred metres ahead of Rhett's team by now.

It could have just been an erratic driver; there were plenty of them. Nervous and hoping to dodge any dangers on the road, many drivers weaved in and out of the traffic. But Rhett had a very bad feeling. He pulled out his phone and rang Dan's mobile.

The grey saloon had got to within three cars of the armoured GMC and had dived back into the slower moving traffic in the right-hand lane. It suddenly pulled out at high speed and raced up behind the GMC, the last vehicle in the convoy. Molly in the back was taken by surprise; he raised his fist and indicated for the driver to keep its distance, but it kept on coming and he fired a couple of warning shots, which flew up over the bonnet of the approaching vehicle. Too late, he realised that the car was not going to back off as it swerved past and accelerated towards Dan's vehicle. Dan suddenly registered what Rhett had been trying to tell him and he yelled into the radio. He checked in his wing mirror and caught sight of the grey car speeding past the rear vehicle and heading towards them as Molly's voice came over the radio confirming a possible hostile. The grey car increased its speed as the driver of Dan's security vehicle took evasive action and veered to the left. Dan had no time to react, the grey saloon was on them. It drove alongside and the driver detonated the bomb, sending himself to Paradise and seventy-two virgins.

Well behind, Karim slammed on his brakes and swerved to a stop on the side of the road as up ahead the grey car exploded next to Dan's Land Cruiser. There was a loud boom as a ball of flames expanded outwards and upwards. The rear armoured GMC was swept off the road by the blast and careered into the central reservation. Dan's car was thrown up into the air as black smoke and fire filled the air. It landed on its roof, the doors flew off their hinges and two bodies were expelled from the blazing wreckage as it smashed to the ground and slid across the tarmac with fumes and flickering flames shooting out of the carcass. Vehicles immediately behind had braked in advance but they were still affected by the blast. Glass and metal shattered everywhere.

Rhett and Marcus sat stunned as a second explosion boomed out and more flames and smoke billowed up into the air. People stood in the road screaming and yelling.

Rhett told Karim to drive forward carefully. Dodging cars that were slewed across the highway, they approached the burning wrecks ahead of them.

***

Dan faced forward. In the distance, he could just see The Winged Man, a statue of Abbas Ibn Furnass, a Moorish astronomer who lived in Spain in the ninth century and was believed to have built an early flying machine. His outstretched, winged arms marked the entrance or exit to Baghdad International Airport, and he was always a welcome sight on the way into the airport perimeter. Dan would be there again tomorrow on his way home to Gemma and Kyle.

He scanned the road ahead automatically, but his thoughts were on seeing Gemma's face again and holding his son. The vehicle slowed as a truck pulled out in front carrying a multitude of boxes roughly stacked and tied down with narrow ropes. He glanced down to his right and saw a white, soft-skinned Mercedes. Suddenly, he recognised Rhett looking inconspicuous, no weapons in sight and he grinned and saluted. He saw Rhett give him a slight lift of the head before his own vehicle picked up speed again and they moved on.

A niggling thought was worming its way through the back of his head. He couldn't quite grasp it and then it came through. Rhett hadn't been saying hello, he had been indicating to look behind.

Countdown

Dan looked at the road behind them in his mirror; a stream of vehicles snaked all the way back towards the city and he saw nothing unusual. He shrugged and turned to face front again as he felt his phone vibrate. He moved his hand towards his pocket as something caught his eye. He checked his mirror again and saw a grey sedan with blacked out windows emerge from behind a van in the right-hand lane. It seemed to accelerate and race towards them. It was twenty metres behind and gaining fast when he yelled into his radio. The grey car overtook the rear vehicle and was now heading straight for the Land Cruiser. Dan could make out the shape of a head swathed in cloth as Molly's voice came over the radio. It was nearly on them. Five metres and his driver swerved violently to the left. Dan watched helplessly as the car came alongside and he heard Harry's voice shout out, 'He's on us, he's on us!'

Time seemed to slow down as Dan curled his body into a ball and he heard the boom of the grey car as it detonated next to his Iron Chariot. Images of Gemma and Kyle flashed across his mind, and he heard himself yelling his wife's name. A blast of intense heat seared across his back and over the top of his head. He felt his body spin as the car lifted into the air as though it were a matchbox toy and then his bones shuddered violently as the vehicle slammed into the concrete road on its roof, the doors blew off and he was flung sideways. He was flying through the air, a memory of being in this body position as he dive-bombed Rhett in the pool flickered in his brain. When was that? He heard screams, horns blaring. Chunks of steel and burning rubber rained from the sky as he realised that it was he who was screaming.

***

Karim made the way through the vehicles blocking the road towards the blackened wrecks and they all saw a body in the road. Telling Marcus to stay in his car behind, Rhett got out of the Mercedes and looked up the road to where the Iron Chariot lay on its roof with flames flaring out of the windows. Molly climbed out of the back of the third GMC with blood streaming down the side of his face. He, along with the other men from his vehicle, walked forwards towards the smouldering vehicles. The security guys from the lead GMC vehicle were making their way warily back towards the shattered, burning remains of their convoy. Holding up his ID and a small Union Jack flag, Rhett moved slowly towards the oncoming guys. As he neared, he recognised Cliff and Baz from the party, and they waved him forward with grim expressions of shock and despair on their faces. The heat even from a distance, scorched his skin. A half-charred body with arms and legs at awkward angles was lying in the road, the face was fixed in an expression of terror and pain. It was as if the flames had grabbed hold of his lower body before he was thrown out and away from the still moving vehicle. With a swoop of gut-wrenching sadness, he saw that it was the contorted face of the singer, Harry. He pressed his fingers to his neck to confirm that he was dead. There was no point in checking the vehicle; flames had engulfed the interior and cremated the client and the driver. Where was Dan? He looked around and ran when he saw another body lying at the edge of the highway, the arms outstretched. A blackened helmet lay a few feet away.

Rhett knelt beside the ravaged, burnt body of his friend. Dan's grey-blue eyes stared upwards devoid of light and Rhett gently closed them with two fingers and bowed his head. Choking back tears, he took a deep breath and stood up with his hands on his hips, fury bubbling up inside him. He saw the tiny figure of a woman dressed in a boiler suit with a helmet on her head walking slowly from the lead vehicle towards him. She tried to hold a camera up to her eyes, but her hands were shaking too much, and she let it drop to hang down on the strap. Michele's eyes met Rhett's and he saw tears stream down her face as she realised it was Dan lying at his feet. Rhett breathed in deeply. Cliff and Baz reassured him that they had things under control, and he turned and went back to his team.

They had to keep moving. As long as they stayed on this road they were exposed to further attacks.

11

Monday, June 27th, 2005
Airport, Baghdad

Rhett's stomach rolled and ached sending waves of grief and guilt churning around his body and his mind. Outwardly, he showed no emotion; he clenched his jaw and stared out of the window. Dan had saved his life and now he had failed to save his. The pulse in his temple began to beat; he couldn't shake off the feeling that the bomb had been meant for him.

They reached the airport and he and Marcus went into the terminal without speaking. The flight had landed but it would be a while before the passengers came through, so Marcus went off to get coffee and something to eat leaving Rhett alone with his thoughts.

He found a seat in the corner giving him a full view of the arrivals' hall. Airport staff wandered around trying to look busy, soldiers in full combat gear patrolled the entrances and a few Iraqis waiting for passengers milled around.

Images of Dan flitted across Rhett's mind. Dan laughing on his wedding day, drinking beer together on nights out in Northern Ireland, huddled under blankets as bombs thundered to earth all around them as they silently ate military rations in the freezing mountains of Afghanistan. The cold terror of the huge black bird swooping down on him, and the sight of Dan appearing over the ridge like a guardian angel, firing at his assailant and saving his life. Rhett closed his eyes; his head was thumping, and he saw the face of a young man with brown eyes like polished conkers staring at him in fear. It wasn't the face of the Taliban fighter that haunted him, it was the face of a young man in London.

May 2003, Ealing, London

Rhett checked the surveillance cameras on his screens in the office at the front of the elegant house in Ealing. A simple, double fronted house with bay windows set back from the road with a gravel driveway sweeping across the front, it was a modest abode compared to the vast country estate owned by his boss Hugh Wormsley. Probably only worth a couple of million pounds. It had four bedrooms on the first floor, an attic that had been converted into a studio, a kitchen with an island in the centre, and a large sumptuously furnished lounge/dining room including extensive, white leather sofas in front of a fireplace, a baby grand piano, a round, rosewood dining table and an antique walnut writing desk. Everything was immaculate and in pristine order like a show home from an exclusive property magazine. The basement contained a well-stocked wine cellar, a fully equipped gym, and a small bedroom with an en suite shower for Rhett and his back-to-back man. Broad stairs swept up from the hallway and behind the staircase was another smaller room that was Wormsley's private office with a side door leading onto the path at the side of the house, apparently so that business associates could come to see him without entering the main house.

As far as Rhett could work out though, this wasn't his boss' London place of work; it was a refuge. Wormsley arrived there on a Sunday morning and was dropped off by a chauffeur and bodyguard who were then dispatched. He spent all day in the house, painting in his studio, reading in the homely lounge or pottering in the garden when the weather allowed. He was picked up again on a Monday morning to resume his busy working life and to spend time at his country estate where his wife and children lived.

Countdown

Rhett was in charge of watching over the house whether Hugh was in residence or not. If Hugh was there, he took responsibility for his personal safety in and out of the house, but so far Wormsley had never gone anywhere. Rhett had expected there to be a lady visitor, a mistress of some kind but the only regular visitor in the five months that he had been doing the job was the pizza delivery man who brought a large pizza with all the works: pepperoni, Italian sausage, peppers, onions and mushrooms.

'The only treat I get,' Hugh had laughed. 'My wife worries about my cholesterol and blood pressure so the rest of the week I have to eat rabbit food and quinoa!'

Hugh usually shared the pizza with Rhett, so he wasn't complaining. After quitting the army, Rhett had been approached by the intelligent services; his unique skills and in-depth knowledge of Arabic were of interest to them, and they were keen to get him on board with MI6 in some capacity. He told them that he wasn't interested in becoming a spook; he wanted a clean break and instead he had contacted an old friend from the forces, Jim Brooks who had set up Aztec Security Company a couple of years earlier. Jim had given him a few short-term security assignments and then a more permanent post had come up providing security for a wealthy businessman. Apparently, Wormsley had liked the sound of Rhett's CV and he had got the job. Rhett took the position seriously, but it was boring, and he was thinking about looking for a change. The invasion of Iraq the previous month had given him a pang of regret about quitting the forces; he knew that many of his old chums would have been in there on the frontline and part of him wished he could have been there with them.

The doorbell rang and he saw a young man of medium height with black hair curling over the top of his jacket looking up at the camera over the front porch. Rhett recognised him as the new delivery guy who had only been coming for a few weeks; a cheerful, easy-going lad. Rhett told Wormsley that the pizza had arrived before going to the door and stepping outside.

Countdown

The young man aged about nineteen or twenty with a spattering of acne over his jaw and cheeks held the pizza box in both hands and grinned at Rhett. He was slim with light brown skin and large, brown eyes that gave him the innocent look of a small boy. Rhett had thought he was of Middle Eastern ethnicity when he had first met him and was going to ask but when he said that his name was Sid, he decided it was unlikely and Sid had told him that his family was from Ealing. He was a cheeky young man, always chatty and friendly, and Rhett liked him.

'Hi, Sid,' said Rhett. 'How are things?'

'Yeah, not so bad,' replied Sid in a strong, London accent. 'Me mum's not feeling too well, got some kind of bug. Says it's the weather. Been complainin' all year about the cold and wondering when the sun's going to come out. She's not happy! You all right, mate?'

'I'm good, thanks,' said Rhett. He looked inside the pizza box and breathed in the delicious smell of cheese, spicy meat, and baked bread, then he moved aside for Sid to go in and take the pizza through to the kitchen. Rhett had been unhappy about this arrangement at first, just as he was about the lack of security in general. Wormsley was a billionaire and his regular visit to the London address would be easy to monitor and attract would be kidnappers. There wasn't even a gate across the driveway. When he'd voiced his concerns, Wormsley had said he was just a businessman, not high profile enough to deserve attention. He had plenty of surveillance cameras and alarms; big gates just made one conspicuous and attracted unwanted burglars and the like.

He liked to tip the pizza delivery boys personally; in they went with the pizza and out they came shortly afterwards with a big smile on their faces as they pocketed a fifty-pound note. Sid came out of the kitchen with his usual cheeky smile as he headed back down the corridor towards Rhett.

'Think I'm in the wrong business,' said Rhett when he saw Sid stuffing a small wad of notes into his jean pocket.

Sid looked embarrassed for a moment and then he laughed and went out of the door with a casual, 'Cheerio, mate.' For some

Countdown

reason Rhett waited by the front door and watched him go. He saw Sid pull out his phone to make a call and his hackles rose when he heard Sid speak and he heard him say, '*As salaam alaykum. Altaslim sayakun al'usbue almuqbil.*'

He had only said, 'Peace be upon you, delivery will be next week.' But he spoke in fluent Arabic. Rhett called out to him, and Sid turned with a look of panic on his face that he quickly covered with a smile.

'What's up, mate?' asked Sid.

Rhett stepped towards him, 'Didn't know that you spoke Arabic.'

'Oh what? Yeah, pizza place, they're all Arabic. I picked it up, you know. Some of them don't speak a word of English. Just confirming delivery next week, yeah?' he added. He couldn't look Rhett directly in the eye.

'Good for you,' said Rhett, 'languages are always useful.'

'Yeah,' said Sid. 'See you then,' he added, and turned to walk back to his motor bike parked on the road outside.

Rhett went back in and wondered whether he should disturb Hugh; he knew that Wormsley hated to be interrupted when he was eating and he waited for a while.

Hugh enjoyed his private ritual of putting on music, setting the pizza box in front of him on the table, placing a napkin on his lap and pouring a large glass of Chateaux Margaux 2000. He had cameras and listening devices everywhere and he had heard the conversation at the front door; he didn't think it would be a problem. For now, he turned away from all the screens, put his music on, settled himself in front of his pizza and swirled the wine in its glass. Eating was the only time he turned his mind off business and relaxed for a few minutes. He was a trim man who prided himself on keeping fit and in his mid-fifties he was still in good shape. His light brown hair was full and neatly styled with only a few grey hairs visible on the sides of his long, oval face. He had hooded, small, brown eyes beneath thick brows and a large, wide nose with deep nasolabial folds running from the edge of his nostrils to the corners of his wide mouth. Long, thin lips added to a reptilian appearance. His clean-shaven

Countdown

face had few wrinkles and only the slight sagging in the skin around his prominent Adam's apple and bluish shadows under his eyes gave away his age. He was wearing expensive chinos and a navy cashmere sweater over a white shirt. Everything about him exuded wealth, supreme confidence and arrogance.

He had just taken a delicious bite to finish his second slice of pizza when he heard a knock on the door. He sipped his wine, turned the music down and with irritation, called out, 'Come in!' Rhett walked in to see Hugh wiping grease from his mouth with his serviette as he finished a mouthful of the giant pizza that he had barely touched. Chopin Nocturne Op.9, No 2 played softly in the background.

Hugh closed his eyes, listening to the music and said, 'Chopin. Many people prefer No.1, but I feel that No. 2 has more depth and emotion.'

Rhett apologised for interrupting and went on to report what had happened with Sid and said that he felt uneasy about it.

'I'm sure it's nothing. We know Sid. He's a bright young boy. All the young people probably need Arabic living anywhere in London these days. Good for him, languages are always useful,' Wormsley said in his slow, refined voice. 'Don't worry Rhett, I've got you to protect me, and I know who to call if there's a problem. Leave it with me.' He picked up another slice of pizza with the long, well-manicured fingers of one hand and pushed the box towards Rhett with the other. 'Here you are, take the rest of the pizza. I've had enough.'

Rhett knew when he was being dismissed and he took the pizza into the kitchen. He did not feel easy; it bothered him that Hugh had used the same phrase as he had, '*Good for him, languages are always useful*'. Had he been listening? Sid's Arabic had been too good for someone who had picked it up from working in a pizza place. The use of the future tense, 'delivery will be next week' just didn't sound right. He was sure that it wasn't referring to pizza, it was something else. Maybe the planning of a kidnap. Delivering Wormsley to someone? Wormsley's lack of concern irked him, but then he realised that

Countdown

maybe it was just him; he was just bored and trying to make things more exciting than they really were.

Hugh Wormsley watched Rhett leave the room and close the door behind him, then he finished the pizza slice and wiped his fingers slowly and thoughtfully on his napkin. He stood up, walked to the window, and looked out across the beautiful lawn and neat borders where rhododendron and azaleas flourished with his hands clasped behind his back. After a while, he took his mobile out of his pocket, dialled a number and spoke to someone on the other end.

'We have a problem with the kid; he is not discreet enough and there is something not quite right about him.' He paused to listen to the voice on the other end, 'I know he is related but I haven't become this successful without having a sense for these things. We cannot take any risks at this stage; the deal must go through next week. Do not contact the buyers, find out what you can. I don't need to remind you that there must be no link to me.' He ended the call and dialled another number.

Rhett polished off the pizza, did his usual checks around the house, and checked all the security cameras. The sun had long gone down when he decided to have his usual evening cigarette and patrol around the back garden. Turning off the motion sensor light on the back of the house, he stepped outside; the light was useful for spotting anyone in the garden who shouldn't be, but he didn't like being lit up like a target when it was him outside.

The evening was chilly, a nearly full moon slid in and out of dark clouds lighting up the long, sweeping lawn in brief moments of brightness and creating eerie shadows from the tall trees that lined the garden walls and swayed in the slight breeze. For May, the weather was miserable; the week before there had even been some snow in London. He rubbed his arms wishing he'd put a jacket on and thought again about changing jobs; he missed the buzz, the adrenalin rushing through his blood, and he decided to discuss it with Lorraine when he called her later. An unexpected glow of love went through him at the thought of Lorraine. She was the only woman who had ever made him feel

Countdown

that way. Maybe it was time to make an honest woman of her he thought as he flicked the cigarette lighter shut and put it back in his pocket.

He stepped off the patio onto the soft and spongy grass and drew on the cigarette as he began his customary walk around the extensive garden. A sound from the side of the house made him stop in his tracks and listen. It could have been the wind, a branch tapping against the wall, but it had stopped, and the wind had not. He stepped back and made his way to the corner of the house putting his cigarette out in a plant pot on the patio. Very slowly, he moved his head around the edge of the house and looked down the pathway into darkness. Then he heard the noise again, a gentle tap tap, and he could just make out the shape of a person moving backwards into the trees opposite the door to Wormsley's office.

Silent as a cat he crept down the path keeping his eyes on the trees opposite the door. A slim figure stepped forward and he lunged towards it putting one arm round the neck and with a sharp kick to the back of the knees the person's legs crumpled. He pushed the body forward so that it landed face down on the concrete with a groan and then brought both arms round to the back as the person began to struggle and fight to get away. They were not strong and had no fighting skills. Holding one arm in a tight grip, he dragged the body up to standing and looked into the frightened face of Sid.

'What the hell!' cried Sid. 'Mr. Wormsley called me, he told me to come to the side door. He told me to wait up the street until he called me and then to come to this door.'

The moon emerged from behind a cloud sending a glimmer of white light through the trees. Sid stared at Rhett, his brown eyes shining like polished conkers for a second before being plunged into darkness once more. He tried to pull away, but Rhett held him firm thinking that it wasn't for women that Hugh Wormsley came to the London house.

Suddenly, the office door opened, and Hugh Wormsley stood in the doorway with a paisley dressing gown wrapped tightly

Countdown

around his body over pyjamas. The light from the office filled the pathway.

'Well done, Rhett. I'll handle this from here,' said Wormsley in his smooth, upper-class voice.

Rhett heard a car turning into the driveway and headlights glared down the pathway blinding Rhett for a second as the sound of tyres crunching across the gravel at the front of the house and coming to a sudden stop reached his ears. Car doors slammed and two large men wearing suits came down the side of the house. They roughly pulled Sid away from Rhett and one pulled the young man's arms behind his back and cuffed his wrists.

'Rhett caught this man trying to break into my office. Take him away,' said Wormsley.

The men dragged Sid kicking and screaming down the path. He turned and stared at Rhett, 'He called me! He said that he had a message for me!'

The moonlight caught Sid's face and Rhett saw his nut-brown eyes, wild and staring, glistening under a film of tears. Then he disappeared around the corner and Rhett heard the car start up and drive away.

Rhett turned to Wormsley, 'What the hell just happened? Who are those guys?'

'Such a promising boy,' said Wormsley smoothing his hand across his hair. 'I expect he thought he could get more money out of me. I knew you would protect me Rhett, and I told you I knew whom to call. We don't need to make a fuss; we don't need to attract any attention. Goodnight, Rhett. Well done.'

Rhett opened his mouth to speak but Wormsley turned away and closed the door. Rhett went back to the garden, lit up another cigarette and stood in front of the kitchen trying to work out what had just happened. *'Was Sid telling the truth?'* He had a gut wrenching feeling that he was responsible for something bad happening to Sid. He consoled himself with the thought that Sid could have been part of a kidnapping plot and he had foiled it, but something didn't ring true. *'Where had those guys come from?'* he thought.

Countdown

Hugh Wormsley left the next morning, as usual. A brief article in the news reported another stabbing in the streets of London. A young man whose name had not been released had been found dead in an alley near Ealing Broadway; he was the victim of a mugging. It wasn't exactly unusual in London, and Rhett dismissed his hunch that it might be Sid. However, the following Sunday a different person delivered the pizza and Rhett went down to the pizza restaurant and asked for Sid. He received blank looks and shaking heads. He asked again in Arabic, and they looked at him as if he was crazy. Nobody had heard of anyone called Sid working there and not one of the staff spoke Arabic. He didn't think they were hiding something; he knew that they were telling the truth. He was sure that the dead boy from the week before must be Sid, and at the same time, he realised that he didn't know what he had got himself involved with and he didn't want to know. Rhett told his boss, Jim that he wanted a job in Iraq; he wanted to be where there the action was and with the demand for security in Baghdad on the rise, a job soon came through. He handed in his notice, left Wormsley on what he thought were good terms and took the job in Iraq.

12

Monday, June 27th, 2005
Airport, Baghdad

Marcus placed a cup of coffee down in front of Rhett and nodded towards the passengers beginning to emerge from the baggage hall. Rhett grabbed the coffee and testing that it wasn't too hot, he gulped it down, flung the paper cup in a bin and caught up with Marcus who was talking to a short, skinny man in his late forties with thick, mousy hair and small, hazel eyes staring through thick-lensed glasses that were perched on a long, prominent nose. He was wiping sweat off his deathly pale face with a cloth.

Rhett joined them and introduced himself to the new client, Gordon Kettle. They led him out of the terminal to where the cars were parked and Rhett quickly explained that there were dangers on the route but that as long as he followed Rhett's instructions, they would be fine. He handed him a flak jacket to put on.

'Jesus Christ!' said Gordon, 'It's hot enough as it is without adding another layer. I might just evaporate in a pool of sweat!' He allowed Abdullah to take his bags from him and reached into his pocket for cigarettes and a lighter. Rhett looked at him and held his gaze with a cool, unemotional stare, 'Normally I'd say it's your choice. You catch a bullet, or some flying shrapnel and it could be the difference between your insides being ripped apart and spread across your legs like a broken jam jar on a picnic or a slight bruise. You do have a choice though. While you're under my watch you wear it, or I'll send you straight back out of the country.'

Gordon grumbled and muttered, but holding the cigarette between his lips, he obediently put the jacket on over his short-sleeved cotton shirt. This was his first time in the country, he was nervous and trying to hide it with bolshiness. He talked incessantly as they got into the car and headed out of the airport and back to the city. When Gordon saw the skeleton of the burnt out, wrangled wreck being removed from the opposite side of the road he swore under his breath. Rhett calmly explained what had happened and Gordon stopped talking until they got off the highway.

'What a dump!' he blurted out as they drove through the once beautiful city now a depressing sight with crumbling, impoverished areas and unsmiling people.

Karim pulled up outside the Paradise Hotel and Said stopped behind him. Marcus, Abdullah and Faris stood watch as Rhett helped Gordon with his bags and walked him over to the hotel. Rhett scoured up and down the street as he walked past the bollards protecting the front of the hotel. He didn't see Tariq.

Tariq was on the roof of a building further up the street mostly hidden by a television satellite dish; he watched Rhett arrive with the new engineer and made a phone call.

Rhett nodded at Sam, who looked Gordon up and down and then grinned at Rhett and, touching his forehead, he said, 'All in order, sir.'

Once inside the hotel, Rhett radioed Marcus to go back to the villa with Faris and to tell Karim to park up and wait for him. He and Gordon walked into the bar area and Malcolm stood up to greet them from his usual table by the bar with a smile. Gordon and Malcolm already knew each other from working together in the UK; they were both highly educated and experienced engineers with qualifications coming out of their ears and they had started working for the same telecommunications company a few years earlier. They had both been drawn to working in

Countdown

Iraq because of the high salaries but for different reasons. Malcolm's twin boys had just finished their first year of A levels and were planning to go to university the following year; one wanted to study medicine and the other architecture. With the introduction of tuition fees, it was going to be an expensive few years and Malcolm and his wife both agreed that they didn't want the boys leaving university with massive debts; it would be worth Malcolm being away on the four weeks on two weeks off rotation for a couple of years.

Gordon was one of those people who seemed to have been everywhere and done everything; although prone to exaggeration, he had worked in many different countries and loved to travel. His journey through life had included three failed marriages by the age of forty-five with three children from the first one; he needed the job in Iraq to help pay alimony and support wife number four.

'Where the heck have you brought me, Malcolm?' asked Gordon, finally cracking a smile.

'To Paradise,' said Malcolm indicating the sign showing the hotel's name. 'I knew the money would interest you and that you would want to see the place that we have spent so much time discussing. Cold beer?'

'Now you are talking,' replied Gordon. 'I feel like I've been chewing a dust sandwich.'

The three men sat down at a table for Rhett to go over the plans for the week and to warn Gordon, as a newcomer, about the dangers of being a Westerner in Baghdad and the potential threat of being kidnapped. Malcolm had heard it before but still paid close attention. When Gordon began to tell Malcolm about the bomb wreck that they had seen on the airport road, Rhett decided it was time to leave. He hadn't told Gordon that his best mate and other people he knew had been killed in the attack.

He left the two men to catch up and said that he would pick them up in the morning. As he left the bar he couldn't help looking around for Michele; he wondered how she was feeling after the terrible attack on Dan's vehicle. Although she had pissed him off at the party, he couldn't help thinking about the almost electric charge that had passed between them and how shaken and upset she had looked after the explosion. There was no sign of her, and he called his team to come and pick him up to go back to the villa.

The death of Dan and the other guys, who they had been laughing and drinking with a few days earlier, was a huge blow to the whole team, but there was no point in dwelling on the incident; they all knew the risks. They raised a glass to the dead men that evening, and then got on with their jobs.

Each day Malcolm and Gordon were taken to the site they were working on in different vehicles, never taking the same route there or back. Nobody had noticed the young man, Tariq hiding on the roof of the building near the hotel watching the daily routine and communicating with the cleaner who worked in the hotel. It was over a week later, on Wednesday the 6th of July that Farouq drove his ambulance to a side street down the road from the hotel and waited. It was time for his carefully laid out plan to be set in motion and he prayed to Allah for it all to fall into place.

13

Wednesday, July 6th, 2005
Paradise Hotel, Baghdad

Rhett escorted Malcolm and Gordon into the hotel and called Karim to go with Abdullah to get something to eat and drink; he needed to discuss the move to a new site the following day with the two engineers. The temperatures had soared in the last week and although it was nearing sundown, the air was hot and oppressive. Gordon and Malcolm headed straight to the bar to order refreshing pints of lager and asked Rhett if he would join them in a drink. The thought of downing a cold beer was tempting but Rhett asked for a lemonade.

On the roof over the road, Tariq was sweating but not just from the heat; it was nearly time to begin. He called the cleaner inside the hotel and told him to keep an eye on Rhett's movements; he needed to know when Rhett was away from his clients.

Rhett enjoyed the sweet, fizzy liquid sliding down his dry throat and watched with amusement as the two older men closed their eyes in the pure pleasure of the first mouthful of cold beer after a long day. They went over the new plans, which involved leaving the hotel at a much earlier time in the morning and both men groaned. Malcolm and Gordon began discussing the technical problems of the actual job and Rhett excused himself to go to the bathroom.

Countdown

He walked out of the bar and into the passageway containing lifts, swing doors that led to a restaurant and another door into the toilets. He stepped out of the way of a cleaner who was pushing a mop around the tiled floor and didn't see the woman coming out of the lift until he bumped into her. They both said sorry at the same time and Rhett looked down into the light blue eyes of Michele. They both stood staring at each other; the mutual attraction and their heightened emotions as they remembered the last time that they had seen each other by the wreck of Dan's body, were almost tangible. The cleaner disappeared around the corner taking a mobile phone out of his pocket and leaving Rhett and Michele alone in the corridor. Suddenly, Michele grabbed Rhett's hand and pulled him into the ladies' rest room.

The smell of sweet disinfectant and vanilla hand lotion filled Rhett's nose as she grabbed his hair and pulled his head down to kiss her. He pushed her back against the door as their mouths met with anger and passion; their hands ran over each other's bodies frantic in their desire to touch one another. Rhett's hand grabbed at her breast and roughly massaged the full softness as she reached for his belt.

14

Wednesday, July 6th, 2005
Paradise Hotel, Baghdad

Tariq received the call from the cleaner, moved to the edge of the roof and looked up and down the street. He dialled the number on his phone for Rahil and said, 'Go.'

Rahil closed his phone and climbed into the truck that had been left outside his house with the keys in the ignition. He turned the key with shaking hands and the engine stuttered and then fired into life. He drove at a steady speed down the main road and turned into a smaller street and headed for the Paradise Hotel. Sweat beaded his face and ran down his cheeks into his beard as he adjusted the white cap on his bald head and slowed to allow two women crossing the road in full burkas, oblivious to the traffic, to walk in front of his vehicle. He could see the hotel up ahead on the right-hand side. There were people walking along the pavements on either side of the road and he saw a man coming out of a bookshop opposite the hotel carrying a plastic bag full of books. He drove forwards, reached the bollards, and turned off the engine. Looking out, he saw the tall, thin doorman step out of the hotel and walk towards him waving his arms. Rahil opened the door of the truck, jumped out and began running away up the street. It took Sam and passers-by seconds to realise what was happening when they saw the man running away from his truck. Sam turned and ran back towards the hotel, people in the street began racing for cover or ducking into buildings and shops.

Farouq sat in his ambulance parked out of sight further up the road and took out his ringing mobile phone.

'Now!' said the voice of Tariq.
Farouq nodded at the man in the passenger seat of the ambulance, and he pressed a button on the phone in his hand.

The truck exploded in the street with a huge boom, it burst into flames and jumped into the air as the doors and the bonnet flew in all directions. A car on the opposite side of the road caught fire and slew sideways, its windows shattering. The roar of the detonation was followed by a searing whoosh of air and people given a chance to get away but still too close were blown over. Limbs were ripped off and strewn randomly across the tarmac, the front of the Hotel Paradise shook and crumbled, glass in the windows of the bar and the restaurant on the other side fragmented into tiny pieces of flying weapons. A pile of books flew up into the air, tore apart at the seams and scattered pages fluttered across the hot sky. Sam, who had made it back inside screaming, 'Get down!' was thrown forward, his gangly body pierced with shards of glass and battered by lumps of concrete. Everyone in the bar dived to the floor with their hands covering their heads as glass ripped at their fingers; plaster fell from the ceiling and the air filled with choking dust. Malcolm and Gordon scrambled under their table covering their faces and were far enough away from the windows to avoid the full onslaught of flying glass. An eerie hush settled on the room swirling with dust and then, before anyone dared move, they heard a siren. Two paramedics rushed into the bar area with scarves wrapped around their mouths and noses and headed for Malcolm. They dragged him out from under the table.

'I'm okay, I'm fine. Look after the others,' he said, completely confused and checking his hands for blood. A gas mask was shoved onto his face, and he vaguely heard Gordon shouting, 'Oy! What are you doing?' before he blacked out.

***

Countdown

Rhett and Michele heard a tremendous noise like a cracking clap of thunder overhead and the sway of the building knocked them both sideways. The room rocked and shook as a section of the ceiling cracked and crumbled down on them; Rhett's head caught the side of a cubicle as he went down, and a small trickle of blood ran down his cheek. They both lay still, dazed for a couple of minutes before warily standing up and looking at each other in shock as the sound of a siren and people yelling and screaming reached their ears. Rhett asked Michele if she was all right and she nodded, brushing white powder from her hair and clothes, and pulling herself up from the floor. Then they both turned and ran out of the toilet.

Dust and smoke filled the lobby and people were stumbling about like ghosts with ashen faces and powdery white hair. Rhett glimpsed two men carrying a body on a stretcher out of what was left of the main entrance and Michele stopped to help Sam lying prostrate on the lobby floor with blood all over him as Rhett ran on into the bar area looking for his clients. The bar was filled with smoke, fragments from the shattered window were strewn about the room and Rhett could make out a number of patrons crouched on the floor under tables; the explosion had not been huge, and the experienced journalists were more worried about a second explosion or an attack than any injuries they had sustained. He saw Gordon scrabbling on the floor looking for his glasses, which were right next to him. Rhett got to him, helped him up onto a chair and handed him his glasses.

'Are you alright? Where's Malcolm?'
Gordon reached for his glass of beer, which miraculously still stood on the tabletop and began picking out bits of plaster before taking a huge gulp.

'I don't know. He must have been hurt. I don't know how, the blast seemed to be on the other side. The noise made us dive under the table, the window shattered, and bits of ceiling fell on the floor and tables. These ambulance men ran in, put Malcolm on a stretcher, put an oxygen mask over his face; I asked them where they were taking him, what was wrong with him, but one of them shoved me out of the way and I lost my glasses,' he garbled, trying to think straight, and shaking violently.

'Wait here,' ordered Rhett as he ran to the entrance and out onto the street where the wreck of the truck stood crumpled and burning in the fading light of day; its front end was smashed up against a bollard and the distinctive smell of cordite hung in the atmosphere. A car parked on the other side of the road was sideways up onto the pavement; glass was everywhere from the shops across the street and from cars parked on the road nearby. A group of women were wailing as they gathered around the body of a woman and gently pulled her dress down to cover her one remaining leg. A man whose trousers had been ripped away from his body had blood over his hands and exposed legs and was being helped by two men wearing old suit trousers and cotton shirts. A lone shoe rested in the middle of the road and an open book lay on the tarmac as if someone had just placed it down to pause in their reading. Loose pages fluttered in the air and floated along the street in the slight breeze. He saw the lights flashing on an ambulance tearing away down the street to the left on Al Senaha Street as more ambulances were only just starting to arrive from the right.

Taking in the truck and the minimal damage to the hotel frontage, Rhett called Karim, 'Where are you? You both okay?'

'Here. We are here. Across the road.'

He looked over and saw Abdullah and Karim running towards him.

Rhett raced across to meet them and asked them where the car was. Karim had parked further up the street outside a small café where they had grabbed some food while they waited for Rhett.

'Let's go!' yelled Rhett and the three of them raced down the road and jumped into the car.

'That ambulance, we need to catch that ambulance,' screamed Rhett.

The ambulance veered off to the right into a smaller street as Karim began to chase it. The traffic was lighter, and Karim sped down the straight road following the flashing lights on the ambulance as cars veered and stopped to allow it to pass. Karim slammed on his brakes as a moped pulled out in front of him; he swerved around it, just missing the back wheel and left the shocked rider waving his arms at them. The ambulance headed for the junction but didn't stop as it shot straight across 62 Street with cars screeching to avoid it and horns blaring. Karim followed catching the front of a battered truck and spinning off course before he regained control, righted the wheel, and followed the ambulance once more; just seeing it turn left on 52 Street. Heading for Tahariyat Square in the inside lane, Karim followed; the traffic was heavier and slowing as it approached the roundabout. The ambulance suddenly cut across the lanes and dived off at the first exit onto Karada. Karim was blocked but managed to manoeuvre through the traffic and follow. Up ahead they saw the ambulance reach Aqba bin Nafi and take a sharp left onto Rashid St.; Karim followed as they realised it was heading for the Dora expressway crossing the Tigris.

The traffic on the highway was heavy and the ambulance sped ahead as vehicles moved out of its way and then moved back to block the road. Below them, the water of the Tigris glittered in the orange light of the huge sun resting on the horizon. The ambulance was getting further away from them, and they just glimpsed it take the first exit after the bridge; it was no longer flashing its lights and by the time they came off the slip road it was nowhere to be seen amidst the stream of lorries and cars in the dimming light.

'Damn it!' said Rhett and told Karim to pull off the main road into a smaller street in the industrial area.

15

Wednesday, July 6th, 2005, Baghdad

Malcolm came round but kept his eyes closed; his head thumped with pain, and he tried to work out where he was. He could hear the men who had taken him talking in Arabic and feel the vehicle jolt over uneven surfaces in the road; his bed slid slightly to right and left when they swerved around corners as they moved at great speed. When they slowed at all, he could hear the noise of traffic all around them in between the loud blaring of the siren. He opened his eyes to a slit and saw that straps over his stomach and thighs were holding him down. The two men who had taken him sat on the other side of the van talking and not looking at him; they looked barely older than his own teenage sons. He felt confused and tried to remember what had happened at the hotel; he had not been injured but the ambulance men had taken him. With a creeping sense of dismay, the fog in his brain cleared and the realization that he had been kidnapped dawned on him with a sharp jab of fear; his heart beat at a terrifying rate and he struggled to control his breathing. He desperately tried to remember the instructions Rhett had given him for this scenario, never believing it would really happen. He knew he had to stay calm, but he could feel panic rising inside him, squeezing the air out of his chest and clutching at his throat.

Countdown

With a brief sense of relief, he remembered that Rhett had put a tracker on his phone, but this was immediately replaced with a sense of horror when he remembered that he had turned it off in the bar. Slowly he slid his hand inside his linen jacket, found the pocket next to the side seam and with immense relief he felt the slender bulk of his phone and gently pulled it up. They hadn't found it. He pressed the on button and slid it back into the pocket keeping his eyes surreptitiously on the men. Everything inside his body was screaming at him to cry out, to leap up and run; he breathed deeply and slowly through his nose and clenched his fists. *'Stay calm, stay alive,'* he repeated over and over in his head like a mantra. Rhett would find him. He tried to claw back the instructions Rhett had given him; he had to stay alert, take in as much as possible about his surroundings and be ready to take any potential opportunity for escape. The longer he was held captive, the more chance there was of him being passed further up a chain and the more time that elapsed after capture, the more difficult it became to escape or, be rescued. The sense of dread remained but he managed to subdue the panic as the vehicle sped, swerved, slowed, and sped up again.

16

Wednesday, July 6th, 2005
Outskirts of Baghdad

Rhett's mobile rang with an unknown number showing and he answered cautiously. It was Michele.

'We need to talk,' she said.

'I don't think now is a good time,' began Rhett, thinking what the hell was she doing, but she interrupted.

'I'm with your client, Gordon. We have tracked Malcolm's phone, we know where he is,' she said. 'He is between Mahmudiya and Latifyah heading west,' she added. 'We are coming to join you now.'

'No!' said Rhett. 'My guys will have Malcolm tracked. I can't risk another client getting caught up in this.'

'He's safer with us and we can use his telecommunication skills. We are already on our way; we've got you tracked as well,' she stated, and hung up.

Rhett frowned. He knew the area around the west of Latifyah and Mahmudiyah; it had become known as the Triangle of Death due to the number of suicide attacks and kidnappings. He called Marcus and explained the situation; he gave him their location and told him to arm up and bring the team with him.

When Michele and Gordon arrived in a jeep, Marcus, Steve, Glen and Rynold were already there with enough weapons and equipment for a small army. The sun had gone down, and the sky was black and still above them. Gordon and Michele were using a satellite-linked laptop and they discovered that Malcolm's phone had stopped moving and was located in a building surrounded by farmland. Suddenly, the red marker on the screen disappeared.

'We have already called it in to our guys,' said Michele and they are looking into air and ground support.'

'We haven't got time,' said Rhett. They'll find his phone and will know that we'll be after them. They could move him or already be planning to sell him to another group. We go in now.'

He turned back to his guys, but Michele pulled him back by his arm and said, 'Listen to me!' in a low, harsh voice.

Rhett glared at her, but he stepped away with her to move out of earshot of the others.

'I am not here to try to recruit you, Rhett. We have been following you.'

He stared at her in confusion; her eyes, intense and beautiful in the ambient light from the city, stared back at him with determination. He felt the frisson of attraction mixed with anger,

'What the hell does that mean? Why?'

'We have been intercepting calls between Iraq and London for the last year, a suspected terrorist group communicating with a cell, and they keep referring to particular names, Rhett Butler, Scarlett O'Hara and the Bull. These names were often linked with the mention of another name, Ali. We presumed that this meant activity planned in Birmingham city centre but managed to trace a few of the calls to Ealing in London. Other than that, MI5 haven't been able to link it directly to any individuals. They are a sophisticated, well-organised group and are very clever with their use of phones. Our guys discovered that a young man named Ali al Siddiq was murdered in the area not far from the home of a man called Hugh Wormsley. Hugh Wormsley is suspected of being involved in a number of dodgy arms deals but he has connections in high places and is extremely careful not to get his own hands dirty, so we have never been able to pin anything on him. We found out that someone called Rhett Millard was working for him at the time that Ali was murdered and began to make connections. We investigated you and, at first, when we found out that you had turned down working for MI6 and then moved to Iraq, we suspected that you were involved with the group and that you were doing deals for Wormsley. About the same time as the calls started, you took on an ex-army colonel named Walid al Siddiq, who you call The General, and he is the brother of Farouq al Siddiq. Whatever the group is planning it has been a long time in the works. We believe that the attack on your villa was orchestrated by Farouq and Walid who then used the money you gave them for their terrorist activities. We know now that you are not involved, but this group obviously believe that you killed Ali and they are out for revenge.' She paused and looked him in the eye, 'Did you kill Ali al Siddiq?'

'No,' said Rhett bluntly. He ran his hand through his hair and stared into the distance, his head spinning. The towers of the oil refinery stood as tall, black outlines against the clear night sky.

'The thing is,' continued Michele, 'We then found out that Ali was working for MI5. He was trying to get evidence that Wormsley was dealing in illegal weapons sales.'

Rhett looked at her in total shock, but Michele continued, 'But, we don't think that this was why he was killed. He wasn't beaten or tortured before he died so we are sure that the group that he was working for didn't have anything to do with it. He was fatally stabbed, and his body dumped by some bins, but MI5 took his body in for an autopsy and found traces of chloroform. They think it was Wormsley, but they don't know why; they told the family that he was mugged and died from his stab wounds. He, along with his mother and two sisters, was allowed into the country in the early nineties; their lives were in danger in their homeland, Iraq; their father was imprisoned by Saddam, and later killed. Ali was ten at the time; he grew up in London and he was studying to be an engineer. His mother and sisters, along with Ali were grateful to Britain for giving them a new life; like many Iraqis they were overjoyed when Saddam was overthrown, and they have worked hard to make their own way there. Ali's death was devastating for them.'

Countdown

'What a mess,' said Rhett and told her what had happened. He ran his hands over his face and walked away from her. Things started linking together in his head. An image of Sid's cheeky, grinning face flashed across his mind but was immediately replaced by his deer brown eyes terrified and pleading. Sid – Siddiq, of course! A knot of pain formed in his gut and twisted and suddenly, he understood his nightmares. He hadn't killed him directly, and although he'd blocked it out and moved on, the guilt had gnawed at his insides. He thought about Walid and felt a great sadness; he liked and trusted the man and he didn't want to believe that he had been set up and used by him. Farouq – ambulance driver, oh God! Tariq – watching the hotel and Farouq covering for him. They hadn't tried to kill him, yet; they were using him and their knowledge of his movements to make a bigger statement with the kidnapping and possibly the murder of Malcolm. They were punishing him by killing his client.

'Bastards!' he muttered. He turned and walked back to the team. 'We are going in to get Malcolm now. If this is where the group is based, you can blast the place to the high skies after we're out, but it doesn't make sense that this is all they have planned. What about the weapons they have been buying from Wormsley? You don't need much to kill a man in front of a video camera and there are plenty of cheap weapons available in the market here. I gave them money, but nothing substantial enough to worry about.'

'If we can wipe them out, it won't matter what else they have planned,' said Michele.

17

Wednesday, July 6th, 2005, Farmhouse near Latifiyah, Baghdad

MALCOLM

Malcolm kept his eyes closed. He was aware of the siren stopping, the vehicle was still moving but at a much slower rate. His body jarred as they went over bumps and tipped into potholes on what he presumed was more of a track than a road. He could no longer hear any noises from outside the car and knew that they were taking him away from the city. Were they taking him out into the desert to kill him? He reasoned that they would need to show proof of life if they were going to ask for a ransom. He forced himself to keep breathing slowly and deeply and not to think about what they had planned; he was sure that Rhett would have tried to track his phone. He and Gordon had often talked about what to do if anything happened to either of them; speculating and planning over a few beers based on other kidnappings that had taken place. The reality was not so easy to deal with.

    The ambulance came to a halt and keeping his eyes closed, he heard the two men climb out of the back and begin talking to someone. He moved his hand slowly to his phone and switched it off. If they found it, he didn't want them to think that he had been tracked and immediately destroy the phone and move him

Countdown

to another place. He hoped that they weren't just stopping for petrol.

The talking stopped and he heard someone getting back into the van. The straps over his body were released and suddenly he was jerked up to sitting and saw a man with a mask covering his face standing over him. He looked out of the back of the vehicle and in light coming from an old, flat roofed building behind them, he saw two more masked men holding automatic rifles standing in a sandy yard before a hood was shoved over his head. It felt woollen and scratchy, and he let out a muffled groan as his breathing became restricted; he concentrated hard on not sneezing. Through the woven material he could only make out shapes around him. The straps across his legs were undone and he was told to stand up and, shaking, he managed to swivel his body and put his feet down on the floor. With the man holding his arm, he edged forward and felt the slope of a ramp under his feet. He shuffled down and once he was on flat ground, he saw the outline of another man step forward and handcuff his wrists together at the front of his body.

He was led forward, and he could just make out a low building. He felt the surface underfoot change from gravelly to firm and was led down a dark corridor into a room with bright lights where he could make out blurry forms moving about around him and hear voices murmuring in Arabic. He was turned and dragged across the room, and he lost his bearings as he was led into darkness once more and led forward, turned around and led forward before turning again; he began to feel sick and disorientated. He was pushed forward again by what felt like the butt of a gun and tried to keep his balance as he moved blindly forward. He heard a door open, low light emerged and then he was nudged to turn left towards the entrance. He stumbled, but a hand caught his arm and led him across what he presumed was a room. He was told to turn around and sit down so he quietly obeyed and as he bent down, he realised that he was next to a wall. He slumped down with his knees bent and leant his head back against the cold, hard surface, straining to see who was in the room with him.

Countdown

Someone bent over him, fastened a shackle to his ankles and linked a chain to his wrists so that he couldn't move his hands upwards without being a contortionist; his wife was always nagging him to take up yoga. The thought of his wife and sons brought the reality of his situation home to him and his stomach clenched in terror.

'Come on Rhett,' he whispered. 'I know you can get me out of here.'

He could just make out a man standing a few feet away from him holding a large gun of some kind across his body.

'Excuse me,' Malcolm said politely. '*Salaam allay kum*,' he continued with terrible pronunciation.

'Wa alaykum salaam' replied the young sounding voice automatically.

'Do you speak English? I'm afraid that's about all of my Arabic.'

'Yes, I speak English,'

'I wonder if I could go to the bathroom,' said Malcolm.

The man moved to the door and opened it. Malcolm heard him calling down the passageway and a harsh voice answered. He came back into the room and moved towards Malcolm. Malcolm held his breath and shrank back against the wall, then the man bent down and undid the chain from his wrist to his ankles and released his legs before hauling Malcolm up. He dragged him across the room and out into the corridor. A door opposite was opened and the man turned the light on, undid Malcolm's handcuffs, turned him to face into the toilet and then stood behind him and pushed him inside leaving the door slightly ajar.

Malcolm stumbled forward, his hands automatically reached out and found the edge of a sink which he held onto until he regained his balance. He couldn't make out a toilet ahead of him, but he could smell it; the fetid fumes of stale urine and raw sewage hit his nostrils and seemed to gather at the back of his throat. He looked back; he could make out the thin man through the crack in the door and wondered if he had his back to him. He turned away from the man, reached slowly up to the hood and

Countdown

pushed it upwards taking in big gulps of the stinking air that relieved his claustrophobia but made him retch. He pulled the woollen cover up further to see a hole in the floor with yellowing brown footrests on either side and numerous mosquitoes hovering around the opening. There was a small window up to the right of the cistern, but he realised with dismay that even if he could squeeze his bulky body through it, his days of sprinting down the rugby pitch outrunning the pack were long over. He scrabbled with his trousers and squatted over the outlet to empty his bowels while desperately maintaining his balance in order to avoid touching the dubiously stained walls.

A scruffy, plastic bucket to the side was half full of brown looking water which he used to clean himself. He stood up again, sorted himself out, flushed the toilet by tugging on a rope attached to the cistern on the wall and rinsed his hands under a small trickle of water from the tap in the sink. He managed to quickly splash some water onto his face and inhaled deeply not caring about the germs he might be ingesting before pulling the hood back down and facing the door with another prayer for Rhett to save him.

The man at the door turned, put on the handcuffs again, took hold of Malcolm's arm and led him back into the room opposite.

'Thank you,' said Malcolm.

The man told him to sit back down against the wall, but he didn't chain him up to his ankles again. He had quite rightly guessed that Malcolm was not going to try any heroics with a man holding an automatic rifle.

Malcolm pulled his knees up to his chest and huddled against the wall. Time went by and then he heard the smack of soft-soled shoes on the tiled floors and loud voices coming down the hallway. The voices were talking in Arabic and then he heard English words spoken in an American accent, shrill and terrified.

'Where are you taking me? Let me go!'

The door into Malcolm's room opened with a crash and there was a commotion in the corridor, then a voice said something in Arabic and the door closed again. Malcolm heard the American accent again, shouting a muffled, 'Let me go!' He heard a thud, followed by a scream of pain; another door banged and then there was silence again.

'We do not need stupid, noisy man in here, eh?' said Malcolm's guard, laughing and lighting a cigarette.

'Malcolm, please call me Malcolm,' said Malcolm. Sweat poured down his face and the material itched and scratched his damp skin.

He lost all sense of time as he was left in the semi darkness of the room, even the slender shape of the guard seemed to blur until he wasn't sure if it were a figment of his imagination; his eyes strained to make out what he could of his surroundings but there was not enough light. The door opened and a dark shape approached him and his whole body trembled as he felt a hand on his arm. Then his fingers were opened, and a plastic bottle was placed in his hands.

'Water,' said a man's voice; the man moved away, and he heard the door close.

Malcolm lifted the hood to just above his nose; there was no way he was going to take a look at the guard. Tentatively he brought the bottle up to his mouth to find the top had been removed and tilted the bottle until a tiny drop fell on his lips and he licked what tasted like water.

'We aren't going to poison you.'

Malcolm shuddered at the thought of what they might be planning to do to him and whatever might be in the bottle, his thirst got the better of him. He gratefully gulped down the tepid water and it tasted like sweet nectar to his parched throat.

He heard strange bangs and knocks and thought he heard muffled screams, but he couldn't be sure. His whole body was tense and his mind whirled. He was still here, still alive. Had they already sent out messages of his kidnapping? Would his wife and sons know? He thought of Pauline, his wife for twenty years; they had been childhood sweethearts and he couldn't remember a time when he hadn't loved her and had her by his side. Did she know how much he loved her? And their sons, Frank and Simon in the middle of their A levels; it was a crucial

Countdown

point in their lives, and this would devastate them. Did they know how proud he was of them? He regretted all the times he had argued with his wife, all the times he had been strict or bad-tempered with the boys. He thought about his parents, his brothers, his friends, the time that he spent travelling and away from home, the mistakes he had made, and tears trickled down his cheeks. He wasn't ready to die. Suddenly, the door to his room opened and he heard a voice say, 'Yalla! Let's go!'

He had never felt such intense fear; his chest ached, and his throat constricted. Footsteps hurried along the corridor outside his room and his guard moved towards him. Malcolm gulped, he found it difficult to breathe and his body trembled uncontrollably. The guard leant down and undid the handcuffs, then he took one of Malcolm's hands and pulled his arm out straight in front of his body with the palm flat and facing upwards. Malcolm felt him place something cold, hard and weighty on the centre of his palm. He was sure it must be a grenade or bomb of some kind; he daren't move his fingers round to feel the object, he daren't move a muscle. The guard stood up and said, 'Goodbye, Malcolm. Thank you for fixing us communication systems.'

Malcolm watched the blurry image of the man leave the room and then the dim light went out and he was left in pitch black. He sat frozen, his hand outstretched, not daring to move. The weight of whatever it was seemed to increase as the time went by; he carefully, very, very slowly drew his hand back so that it was resting on his knee. His heart galloped, his mouth felt as though it was filled with sawdust, and he tried to concentrate on breathing slowly. Time seemed to stand still as he waited for the explosion, for certain death.

18

Wednesday, July 6th, 2005
Outskirts of Baghdad

Rhett and the team looked on a satellite map of the area and found a route that meant that they could drive to within five kilometres of the farmhouse to a place where they could covertly create a base.

'We can't drive any closer without attracting attention and there could be militia out looking for us who would be only too happy to take on a group of westerners, and alert the kidnappers to our presence,' said Rhett.

They all agreed on the plan and Rhett and his team armed themselves up. Marcus reached into a holdall and threw a pair of night vision goggles over to Rhett. He caught them neatly and said, 'Where the hell did you get these?'

'Everything is available in the market here. Nizam picked them up a couple of months ago when I sent him to get supplies. I gave him a right bollocking at the time.'

They each got a pair of the goggles and Rhett told Karim to stay with his vehicle and wait for instructions. He, Gordon and Abdullah got into Michele's jeep while Marcus, Rynold, Steve and Glen got back in their Nissan Patrol. They set off along the tracks and small roads that they had marked out on the map and eventually stopped on a deserted lane that ran through an apple orchard. The shell of an old villa stood back from the road, and they parked the vehicles out of sight in the trees. Gordon and Michele set up with the laptop and radio transmitter in the crumbling ruins while Rhett outlined the route and plan of action when he reached the farmhouse with Marcus, Steve, Rynold and Glen. They had canals and irrigation ditches to cross on route and they worked out roughly when they would be in position. From the blurry satellite picture of the farmhouse, Michele could monitor the movements around the building and reported that the ambulance had gone. There were two smaller outbuildings with a small group of palm trees clustered between them. Gordon handed each of them a small, plastic object which they all looked at carefully.

'What the *fok* is this?' asked Rynold picking up the tiny bud in the palm of his hand.

'It is a wireless earpiece with microphone,' explained Gordon. 'State of the art, no wires required.' He then took five, more recognizable earpieces with wires attached and handed them out.

The five big men looked down at the skinny Gordon and frowned. He pushed his glasses back up his nose and gave a nervous cough before speaking.

'So, Malcolm and I spent a lot of time discussing various scenarios.' He glanced at all of them to see looks of scepticism on their faces and continued quickly, 'Don't look at me like that, I'm not a bloody moron. We have no real understanding of military or secret service activities, but in our spare time we devised some things between us in case of any unfortunate circumstances. The small bud is the prototype for something I have been working on in research and development. As you can see, one of the pieces has the usual coiled wire which runs down the side of your neck, but the other does not. We thought that in a certain situation where, say you were captured, it is likely that your captors would look for an earpiece and remove it. If you had one obvious one and another very discreet piece in the other ear, they would remove the first one and be unlikely to look too closely for another one.'

He saw them all thinking this over and continued, 'Of course, it is unlikely in today's scenario that you will be captured but,

Countdown

well, um better safe than sorry as they say. Unfortunately, Malcolm and I hadn't foreseen him getting taken today.'

'Bloody right, we are not going to get captured!' said Glen.

'So, we can speak to you using one or both of these,' said Steve.

'That's right,' agreed Gordon. 'And to each other.'

'We are not going to be captured!' exclaimed Rynold.

'We'll use them,' said Rhett. 'It avoids any of the crackle that you get using our radios when we are close.'

'It also means that we can easily talk to you if we need to let you know about anything that we see on the satellite picture,' said Michele, and Gordon agreed with her.

'Prototype?' asked Marcus. 'How do you know if it works? Don't tell me, you have tested it on animals.'

Glen let out his high-pitched laugh and Steve dug him in the ribs.

'Um, well, we have done extensive testing, but not in the field, as yet,' admitted Gordon.

'We'll take them. If they work, they work. If they don't then we're no worse off,' said Rhett.

The rest of his team shrugged and put the earpieces into their ears.

'Can we still hear what's going on around us?' asked Glen.
Steve mouthed, 'You are an idiot,' at him without making a sound and Glen said, 'I can't hear you,' and took the ear bud out.

Everyone laughed and, realising what had happened, Glen laughed too and mock punched Steve.

'We are wasting time,' said Rhett. 'Let's go. Abdullah, you keep guard up here with Michele and Gordon.'

They knew where Malcolm was for now but that could easily change.

Countdown

19

Wednesday, July 6th, 2005
Hereford 5.00pm // Baghdad 7.00pm

Lorraine pulled a pair of black leggings up her long, fit legs and over the ever-increasing bump, which she called Pom. She threw on a floaty cotton top, slipped her feet into her trainers and lifted one foot after the other onto the edge of the bed to tie the laces. She brushed her hair and put on a little make-up. Her skin was glowing and despite not having her usual flat stomach, she felt beautiful and healthy.

Her eyes fell on a box in the corner of the room containing photos and other memories of Rhett which she couldn't bring herself to throw out. She took out a framed photograph; it was an unposed, natural shot that her father had taken of her with Rhett at the beach in Weston-super-Mare. The picture captured them both laughing as Rhett held her in his arms about to throw her into the sea. Holding up the framed picture, she looked at Rhett's laughing face; he had been so carefree and happy that day. She stroked his face with her finger and felt the usual surge of sadness and a hollow pain. God, she missed him. She knew she had to tell him, but she had brought his number up on her phone so many times and then not pressed call afraid of disturbing him in the middle of something dangerous. It wasn't fair to distract him; she had to wait until – until when? If he

Countdown

were still on the same rotation, she worked out that he would be back around August.

She had no idea that at that moment in time Rhett was in the outskirts of Baghdad in pursuit of his client's kidnappers.

'That's your daddy, Pom,' she said running an affectionate hand over her stomach. 'I hope you'll get to meet him.' She jumped when her phone rang, and she put the photo down on her dressing table before answering the call.

'Hi Mum. I'm just going out,' she said.

She walked out into the hallway listening to her mum chatter away and ask her how she was and where she was going.

'Yes, I'm feeling wonderful, thanks. Pom is growing fast,' she said. 'I'm going over to my friend Sal's house for dinner with her family. She lives in some out of the way place near the dog kennels in Brampton Abbotts; I'd better go as I'm not sure I know the way. I may just have to listen out for dogs barking!' She laughed and said, 'I'll call you later.'

'Have a lovely time, dear. Speak later. Love you,' said her mum.

'Love you too. Bye, bye,' Lorraine put the phone in her bag, picked up her keys and left the house. 'Let's go and meet your Aunt Sal and her family,' she said, patting her tummy.

Salma had invited her over for dinner to meet her mother and sister. It was the first time that she had been to her house; they always met in town to go to the cinema or the theatre, sometimes just for a coffee or a bite to eat.

Lorraine drove slowly down a long, quiet country road and arrived a few minutes earlier than planned outside the address to which Salma had given her directions. It was quite a big, old house set back from the road with a driveway leading to a small garage and a scruffy front lawn. She checked her phone to see that she had got the right house number and decided to park in the road in case she ended up blocking the driveway. The house looked shabby and neglected from the outside with cracked and peeling paint on the window frames and the front door. Heavy looking brown curtains were drawn in all the windows despite it being an early evening in July with the sun still shining brightly.

Countdown

Putting her car keys into her small bag and hanging it over her shoulder, she walked up to the front door and pressed the bell. She couldn't hear a ring inside and after waiting a few moments she knocked on the letter box and waited. In the distance, the forlorn sound of dogs barking broke the peace of the countryside.

Lorraine heard murmured voices and people moving about inside and then the door opened and Salma stood there smiling.

'Hi! You are early,' said Salma, sounding flustered and a bit annoyed.

'Oh, sorry,' said Lorraine, taken aback by the sharpness in Salma's voice. 'I found it quicker than I expected.'

'Don't worry, don't worry!' said Salma resuming her normal easy going self. 'Glad you found it okay. Come on in.'

Lorraine stepped into a dim hallway and although it looked a bit dusty and dirty there was an underlying smell of bleach. Salma led her down the hall past two closed doors and into a large kitchen. This room was light and airy with sunlight pouring in through an open window at the far end. Two women, one who looked to be a few years older than Salma wearing jeans and a T-shirt, and an older lady in a long dress with a print in different shades of green with a hijab covering her hair, were busy at the oven and sideboard. They turned and smiled when Salma and Lorraine entered.

'Welcome!' exclaimed the older lady in Arabic, 'We have heard so much about you,'

'Speak in English, Mama,' said Salma.

Lorraine laughed and said, 'I'm sorry, my Arabic is not very good. It's lovely to meet you.'

Salma introduced the women as her mother, Reem and her sister, Sawsan and invited Lorraine to sit at the large wooden table in the centre of the kitchen. Lorraine took in the appearance of the other two women. Sawsan had long, flowing dark hair and an attractive, lightly tanned face; both she and Salma were beautiful. Reem was tall, slim and serious looking; she could see the resemblance to Salma, but there was a weariness about her skin and a bitter downturn of the mouth.

Lorraine was sure that Salma had described her mother as a happy, bubbly woman always pretending to watch her figure, but who enjoyed her cooking and eating too much.

She dismissed her thoughts and smiled at the women; she was so pleased to finally meet Salma's family who had been through so much. She moved across the room and looked out of the window at a large, unkempt garden; it was completely overgrown with long grass and bushes. A rickety fence went around the outside and one section was leaning precariously inwards with a hole in the rotten, broken slats. She guessed that Iraqis weren't into gardening.

'You've got loads of blackberry bushes!' she exclaimed, trying to find something positive to say. 'They'll be ripe in a couple of months. I'll come over and make you blackberry crumble if you like.' She turned back to the room, 'What a lovely, big house you have,' she said.

Sawsan and Salma exchanged glances.

'Yeah, it's great,' said Salma.

Sawsan invited her to sit down in a wooden armchair next to the table and gave her a cup of tea.

'Is it just the three of you living here?' asked Lorraine, in an attempt to make conversation more than being nosy and she was conscious of trying too hard; always a sign that she didn't feel comfortable.

'Our cousins are also here, you will meet them later,' said Reem. 'Now, how are you feeling? I hear congratulations are in order; it must be difficult for you without a husband, but it is not so unusual in this country.'

'Mama!' interrupted Salma.

'It's fine,' said Lorraine placing one hand gently on her stomach. 'Different cultures. It must have been so hard for you when you came over alone with your children.'

Reem sighed and said, 'Oh yes. It was hard but there were other Iraqis who helped us a lot. Our new family.'

'I would be a lot happier with a husband,' Lorraine said honestly. She smiled and took another long sip of tea. She watched the women busy preparing food and wanted to offer to help but the sun was shining on the back of her head, and she suddenly felt very warm and sleepy. 'Oh, I'm sorry. I feel so tired.'

'It's okay, you just sit there and relax,' she heard Salma say.

20

Wednesday, July 6th, 2005
Farmhouse, near Latifiyah, Baghdad

FAROUQ

The ambulance, with Malcolm in the back, arrived at the old farmhouse and Farouq gave the driver instructions to return to the hospital with the vehicle. He moved to the back doors and spoke Arabic in a low voice to the two men who had emerged.

'Cover his head and bring him into the house,' he ordered.

'Tariq, you will guard him. If he causes any trouble, knock him out.'

Farouq turned towards the flat roofed farmhouse with its stone walls and headed for the wooden door with fading blue paint and an ornate but rusting metal overlay. He left the door open and walked down the corridor into a large, well-lit sitting room where numerous men lounged about on shabby, sagging settees. A television was on in the corner. They jumped up as Farouq entered, gathered up their guns which were leaning against the walls or lying on the floor and tried to look efficient.

He greeted everyone with *'As salaam alaikum'* and they gave the customary reply, then he pointed at two of the young men wearing the uniform of ill-fitting jeans and football shirts with shemaghs wrapped around their necks and told them to take positions guarding the front and back of the building. The two men hurried outside.

At the far side of the room was a sturdy wooden table with two men working on computers and he walked over to them as Tariq and the other guard from the ambulance came in with Malcolm and he gestured angrily for them to take him out of the room.

'Where are they?' he asked the men at the computers. 'Did they track his phone?'

One of the men wearing round, black rimmed glasses on his prominent, hooked nose looked up at him and smiled, 'Yes. They tracked his phone and now we are tracking them. They have stopped in the industrial area where you lost them.'

'Good. They will be gathering forces and then coming here. Where is the girl, our little Scarlett O'Hara?'

'We have received the first video; it is now on a loop and ready to put onto the USB,' he said, indicating the laptop he was working on.

'Excellent,' said Farouq. 'Hereford is ready, and London is ready.' He turned to the remaining men in the room. 'Zayed, check the explosives.'

'I have already checked, sir,'

Farouq's eyes narrowed, 'Zayed, check the explosives,' he repeated with venom in his voice.

Zayed ran out of the room and Farouq turned to the remaining two, 'Let's keep our guest amused. Ahmed, you have a good American accent. I need you to pretend that you are a prisoner shouting and upset, and Malik you will make noises of beating and yelling at him to keep quiet as you move to the prisoner's room and then down the corridor to the end room. Do you understand?'

Ahmed and Malik looked at each other and grinned. They left the room and Ahmed began shouting in a New York accent which he had learned from the many American films he had watched and bounced noisily against the walls of the corridor. Malik followed telling him to keep quiet and insulting him in Arabic. They burst into the room where Malcolm was being held and then moved back out into the corridor. When they reached the end of the hall, they slipped a catch near the ceiling to open a hidden door into another room. With the door closed, Malik threw an old chair across the room and Ahmed cried out and screamed as if in pain.

In the dark cell, Malcolm's terror increased, and he determined that to stay quiet and acquiescent was his best chance of survival just as Rhett had advised him.

In the living room, Farouq inserted the memory stick into the side of the television and flicked through the options on the remote control until he matched the correct channel. A clear picture filled the screen and the voices of women talking in a mixture of Arabic and English spilled into the room.

'They are on the move,' said the large man with chubby fingers and a round face working on the other laptop. 'Two vehicles using the back roads and heading southwest.'

'They will come on foot for the last part, which gives us time to finish here,' said Farouq.

'They may have called in for air support.'

'Nothing will happen while we have the hostage here. They plan to rescue him themselves,' replied Farouq calmly. 'Let's pray and then we will eat before we leave. We have a long night ahead.'

21

Wednesday, July 6th, 2005
Farmland, near Latifyah, Baghdad

Rhett and his team spread out with a tactical distance between them and using the contours of the ground to stay as low as possible, they began to make their way across the terrain towards the farmhouse. The warm air, slightly moist due to the humidity coming from both the Tigris and the Euphrates as well as the numerous irrigation systems quickly created runnels of sweat that ran down their faces. They stayed low to avoid being silhouetted against the horizon, traversed fields of crops and dodged through orchards moving at a steady pace. Rhett felt strong and calm, all of his training kicked in and his mind became totally focused on their objective. They reached numerous canals and irrigation ditches with Michele guiding them remotely from the makeshift base. Giant reeds nearly as tall as them lined the waterways and they pushed their way through before wading across the channels until they reached a small palm grove just outside the farmhouse perimeter; their clothes were drenched but not one of them paid attention to any discomfort. The sliver of a waning moon provided little light on the ground and the flat-roofed one-storey buildings seemed silent and unoccupied from the front.

'Two guys outside,' came Michele's voice. 'One at the front and one at the back.'

'Roger that,' said Rhett.

Countdown

Rhett gathered the team around him to deliver their instructions. Steve and Glen were to take care of the guards outside and then keep watch and provide support weapons while Rhett, Marcus and Rynold went in.

They pulled on their night vision goggles and moved forward silently. They reached the edge of the grounds bordered only by a sparse hedge and a few trees as the grounds merged into the arable land around. Steve and Glen separated and headed for their targets crawling silently along the damp earth on their bellies.

Steve whispered, 'Target in sight and Glen responded, 'Roger.'

Almost simultaneously, they crept up behind their targets, one on either side of the main building and slit their throats with slick efficiency, holding the bodies as the life left them and lowering them silently to the ground. Both men then dragged the bodies into the surrounding field out of sight and crouched low, one on either side of the farmhouse with eyes on the front and back entrances. Rhett waited for Steve who was watching the front, to give him the all-clear before leading the way across the sandy ground to the side of the property. With Marcus and Rynold following, Rhett edged along the outer wall and glanced around the corner. Suddenly, Steve's voice whispered in his ear and at the same time he heard the door to the house open and he dodged back out of sight.

Rhett moved forward again and watched from the darkness as a young man with a full beard and black unkempt hair stepped into the yard and lit a cigarette. Malik walked forward from the farmhouse looking for his friend and was about to call out his name when Rhett silently approached him from behind with his knife held ready. With a violent thrust into the side of the neck and a decisive pull from left to right, Malik was dead before he could make a sound. Rhett pulled him back across the sandy ground and leant him sitting up against the farmhouse wall; Malik's head rolled forwards and blood soaked into the football shirt that he was wearing. Rhett signalled for Marcus and

Countdown

Rynold to get behind him. They removed their night vision goggles and stood ready.

Gently, Rhett pushed against the door, and it swung inwards. The hall was in darkness, but they could see light coming from a room straight ahead and heard indistinct voices. A passageway went off to the right of the door and Rhett indicated for Marcus and Rynold to follow him, covering each other as they moved towards the room in front of them.

Rhett checked the corridor to the right, stepped forward and shoved the door ahead open and moved into the room holding his weapon up and ready to fire as he dodged to his left; Rynold followed, moving to the right, while Marcus covered the door and hallway. Rhett and Rynold swung their weapons from left to right and scoured the room. There was nobody there. A television was on in the corner showing some kind of soap opera with the volume down low. They checked the whole room and called, 'Clear!' then they moved through another door into a small kitchen and found it empty. Marcus joined them in the kitchen looking at the remains of a recent meal scattered across a small table along with empty plastic water bottles.

Rhett indicated for Rynold to stay in the room and for Marcus to follow him. They stepped out into the corridor and heard a movement to the left. Rhett swivelled round to see a man coming towards them and fired. Ahmed screamed and fell to the floor before he could even get his finger to the trigger. Rhett swiftly reached Ahmed's prone body and fired another round into his forehead. They reached a door on the right and Rhett turned the handle slowly and then pushed it open with force before following inside with his weapon ready. The smell made him gag and his hand went up to cover his nose and mouth as he discovered a stinking bathroom with no occupants. He stepped back into the corridor and moved towards the door opposite which was open. He edged in and swung his weapon around the seemingly bare room and then a hoarse voice called out.

'British hostage!' Then more loudly, 'British hostage, Malcolm Johnston, please don't shoot!'

Countdown

Marcus flipped on the light switch and he and Rhett saw a man with his head covered by a hood crouched up against the wall with one hand flat on his knees. On the palm of his hand was an apple.

'I've got Malcolm,' Rhett said quietly and moved towards him. 'You're okay, mate. It's Rhett,'

He knelt beside him, took the apple off his hand and pulled the hood off his head. Malcolm looked up into Rhett's face, then he looked down, saw that Rhett was holding an apple, not a grenade, and passed out.

Once they had cleared the main building and checked the outhouses and found that there was nobody else there, Rhett told Michele to call off any air strike and to come to the farmhouse to collect them. Marcus and Rynold carried Malcolm into the lounge area and put him down in a chair, while Rhett got some water from the kitchen. Malcolm came round and took the glass from him, 'I'd prefer a beer,' he said with an attempt at a smile; his face was grey, and he looked ten years older. 'Where is the other guy?'

'What other guy?' asked Rhett.

'I heard them bring someone else in, they took him down the corridor past my room. An American, I think.'

'Look after him,' ordered Rhett as he went back down the corridor. When he reached the roughly plastered wall at the end, he banged on it. In the centre, he heard the hollow sound of a doorway. He felt around the edges and found the catch in the bricks at the top and the door in the wall opened into what appeared to a be small storage room with a rough, sandy floor, open brick walls and no windows. On the floor in the centre was an incongruous, well-worn rug, and a broken chair was lying on its side in the corner. He bent to move the rug and found that it was nailed down. Pulling it upwards, it rose along with the trap door to which it was fixed, and he looked at steps leading down into a tunnel below.

'Where the *fok* did they go?' Rhett heard Rynold saying as he went back into the lounge.

Countdown

'There's a tunnel out of the back room,' he told them. We'd better get outside. There could be booby-traps rigged up to timers,' said Rhett. Then his eyes fell on the television, which was still murmuring in the background. He stopped still and stared at the screen. There were three women moving around in a kitchen, one was talking in Arabic. As the women moved, they revealed another woman sitting on a chair facing the camera sipping tea. The scene played for a few seconds and then repeated on a loop. The other men saw Rhett staring at the screen and followed his eyes.

They heard cars pull up outside and Gordon, Abdullah and Michele ran into the house to find them all staring at the television. Michele stared at the screen, 'That is Ali's sister, Salma, and I think that the older woman is his mother, Reem. I can't see the other two clearly, but one must be his other sister, Sawsan.' Suddenly, she gasped as the fourth woman was revealed. She put her hand to her mouth looking at Rhett in horror, 'That's Lorraine.'

Rhett met her gaze and she saw the pain in his eyes as she whispered what he had already guessed, 'That's Scarlett O'Hara.'

Everyone stared at Rhett.

'Who are they?' asked Glen.

'I'm going after Farouq,' announced Rhett.

'We're coming with you,' said Marcus.

'No, it's me he wants. I am going alone; I've got coms, you can track me. Michele, find out where they have got Lorraine and get something sorted! Farouq will be expecting me to go after him. He wants me to suffer so I doubt that he'll shoot me straight away. You've got time to find out where they take me and maybe this time, we'll catch the whole lot of them and find out who they are linked with in the UK.'

22

Wednesday, July 6th, 2005
Brampton Abbots, Hereford, UK

Lorraine woke up in utter confusion to find herself sitting on an armless chair in the middle of an empty room; her mouth was gagged tightly with a scarf and her arms were stretched behind the back of the wooden chair and tied at the wrists. Her neck was stiff from hanging forward with her chin on her chest and as she lifted her head it was as though someone was swinging a sledgehammer in her brain; her vision was blurred, and she took a while to register where she was. The room was completely bare of furniture but as her eyes focussed and the throbbing ache abated, she could see the drawn curtains and recognised them as being the ones she had seen in the front window earlier. Sunlight edged through tiny gaps, but she didn't know how long she had been out of it. She was still in Salma's house but was it the same evening? Where was Salma? Who had done this and what had they done to Salma and her family? She fought to remember what had happened but there was nothing but a blank after sitting at the table and drinking a cup of tea. She felt completely disoriented, confused, and frightened; she struggled to free her hands and tried to call out.

Suddenly, the door opened behind her, and she looked over her shoulder to see two men come into the room. They had short, black hair and were wearing scarves around the lower part of their faces so that she could only see their dark, almost black eyes. They did not look at her. One was carrying a video camera attached to a tripod, and he set the tripod down a few feet in front of her, adjusted the camera to face her and looked through the eyepiece to check its position. The other man moved to stand directly behind her where she couldn't see him. She was gripped with terror and tried to speak, but all she could make were muffled grunts. Every nerve in her body buzzed and she tried again to tug her hands free; she desperately wanted to fold her arms protectively across her stomach, but she was forced to sit there with her swollen belly pushed forward, obvious, and vulnerable. The young man behind the camera lifted his head and stared at her. He was enjoying his position of power over her and felt the need to speak, to tell her something about this huge thing that he was a part of; he didn't know anything really, just what he'd been told, but he wanted her to know that he was part of something important. It didn't matter what he told her; she was going to die.

'We are sending a message to the West,' he began. 'What we have planned will make the Twin Towers fade into insignificance, the IRA attack on this site will seem like an indoor firework in comparison and there will be more bones than one little Roman girl to find.'

He faltered, not sure what else to say and saw that his partner, Aziz was waving the gun at him and looking angry. 'What are you doing? You haven't even got the camera on. Shut up and let's get on with it,' snarled Aziz.

Sultan felt good about what he had said, even if it hadn't been recorded and he moved back behind the camera feeling empowered.

Lorraine heard a strange click of metal behind her and then felt something hard press against the back of her skull. On the side of the camera a red light went on and she stared at the lens, her eyes wide and her body petrified with terror.

23

Wednesday, July 6th, 2005
Farmhouse, near Latifyah, Baghdad

'You are not going alone,' stated Marcus blocking the door out of the sitting room.

'Get out of my way!' shouted Rhett moving forwards with his gun aimed at Marcus; his golden eyes blazed with fury and helplessness.

Rynold, Steve and Glen grabbed him, pushed the gun down and held him still. Rhett relaxed and pulled away saying, 'Okay, okay,' with his hands in the air and paced around the room, rubbing his head with his hands, and causing the thick, black hair to stick up in tufts. He regained his composure and turned to them all, 'We can't bulldoze in anywhere; we have to find out who has got Lorraine, where they have got her, and then make sure she is safe. Farouq wants me, so I will have to let them take me. They know I will follow them down the tunnel, and they will be waiting for me.'

The others started to argue but he held up his hand.

'Michele, get a team to come in here to gather forensics and deal with the bodies. See what you and Gordon can get from the video.' He walked over to the television pulled out the memory stick and threw it to her. 'Glen and Steve, you go with Michele, Malcolm and Gordon back to the villa, you can track us, and Michele you can get MI5 on board with finding Lorraine. If I can talk to Farouq, we may get some clues. It seems he likes to

Countdown

play games and he seems extremely confident about whatever is planned. I don't believe that this is just about getting revenge on me, and we may be able to use that to our advantage.' He had switched into operational mode, burying his pain and fear. 'Glen and Steve get Walid and find out what he knows. If he has betrayed us, he is going to know about it. Marcus and Rynold you come with me, but you stay back when they try to take me. Got it?'

Everyone nodded in agreement and began making their way out of the farmhouse. Michele made a call and followed Steve and Malcolm to the jeep while Gordon went towards the Nissan Patrol with Glen. Rhett, Marcus and Rynold headed for the back room where the trap door stood open.

Rhett went down the steps first and looked down a long tunnel about eight feet high and three feet wide with electric bulbs lined along the roof and lighting the way ahead with a dim yellow glow. Marcus followed him and Rynold came behind but just as he stepped onto the final wooden stair, they all heard an ominous, recognisable whirr, followed by a steady clicking. Rhett shouted, 'Run!' and began racing down the high but narrow tunnel.

The underground passage turned sharply to the left and Rhett and Marcus dived to the ground around the corner as an explosion echoed above and behind them, shaking the walls of the tunnel and showering them with clumps of dried mud from the ceiling. Another explosion followed ripping the trap door off and sending a fireball into the opening of the passageway which roared and billowed into the tunnel. Rynold screamed and leapt around the corner landing on top of Marcus as the heat filled the corridor beside them and devoured the oxygen in its path. Lightbulbs exploded and the fire retreated like a ravenous monster to attack the wooden door and struts supporting the roof. The three men scrambled to their feet and ran as the tunnel behind them collapsed in a crashing and heaving of splitting wood and earth.

The subterranean path twisted and turned, and they slowed and came to a stop when they realised that they were safe.

'What's that smell?' asked Rynold.

A sulphurous odour filled the enclosed space and Marcus and Rhett looked at Rynold.

'It's you, mate,' said Marcus.

He turned Rynold round to reveal that the hair on the back of his head was a tight mass of frazzled, rust coloured fuzz. Rynold ran his hand through his hair and looked in horror as a mass of shrivelled, burnt strands came away in his fingers and fluttered onto his shoulders.

'You can get shampoo for that,' said Marcus.

'Jesus!' exclaimed Rynold. 'That was close.'

'Anybody on comms?' asked Rhett to see if he got a response through his earphones but there was nothing. He tried contacting Michele on his phone but there was unsurprisingly no signal.

'We'll just have to hope they pick us up when we get out of the tunnel,' he said. 'Let's keep going.'

None of them wanted to think about whether the others had been far enough away when the explosives detonated, or not.

***

Michele climbed into the passenger seat in mid conversation on her phone explaining the situation to her boss at MI6, Leyton Lewis. She finished the call and nodded at Steve who put the jeep in gear and began to drive out of the yard with Glen following in the Nissan. A flash of light was followed by a loud crack as the kitchen area of the house exploded. Michele instinctively ducked down and both Steve and Glen turned their vehicles away from the buildings and accelerated across the adjacent field as a second explosion, larger than the first, resounded with a deafening boom and great plumes of smoke and fire rushed upwards and outwards followed by a terrific blast of air which caught the backs of the retreating cars and threw them forward. Steve maintained control and carried on going, but Glen's vehicle hit a rut in the soil and the car somersaulted and smashed down on its roof. Steve stopped and he, Malcolm and Michele ran over to the other car to see Abdullah crawling out of the passenger door wiping away streams of red running down his cheeks with his scarf. The windows were covered in red that clung or slid down the glass and Michele shouted, 'Gordon! Steve!' as she crouched down and looked inside. Gordon hung from his seat belt his head dangling in space, covered in chunks of red. He opened his eyes, looked at Michele, and groaned, 'Get me out of here!'

Michele helped release Gordon and she and Abdullah pulled him out through the car window. On the other side, Steve had got Glen and they walked round the vehicle to look at Gordon sitting on the ground wiping his face with a handkerchief. Malcolm offered his handkerchief to Glen and said, 'I think you might need this.'

Glen, Gordon and Abdullah wiped the red gunk from burst watermelons off their faces and clothes as they all stood and watched the blazing farmhouse which cast an orange glow across their faces and the sky.

'Let's move out,' said Steve. The five of them piled into the jeep and headed back to join Karim. Michele and Malcolm got into Karim's car with Abdullah and both vehicles raced back to the company villa.

***

The air was thin, and the smell of wet earth filled Rhett's nostrils, but the tunnel was well built with sturdy wooden supports. Rhett worried that Farouq and his group had made chambers below the ground for their nefarious uses, but the slope of the floor changed to an incline, and they began moving steadily upwards. As they progressed, the tunnel got smaller, and they had to bend their backs and knees as they moved forward crouching. Rhett reached an opening and stepped into a small cell with a high ceiling; rungs going up the side of the wall led to a hole with a metal grating across the top through which he could glimpse the night sky.

He stepped into the space and Marcus and Rynold followed stretching out their bent, strained backs. Suddenly they all put a hand up to the side of their heads and smiled as they heard the familiar lilting Welsh voice of Glen calling in their ears. Rhett held up his hand for silence and pointed up at the open roof. He coughed gently, not willing to risk speaking without knowing who or what was waiting for him at the top. Glen understood that Rhett couldn't answer, 'Back at base. We've got you,' he said.

Rhett signalled for them to go back into the tunnel, and they crouched in a cramped semi-circle as Rhett told them the plan.

Rhett scaled the ladder running up the side of the wall and reached up to the metal slats above his head. The grating slid to one side easily and he kept his fingers wrapped around the metal as he climbed silently out into an olive grove and remained low. The ground was strewn with fallen fruit and the eerie, crooked branches of the ancient trees surrounded him. He heard a movement behind him and swung around throwing the grating in the direction of the noise. He heard a thud as the grating hit something solid, followed by a groan and the sound of a body dropping in the darkness, but more figures loomed into view. He moved quickly to his left into the trees and heard crunching steps behind him as he tried to increase his distance from the tunnel entrance. He dodged past a tree and a man stepped in front of him pointing a gun directly at his chest. He sprang forward kicking the gun out of his hands and then spun round and brought his elbow into his neck; the man fell sideways but two more men appeared. Rhett grabbed the closest round the neck, took control of his gun and aimed it at the second man; he forced the man's fingers to pull the trigger and let a round fire into the other man's guts.

Marcus heard the blast of gunfire and a cry of pain to the left as he lifted his head above the edge of the manhole and looked around into the darkness making out the shapes of the olive trees set evenly apart. The sound of heavy footsteps running across the ground was all to the left and he crawled out onto the ground to the right of the entrance followed by Rynold. They heard the rumble of an engine starting and suddenly lights flooded the wooded area over to the left of the wood as the headlights of two vehicles came on and the silhouettes of at least a dozen men moved forward and surrounded Rhett. With practised stealth Marcus and Rynold circled round to the back of the vehicles in darkness. There was a Land Cruiser and an open backed transport vehicle, and they waited for Rhett to begin fighting again before moving in and attaching trackers to both and then fading away to hide behind trees fifty metres away. They watched as Rhett threw one man over his head ducked down and then sprang up to clock another in the face and at the same time shoot his foot out to crunch another man's knee. Trusting that they wanted him alive at least for the time being, Rhett was determined to inflict as much damage as he could on his assailants and to make as much noise as possible to distract from Rynold and Marcus. Four men approached him, and he dealt with two; twisting the arm of one until it snapped and shoving him into the next man whose nose he smashed with a quick burst of power from his right arm, but a third grabbed him round the neck and he fell to his knees as something hard hit him between the shoulders and he felt the sharp point of a needle enter the side of his neck.

24

Wednesday, July 6th, 2005
Farouq's Villa compound, Baghdad

Rhett came round in a brightly lit room with TV screens set up on a desk and a video camera on a tripod facing him. He realised that he was wearing only his boxers and was tied by his ankles and wrists to a chair, which stood ominously on a large, plastic sheet. The windows were boarded up and the room smelled musty and damp but as he looked around, he had the impression that this was a once comfortable and loved office. The desk was solid and made from sturdy, polished mahogany with a matching, high backed chair behind it; as well as the computers there was an ornate desk lamp and office paraphernalia. On the wall behind the desk was a large picture of Farouq standing proudly in army uniform shaking hands with Saddam Hussein. He turned his head and saw that on the wall behind him were two crossed swords emulating the famous crossed swords of the Victory Arch near the Republican Palace. He could feel that the wire from one earpiece was no longer there and hoped that the other bud was still in place. He coughed realistically in case he was being watched and was relieved to hear Michele's voice coming through as though she was right there by his side.

'Better than the snoring,' she whispered, 'Glad you are awake,' and he forced himself not to smile. 'Everybody back at base,' she said, letting him know that they had got away from the farmhouse safely.

Countdown

A door opened and four men wearing black trousers and shirts with ski masks over their faces, stepped into the dimly lit room carrying assault rifles. They spread around him with two on either side and then another figure came through the doorway in army fatigues, and he recognised Farouq.

'Hello, Rhett, thank you for coming,' said Farouq walking up to stand in front of the desk.

'If I'd known you were going to take my clothes, I would have worn my best boxers,' replied Rhett.

'You know why you are here, of course,' said Farouq ignoring the comment. 'You killed my nephew, Ali. An innocent in all of this fighting and destruction.'

'He was dealing in the buying of illegal weapons,' said Rhett, 'so I don't think you can call him innocent.' He wasn't going to tell Farouq that Ali was working undercover for MI5.

Farouq strode towards Rhett and swiped the back of his hand across Rhett's cheek. The force knocked Rhett's head sideways and the heavy ring on Farouq's finger cut into the skin of his cheekbone.

'He knew nothing of that. He thought that Wormsley might be buying drugs, but he never asked. He was happy to earn some extra money to help with his studies; deliver pizza and pass on simple messages. He didn't deserve to die,' stated Farouq walking back across the room to his desk.

'I didn't kill him,' said Rhett simply.

Farouq perched on the edge of the table and eyed Rhett with his head on one side, 'Wormsley told me how you attacked him and stabbed him with unnecessary violence thinking that he was a kidnapper. You Special Forces people don't know how to control yourselves.'

Rhett shook his head, 'Let Lorraine go. She has nothing to do with any of this.'

'Ah, the lovely Lorraine. It is your fault that she is involved, and I have to thank you for the part you have played in all of our plans. When you killed Ali, it seemed as if you had ruined everything we had planned. Wormsley backed out of the deal they were making with him; he told them that he could no longer be associated with the group. Members of my mosque approached me and told me that Ali had been murdered by Wormsley. I was not involved at that point but when I investigated and finally got hold of Wormsley he told me the truth. He had to cover up your murder of Ali and sent you to Iraq to get you out of the country. Your actions left him open to suspicion and he had to get you away. When he told me that you were still in Iraq, all I wanted was to exact revenge by killing you, but then I saw a way to not only make you suffer but to also make you part of a new plan. You have helped us so much Rhett.'

Farouq reached into his pocket and took out a packet of cigarettes and a lighter.

'What plan, Farouq?' asked Rhett. 'A plan to kill more innocent people? The attack on my villa, the car chase, the suicide bomber killing my friend, Dan, the men...'

'Ah yes, Dan!' interrupted Farouq looking animated. 'This is when I knew that Allah was on my side. The driver of the vehicle with the bomb had instructions to find you and then detonate ahead of you in the road. We could not know that your friends would be there at the same time, it was just a lucky coincidence or a sign from God that I was on the right path. Everything was just part of the process of upsetting you and leading you here.'

'You have allowed your own men to be killed and injured for what? Just so you could get some money from me and lure me here in some elaborate game of vengeance?'

Farouq waved the cigarette packet and the lighter in his hands, 'They were soldiers, Rhett; prepared to die for a cause. Just as your friends and your client had to die at the farmhouse. Poor Malcolm, I expect he thought he had had a lucky escape only to be killed a few moments later. You understand that as a soldier, but I want you to also understand responsibility.' He paused, took a cigarette out of the packet, and lit it.

Rhett realised that Farouq didn't know that his team had got away from the farmhouse.

Countdown

Farouq took a deep draw on his cigarette, squinting as the smoke wafted over his face, and put the lighter and packet back in his pocket. 'Your governments of the West are responsible for sowing the seeds and nurturing our so-called terrorism. They invade countries and cause widespread death, destruction and poverty under the guise of liberating oppressed people, but they don't care about the ordinary people, they only care about the political and financial gains for themselves and then they are surprised when they discover new enemies.'

He began pacing up and down in front of Rhett as he talked, as though he was a lecturer in front of a great auditorium of students.

'I am a simple man, I worked hard to provide for my family and under Saddam Hussein I was able to live a cultured, decent life. Yusef, my older brother, caused his own death and consequently the death of our mother when he sent his family away. Yusef was a traitor and he deserved to be punished. I was deeply affected by Saddam's overthrow and the chaos that followed with the troops remaining in our country. The army was disbanded, thousands of us lost our jobs, and our homes were invaded without reason. While sectarian groups were forming, initially I remained peaceful but then my son Jamil was caught in the crossfire from trigger-happy troops. My little boy bleeding and in pain; he had to go through numerous operations to remove shrapnel from his head and back. Scarred for life, he will never play sport, he will never run and jump and climb with the other boys. We have yet to find out how badly his mind has been affected. Discovering that Ali had been deliberately murdered was the final straw. I suddenly saw the truth; Saddam was a good leader, a great leader. I was persuaded that it was time to join others who want to fight back, to let the people of the West know what it is like to suffer great loss and to get the message across that we want all foreign influence out of our country. I am not alone; our numbers are growing, not just here but across the world. I belong to a group who are not religious fanatics, we do not see ourselves as terrorists but as freedom fighters, Brothers of Truth. We are the resistance fighters of this war, and we will take revenge on those countries who have brought this new terror to our land.'

'Killing Lorraine will not help you in your cause. She is like Ali and Jamil an innocent person,' said Rhett. He paused and then added, 'What about her parents? Think about her parents. Her parents will be devastated.'

Listening in, Michele frowned and turned to Gordon, Malcolm, and Steve.

'Why does he keep mentioning her parents?' asked Steve. Michele's eyes suddenly gleamed, 'Her parents might know where she was going. He is telling us to contact her parents!'

She returned to the microphone and whispered, 'Roger that. Marcus and Rynold in position. Waiting for your order.'

'Where is she?' Rhett continued, 'Let her go and…,' he took a breath as though upset, 'Once I know she is safe.' He paused again, 'Then you can use me for your message. Do whatever you want for your video audience.'

Michele understood that he was telling them to wait until he knew that Lorraine was safe before coming to get him, but she wasn't sure if she could take that risk.

'You don't have any bargaining power,' said Farouq. 'As I said before, you are just part of the plan. A play within a play, a sideshow to divert from the main attraction; it has taken a lot of slow and careful planning to get everything into place. What we have planned will make the world sit up and pay attention more than anything that has gone before.' He paused and a sly grin spread across his face, 'It will certainly leave a sour taste in everyone's mouths.'

'Ali, his mother and his sisters, all of them were given a new life in the UK. Why would you want to hurt the country that gave them that?' asked Rhett.

Farouq leaned back on the edge of the table, 'I could not reach my sister-in-law, Reem or the eldest daughter Sawsan at first. They were too westernized and grateful for the life that they were given in your country, but Tariq and Salma, they were easy to persuade; young, disaffected and struggling with their torn family. They have been especially useful in setting everything up. With their help we soon brought Reem and Sawsan to share and understand our feelings; they were so angry about Ali's death after I explained what had really happened to him. Once Sawsan saw the truth she committed totally to the cause and has shown herself to be quite an impressive leader; everything in Hereford has been her plan. Salma, well, she is the most determined and brave young soldier. I am immensely proud of them all and Tariq is here waiting for his opportunity to exact the final revenge on you and then the West.'

Rhett twigged that the Sal whom Lorraine had so often mentioned must be this Salma. He closed his eyes briefly, wishing, as he had so many times before, that he had paid more attention to her life. *'Come on MI5, do your job and find out where she is,'* he thought.

'You like to call us violent and despicable, but it doesn't even come close to the actions of the West. I expect you have Walid now in a room very similar to this. What will you do to him, I wonder? Let me save you the bother and assure you that he knows nothing about our plans.'

Michele turned to Steve, and he ran out of the room and downstairs to the safe room at the back of the villa. He burst in on Glen who was sitting facing Walid across a table; Abdullah stood inside the door with a rifle in his hands. Walid's face was pale and desperate as he said, 'Please believe me, I don't know anything, just that something big is planned to strike at the Western intruders.'

'Just tell us everything that you do know,' said Steve giving Glen a small shake of the head.

Farouq threw his cigarette down and left it glowing red and slowly dying on the stone floor. 'The politicians are manipulated and controlled by the men with the money. Men like Hugh Wormsley who control and corrupt the course of politics and the law to ensure that they can get richer. They don't have any patriotism or any moral fibre, they are driven by power and greed, and they control the politicians who need their financial backing. The politicians who decided to invade Iraq based on lies that served their own goals should be rotting in jail for crimes against humanity, but they are free and wealthy men. Men like you with your extreme skills and abilities are brainwashed to fulfil the desires of these men. We will strike at your heart; we will strike at their heart. Lorraine is just one of many who will suffer.'

'Just kill me,' said Rhett. 'Take your video and send your message to the world.'

'Rhett, Rhett, be patient, your time will come.'

'If I am to die, you might as well tell me how you think you are going to send a bigger message.'

'We are going to… How do you say it? Hit the Bull's eye and the Lion's heart.'

Rhett suddenly clicked onto what he was referring to, 'You mean the Hereford bull. You are planning to strike in Hereford.'

'Very good. It is too late for anyone to stop it; everything is in place, but Hereford is only the beginning.'

'You are just scum, Farouq,' said Rhett trying to keep the conversation going. 'You say that you and the people you are connected to are acting out of revenge for things the West has done, but you are just cowards killing and injuring innocent people of all different nationalities including your own under the pretence of a valid cause.'

Farouq dismissed him with a shake of the head. 'I expect you are hoping that your team will somehow find Lorraine, but I am afraid I got rid of them all after you came after me down the tunnel, as I knew you would. Nobody will find her or you, until it is too late,' he said with a smile. He turned to the TV screen on the desk. 'Did you enjoy the little show I left you at the house? That was just the trailer, now let me show you more. There is a lovely surprise for you.'

Michele's voice came into his ear, 'We've located the house. We know where she is, team getting ready.'

Farouq turned to the screen and pressed play. The screen filled with the same kitchen that Rhett had seen on the television at the house and the video played without sound. Lorraine walked in and he watched her smiling and laughing with the three Iraqi women; she looked radiant in the floaty top and tight leggings. He saw her look out of the kitchen window and then turn back saying something with animation.

Rhett watched as Lorraine sat down at the kitchen table holding a cup and drinking from it. The camera zoomed in, and he saw her eyes begin to flutter; her head drooped, and the mug fell out of her hands and smashed on the floor. The screen went black for a second and Rhett looked up at Farouq with venom in his eyes, 'What have you done with her?' he shouted.

Farouq smiled, 'Wait, wait, it's not over yet.'

The screen flickered and another image filled the screen and Farouq turned up the volume. Lorraine was now sitting in a chair with her mouth gagged. Her arms were tied behind the back of the chair and her floaty top clung to her stomach. Her distinctively round stomach. Rhett leaned forward in shock and a lump formed in his throat making it difficult to swallow.

'Oh, didn't you know?' asked Farouq. 'She's pregnant. Six months apparently.'

'You bastard!' cried Rhett squirming in his chair and trying to free himself. The film continued and Rhett watched as the camera zoomed in on her terrified, pleading eyes and he heard her muffled cries. Behind her, a man with a pistol stepped forward and held the nozzle to the back of her skull and then stepped back slightly before firing. There was a bright flash, and the screen went black as the sound of a shot rang out from the monitor and resounded around the small office.

25

Wednesday, July 6th, 2005, Brampton Abbots, Hereford, UK

Lorraine was frightened and bewildered, something hard pressed briefly against the back of her head and then an earth-shattering bang resounded in her ears; she jolted in fear and ducked automatically. It sounded like a car back firing inside the room; she had no idea what a gunshot really sounded like or felt like, but she was sure she would know if she had been shot or, come to think of it, not know anything.

Her ears were ringing, and her heart was pounding; she was terrified but felt very much alive as she heard the men laughing and then one said, 'Get the footage.' She raised her eyes and saw one of the men take the film from the camera and walk past without looking at her.

She turned her head and watched the two men leave the room. One of them stopped at the door and said, 'Wait here. We haven't finished with you yet.' She heard them both laughing before the door was closed behind them.

She screamed for help, but no sound came out of her mouth apart from a low moan. She strained her hands against the rope around her wrists in desperation, the rough sisal cut into her skin, and tears streamed down her face. All-consuming terror constricted her throat and tightened her chest as she tried to make sense of what was happening. Then she stopped struggling, *'Never panic, the worst thing you can do is panic. Stay still, breathe deeply, assess the situation.'*

She could hear Rhett's voice in her head. The self-defence lessons and his words came back to her now, *'You won't be as strong as most men, so you are not looking to fight; you are looking for an opportunity to run.'*

She sat still and calmed herself as much as she could, then she realised that the men had been careless. Viewing her as weak and pathetic, they had only tied her wrists behind the back of the chair; her legs were free. She looked around the room for anything with which to cut the rope; the camera and tripod were the only items in the bare room. She could smash the camera but that would attract attention and there was no guarantee that anything sharp enough would result from the breakage. There was a radiator under the window, the edges fairly thin and rusting, on the other side of the room. Slowly, she moved her arms backwards, up behind her back and by moving her body to one side and then the other she released one arm and then the other over the wide back of the chair.

She could stand but she didn't know how much time she had before the men came back. She ran over to the radiator and tried forcing the rope up and down against the metal side, but she couldn't get enough pressure with the narrow gap to the wall, and it was too thick to provide a cutting edge any time soon.

She nudged the curtain aside with her head and looked out onto the scruffy lawn and driveway through the plain glass window, but there was no way that she could open the window with her hands behind her back. A narrow sill ran under the window about waist high and she tried to hoist herself up onto it, but she couldn't get enough leverage to lift herself up and stay on it.

She rushed back to the chair, picked it up behind her and carried it back to the window ledge where she managed to stand on top of it with her side facing the curtain. It was her only chance; she was sure that they would be back any moment and that the next film would be of her dying for all the world to watch.

Countdown

'I love you, Pom,' she whispered. 'Stay strong, baby.'

She leant sideways away from the window and bent her knees, then she flung herself against the curtain with all her strength. She heard the thud of her body hitting the window through the curtain followed by shattering glass; her body carried on forward through the gaping, jagged hole ripping at the curtain as it let her go and then her shoulder smashed onto the hard, dry grass below. She didn't feel it, she didn't notice the gash across the top of her arm or the cuts on her ankles; she pitched over on fragments of glass, picked up a long, thin shard with her fingers, and rolled up onto her knees. She staggered to her feet and, with adrenaline coursing through her body, she ran across the lawn, down the driveway and blindly turned into the quiet, country lane.

She knew they must have heard the crash of the breaking glass but hoped it would take them a while to realise where the noise had come from; they wouldn't be expecting her to escape but once they found out, they would soon be after her. There were no houses in sight and the sun, no longer high in the sky, still shone brightly on the green trees and fields. There was her car, but she didn't have the keys. To her left was civilization but the road to the right curved around a bend and she ran along the verge in that direction. As soon as she was around the bend she veered off and crashed through a tiny gap in the hedge that lined the road into a field. The grass was long and thick along the edge between the hedgerow and lines of ripening wheat rippling in the soft breeze, and she kept down low as she made her way back towards the house. Her hands were wet with blood as she held the broken shard against the rope as she moved. Reaching the corner of the fence that surrounded the house she heard the men shouting and crouched down trying to control her breathing; she felt the rope slacken and squeezed her hands out of their bondage. She tried to untie the gag, but her hands were too shaky and slimy with blood, so she tugged it down under her chin and breathed in great gulps of air. A woman's voice screeched, 'Bring her back, she can't have gone far!'

Countdown

She heard footsteps in the road on the other side of the bushes run past her and she began to edge along the fence at the side of the house. Looking over her shoulder to check that nobody came into the field, she kept as low as she could while moving as quickly as possible. Finally, she reached the broken fence that she had seen when she had looked out of the kitchen window; she crawled through the hole and fell sideways into the long weeds. Not caring about the pain, she pushed herself deep into the brambles of the blackberry bush; the thorns scratched and ripped at her clothes and skin, but she didn't stop until she was sure she was hidden. A startled blackbird flew up into the air with flapping wings and she lay still as the sound of rushing blood pumped through her ears. Rhett's voice came into her head again reminding her that any movement attracted attention and kept as still as possible with all her senses heightened, trying to concentrate on looking for an opportunity to rescue Salma.

She had to find Salma; whoever they were, they must have taken her and her family prisoner as well. Suddenly, her heart seemed to stop, and she stifled a sob as she realised that she could hear a voice coming from the house. She curled silently back into the sharp, prickly bushes and listened. From the pauses, she guessed that whoever was talking was on the telephone and very slowly she moved forward and crouched up onto her knees. Through the thorny branches and long grass, she could see the open window and now she could hear clear voices coming from the kitchen.

'They have our location,' said Sawsan's rough voice. 'We have to get out of here now. I have called Aziz and Sultan and told them to forget about Lorraine. We move into position tonight.'

'Sawsan, listen to me. We can't leave the girl,' said the voice of Reem brusquely, 'she has seen our faces.'

'She won't have taken much in, Mama, and she will be in shock,' said Sawsan. 'Salma, here is your ticket to London, the case is in the hall; find Sultan and go to your first position. I will call to tell you when to detonate the charges in the house.

Countdown

Mama, you get the rucksacks ready; we all know what to do. When they come for her, they will get a nasty surprise; tomorrow we will give them more surprises and then at ten o'clock tomorrow morning Salma will show the world what it is really like to live in fear.'

Lorraine couldn't believe what she was hearing, but then the hard truth hit her; they were all in it together and Salma was one of them. She sank to the ground in sorrow and confusion. *'What the hell was going on?'* She knew that, somehow, she must remember everything she had seen and heard.

***

Reem and Sawsan quickly changed into walking gear; to all intents and purposes they looked like ramblers with long shorts, scruffy tops, walking boots, floppy hats, and rucksacks on their backs. Sawsan slung a pair of binoculars round her neck then they left by the front door and moved quickly down the road until they came to a gate leading into a field. By the side of the gate was a pathway and a tall signpost indicated directions to the next village. They went onto the bridle path and began to saunter along as if they didn't have a care in the world towards some woods up ahead.

Aziz changed into long shorts, black trainers, and a navy-blue top with a sleeveless visibility jacket on top. He went into the garage where there was a car and a bicycle. Salma and Sultan followed him inside. They were dressed as before in jeans and T-shirts, although Sultan had removed his scarf. Aziz took the red Pashley Mailstar postman's bike leaning up against the wall complete with full saddlebags and another bulging sack in the front holder and opened the garage doors.

Salma and Sultan climbed into the car, a used Ford Focus in light sapphire blue and, with Sultan driving, they headed out into the lane and turned right. Behind them Aziz climbed onto the bike and headed left from the house. A few hundred yards down the road, Sultan pulled into a lay-by and for anyone passing they looked like lovers smooching in a country lane.

Lorraine heard a car engine starting up and a vehicle pulling out into the road and driving away. There was silence from the

Countdown

house. Around her, birds twittered and chirped; a light breeze rustled the leaves in the trees and the overgrown grass. She dared to breathe and thought about what she had heard. *'They have our location', 'They will get a surprise – charges are ready. I will tell you when to detonate.'*

'They must mean the police,' she thought. *'They are planning to blow up the house when the police arrive. I must warn them.'*
She pushed her way back out of the brambles, snagging her hair and scratching her face even more before she could manage to stagger up to standing. She turned and screamed as she came face to face with a man dressed completely in black combat gear holding a weapon.

'Lorraine? Are you Lorraine?' asked the man gently. He held her by the arm with a firm grip as she struggled to get away.

She stopped and looked at him and he smiled, 'It's okay, it's okay. I am here to help. My name is Andy.' He talked into a microphone on his chest and said, 'I have secured the principal.'

'They have put charges in the house,' said Lorraine, garbling, 'they said they are going to detonate remotely. They left in a car, but I don't know where they went!'

'House rigged,' Andy said to his chest, 'I repeat, house is a no go. Need bomb disposal and,' he looked at Lorraine's torn face and bleeding hands and arms, 'need medical assistance.'

He seemed to signal at the grass around them and five previously invisible men emerged from the undergrowth wearing the same black outfits as Andy and retreated out of the garden by another hole in the fence at the far end. Andy turned back to Lorraine and said, 'Well done. How many of them?'

'Five I think, three women and two men.'

'Five suspects in car, three women and two men,' he said to the person at the end of the mic on his chest.

'Right, let's get you away from here,' he said to Lorraine. 'We need…' but she had fainted before he could finish.

139

26

Wednesday, July 6th, 2005, Farouq's villa compound, Baghdad

The sound of the gunshot still rang in Rhett's ears, and he was filled with an all-consuming horror and rage. He screamed, 'No-o-o!!!' and threw himself backwards; tucking his head forward, he smashed down on his back and the chair disintegrated beneath him. He did a complete roll and sprang to his feet leaving him with two broken chair legs still tied to his ankles and his wrists bound with duct tape behind his back. He bent forward lifted his arms as high as he could behind his back, brought them back down with force as he pulled his elbows away from his body and the duct taped ripped apart. He instantly dived into the man immediately to his left as the men on the other side of the room raised their weapons to fire. The first man fell against the other, and they lost their balance. Rhett chopped the side of his hand down hard on the side of the first man's neck and he crumpled. Rhett grabbed his gun and stomped with all his strength down onto his groin, before swinging the butt of the gun backwards and smashing the second man in the face. He turned and moving fast across the room, he fired at the other two henchmen as they fired at him. He bent down and pulled a jagged piece of wood from the bindings on his leg and threw the missile across the room at one of the guards. The point sliced into the man's eye, and he screamed in agony as Rhett slammed

bullets into his comrade and then finished him with a round to the head. Both men collapsed on the floor in a bloody heap.
Rhett felt cold steel against the side of his forehead and stopped.

'Drop the gun, soldier,' ordered Farouq.

With a swift upward jab of his elbow Rhett knocked Farouq's gun arm upwards and the gun exploded as it flew across the floor. Rhett turned but Farouq was ready for him and punched him in the face and knocked the gun out of his hands. Rhett returned the blow and then flew at him. Both men landed on the desk sending the computer and screens sliding and crashing to the floor. Rhett put his hands around Farouq's throat and began squeezing as he stared into the bitter hatred emanating from his black eyes. Farouq reached down to his pocket and with desperate, fumbling fingers he managed to retrieve his lighter. He pulled it out, flicked it on and held the bright flame against the bare skin of Rhett's shoulder. Rhett flinched and Farouq rolled out of his grip, grabbed the heavy based lamp, swiped it against the side of Rhett's head and scrabbled off the desk. Rhett leapt around with blood oozing out of a gash above his ear and fired his heel into Farouq's knee; he stumbled but carried on forward and bent down to grab the weapon lying next to one of his fallen men, but Rhett was right behind him. As Farouq stood upright and turned to fire, Rhett grabbed one of the swords on the wall and brought it swiftly down on Farouq's arm, slicing through the material of his army shirt and through the flesh on his upper arm to the bone. Farouq screamed in rage and dropped the weapon as he tried to hold his arm together with his other hand. He fell to his knees and Rhett took hold of the hilt in both hands and raised the sword above his head with his eyes blazing. Behind Rhett the door burst open, and the blast of a round echoed around the room.

27

Wednesday, July 6th, 2005
Olive Grove, Baghdad

Marcus and Rynold made their way through the olive grove to the track where the vehicles had left; they had taken their dead and injured with them, as well as Rhett.

'Vehicles tracked?' he asked Steve on comms back at the villa base.

'We've got them. They are heading back towards the city, still moving. We are sending a support team to pick you up now. We've still got Rhett, one comm gone but that ear bud of Gordon's is still in place. His snoring has been keeping us awake.'

'Yeah, they injected something into his neck before they took him. He caused quite a lot of damage before he went down,' said Marcus.

The familiar sound of a Humvee could be heard coming towards them and the lights of a huge vehicle lit up the path just ahead of them.

'Support has arrived, keep us informed of location,' said Marcus.

'Will do,' replied Steve.

The massive beige, armoured vehicle pulled up beside Marcus and Rynold and a large man jumped out of the front and saluted them. He looked like Rambo with massive bulging arms, a wide chest, and strong, powerful legs that made Marcus look small in comparison. He strode towards Marcus and Rynold and saluted. 'Sergeant Dick Brentwood, Delta Force. I've been told to liaise and support with Marcus Jackson,' he said in a mid-western drawl.

'Good to see you, Dick. I'm Marcus and this is Rynold.'

'Sir!' said the US sergeant, 'I've been told to follow your orders and support your rescue mission.'

'Great. How many men have we got?'

'Eight, sir.'

'Okay, let's get going. I'll fill you in on the situation and the plan on the way, we don't have a second to waste.'

'Yes, sir!' said Dick and led them back to the jeep.

Marcus raised his eyebrows at Rynold who grinned and saluted him.

***

Malcolm, looking a little less pale but exhausted, sat next to Gordon as they both tracked and traced the vehicles carrying Rhett. He said that he would prefer to be involved rather than to rest.

Gordon announced that the vehicles carrying Rhett had stopped and Michele got word from her intel that they had stopped at a villa compound that was the old home of Farouq before the dismantling of the army. It had been abandoned for the last couple of years but now they could see a large amount of activity.

Steve passed the information on to Marcus, 'Heavily guarded villa compound; at least fifteen men outside and more inside. Sending location through to your team now.'

Along with the Delta Force team Marcus and Rynold made their way to a street adjacent to the villa compound where Marcus went over the final plan with the Delta team and gave a quick set of orders. A sniper pair went to the roof of a derelict building in the street opposite the compound from where they had direct line of sight to the target area and could provide cover for the impending assault. The villa was in an unlit road with a few walled villas spaced out along it. Around Farouq's villa was a large expanse of empty sand; men stood on the corners of the walls and on the flat roof of the two-storey building as well as in the courtyard in front of the villa; large wooden doors marked the entrance to the compound. They waited in silence.

'Go, go, go!' yelled Steve into Marcus' ear.

Marcus indicated for the driver of the Humvee to start moving. They drove slowly down the dark street and into the adjacent road where the villa was located with their lights down low. Going at a very slow pace as if on patrol, they came alongside the villa, then suddenly the driver turned sharply towards the compound doors, turned the vehicle lights onto full beam and put his foot down. The jeep hurtled across the sand and smashed through the wooden gates, taking the men on watch by surprise.

The guards on the wall began firing ineffectually at the armoured vehicle as it came to a screeching halt in front of the house and the remaining six members of Delta leapt out, rolling and firing at their specified targets and the sniper team provided covering fire. Bodies fell, fatally wounded, from the roof and the walls, then more men came running out of the front door and Dick's men took them out as they in turn provided cover for Marcus and Rynold to go inside. Four men began firing at them from different sides of the large entrance hall but Marcus and Rynold took them out. They heard more gunfire and then realised that the noise was coming from inside the house as well as outside. They made their way down a hallway and heard a gunshot come from the room at the end. A man jumped out from a room to the right and Rynold kicked the gun out of his hands and fired one round into his head.

Crashing and banging could be heard from the room at the end and checking two more rooms off the corridor they moved fast towards it. Rynold covered the corridor behind them as Marcus opened the door at the end. He took in Rhett standing over Farouq with a sword in his hands then a slight movement to the right brought his attention to a man getting to his knees and raising his weapon; Marcus fired one shot, and the man fell back on awkwardly bent legs, dead.

Countdown

Marcus looked at Rhett with the glaring red mark on his upper arm, his bare back scratched and streaked with blood and more blood running down the side of his head and said, 'Got complaints from the neighbours about a disturbance. Can you keep the noise of your sex games down, please?'

Rhett lowered his arms with a shake of his head, he let the sword clatter to the marble floor and walked past Marcus and Rynold into the hallway.

Behind him Farouq shouted, 'You and I are just tiny pieces in the big picture, Rhett. The West are responsible for creating a monster you can't contain. Do you know where the money has come from for our war? From the American government. Their ears will be ringing with the sound of Arabic music in Washington. You cannot stop it!'

Rhett heard a single shot and carried on walking.

More gunfire came from upstairs as Delta Force cleared the building room by room and Michele's voice came into his ear, 'Lorraine is safe, she's on her way to hospital.' She paused and he could hear her breathing before she continued in a gentle whisper, 'And the baby is fine.'

Rhett leant against the wall and slid slowly down until his head was resting on his knees. When he raised his head and ran his fingers through his hair, his cheeks were wet.

'Get me on a plane to the UK, now,' he said.

Countdown

28

Wednesday, July 6th, 2005
Farouq's Villa, Baghdad

While Farouq was downstairs in the room with Rhett, Tariq was in a bedroom upstairs in the villa. He paced around the room brandishing a pole which he swiped across his body in a horizontal line. He was excited; this was his time to take revenge on his brother Ali's killer. He waited impatiently for Farouq to call him down to the room where they had Rhett. It had been fun tormenting him; planning the attacks on the villa and the car, the destruction of Rhett's friend, Dan and the other infidels on Death Street. Now he would be the one to cut the head off his brother's murderer; his first act of violence in the war for freedom before his second and biggest challenge could commence.

Suddenly, he heard a massive crashing noise and the squeal of tyres in the courtyard below followed by shouting and gunfire, and he rushed to the window and peeped through the thick curtains. He saw soldiers jumping out of the vehicle that had smashed through the gate and killing each of the guards on the walls. There was shouting outside his room now and rounds were being fired downstairs.

Zayed ran into the room and said, 'Come with me now; bring your things.'

Tariq went to a large cupboard and took out a holdall and a large, hard case in the shape of half a pear with a long, bent stalk, which contained his oud. Zayed took the instrument case from him and told Tariq to follow. They stepped out onto the landing where they could see their men shooting down into the lobby below; blood spurted from the head of one of them as his body collapsed onto the bannister and dropped to the floor below. Zayed pulled at Tariq's arm and the two of them headed for the stairs leading up to the roof. They stepped out onto the flat concrete and saw bodies strewn along the edge; two more men were lying on their bellies popping forward every now and then to fire at the intruders below and dropping quickly back and moving along the edge of the roof.

Zayed led Tariq to the back edge and began climbing down the metal ladder fixed to the wall with the oud slung over his shoulder. Tariq edged backwards over the side of the roof and put his feet down onto the rung just above Zayed's head and lowered himself until he could grab the top rung and begin climbing down. On the ground, Zayed signalled for Tariq to follow him across the back yard to a small gate in the villa wall. The battle raged behind them, and Tariq briefly looked back with regret at not being able to kill Rhett Millard, then he slipped through the gateway and followed Zayed into the street backing the villa.

Zayed led the way through dark alleyways until they came to a small square where he opened the doors of a reasonably new Mercedes. They stowed their bags on the backseat and covered them with a blanket before getting into the front seats. With Zayed driving, they headed away from the villa area towards the major highway leading to the Jordanian border over five hundred kilometres away.

29

Wednesday, July 6th, 2005, Brampton Abbots, Hereford, UK

Special Forces fanned out through the woods above the house in Brampton Abbots; Sergeant Mike Rudd spotted two ladies standing at the edge of the trees and saw that one of them was looking through binoculars. He shared the information with his team and said he was about to approach them to tell them to move out of the area. As he came up behind them, he realised that they were looking at the house below and called in, 'Possible hostiles.' He walked towards them and called out, 'Good evening, ladies.'

Reem's breath caught in her throat, but she managed to turn and smile sweetly at the soldier, 'Gosh! You frightened me,' she said holding her hand to her heart.

'Any interesting birds in that direction?' asked the soldier, staring at the heavy-looking rucksacks he had just noticed on the ground at their feet.

Reem panicked and shouted, 'Run!' She and Sawsan sprinted away into the woods and Reem's phone rang. She took it out and seeing that it was Salma she answered it as she ran.

***

A police car stopped next to Sultan's car and an officer got out and tapped on the window. Sultan released Salma from their mock embrace and grinned at the man. The officer signalled for him to open the window and said in a sarcastic voice, 'Sorry to

Countdown

disturb you, sir, but you can't loiter here. Move along now. We are blocking the road this way,' he said, indicating in the direction of the house, 'so you'll have to go the long way round to get back into town. Give you a bit more time together.'

Sultan glanced at Salma and they both looked at the phone sitting between them. It remained silent and deciding that they had bigger tasks to complete, Sultan didn't think it was worth the risk of getting arrested.

'Yes, sorry officer. Going now,' he said politely. He started the car up and drove away down the road. The police officer shook his head and smiled as he took down the number of the car.

Salma picked up the phone and called Reem. 'We've had to leave,' she told her.

'Finish your task in London, Salma. Whatever happens you must finish your job. It is the most important. Do you understand?' Reem said, sounding breathless.

The line went dead, and Salma frowned at Sultan. 'I think they are in trouble,' she said, and she took the sim card out of her phone and threw it out of the window.

***

Reem and Sawsan split up and dived through the undergrowth in different directions. Reem heard the stomp of heavy feet crushing the undergrowth behind her as she threw the phone away and pushed her way through thick bushes off the path. Her breath rattled in her chest as she ran on blindly and then suddenly her foot snagged on a fallen tree and she collapsed under a twisted ankle. She scrabbled to get up and hobble forward, but a burly figure appeared in front of her holding a gun aimed at her chest. To her right she heard the echoing report of a gunshot.

***

Sawsan rolled down a steep bank with stones and branches battering and bruising her body. She reached a narrow path and scrambled to her feet before hurtling along it not knowing where she was heading, but suddenly she could make out a road up ahead and she turned and ran with long strides in the opposite direction. A voice called out for her to stop, but she dodged back into the woods and ran between the dense trunks. A shot rang out and her shoulder exploded with excruciating pain; the force of the bullet spun her round and she crumpled to the ground like a puppet without strings.

***

Aziz cycled madly up the hill not really knowing where he was to go but wanting to get away from the house and into a position where he could hide the postman's bike until morning. He knew he would look odd being out and about at this time of night and made it as far as the T-junction at the top of the hill before he was stopped by police who thought it was a little late in the evening for a postman to be doing his rounds.

Aziz stopped obediently when the police car pulled up alongside him and smiled at the officers.

'Evening young man,' said one officer. 'Bit late to be making so many deliveries,' he said eying the bulging saddle bags and the full sack on the front.

'Oh, sorry officer, I had to go to see my mother who is suffering from cancer, and I got delayed in making my round,' he said hoping to get some sympathy.

Sergeant Frimlow asked Aziz to lean the bike up on its stand and to step away while his partner, Constable Higgins took him to one side to take his name and address. Sergeant Frimlow opened one of the saddle bags and drew a sharp breath when he was confronted with the sight of packed explosives. With his heart pounding, he calmly turned to Aziz and quickly put him in cuffs while telling him his rights. Aziz protested and gave a brief struggle, but he knew it was too late to get away. No sooner had Frimlow called it in, than an armoured vehicle followed by a smart looking BMW swung into the road and drew to a stop in front of them. Frimlow was commended for his actions and ordered to leave the area. Bomb disposal went into action with the bike while Aziz was bundled into the back of the BMW and whisked away.

***

Countdown

Sultan followed the country lanes until they brought them back up to the main road and headed towards Gloucester. Half an hour later he dropped Salma off outside the train station as she had requested; he had no idea where she was heading. She went to the boot of the car and ignoring the rucksack sitting to one side, she lifted out a bulky cabin bag and a small holdall. She looked in through the window at Sultan and they nodded at each other.

Salma put on a baseball cap and made her way to the station toilets. She went into a cubicle where she took off the cap and discarded her jeans and T-shirt; she strapped on a false pregnant belly and put on a frumpy maternity dress and a shapeless woollen cardigan. Finally, she tucked her shiny, black hair up inside a dull blonde wig. She took a small handbag from the holdall and checked inside for a new passport, money, and an open return train ticket to London. She waited until the toilets were empty before emerging from her cubicle and stood in front of the mirrors to plaster her face in pale beige foundation, carefully shaded in bluish bags under her eyes and inserted grey contact lenses. She stepped out onto the platform as a plain looking, pregnant woman, stuffed the holdall into one of the big bins and made her way to the platform with her case.

***

Sultan drove back into Hereford and wondered where to go. They were supposed to stay at the house until the following day; their instructions were for them to act in the morning. He guessed that Reem and Sawsan had been caught and he didn't dare ring Aziz in case he was also compromised. He didn't have anyone else to contact; Sawsan was in charge, and she never told him anything unless it related to what he had to do. He had been so sure about what they were doing; for the first time in his life, he felt important, and he had enjoyed staying in the house for the last few days with like-minded people. Tying up the girl and videoing her had made him feel immensely powerful. Normally, he might have felt sorry for her, but Salma told him that she had been involved with the murder of her brother and so he hated her, along with all the Westerners who had made him feel second class and were responsible for the destruction of his homeland.

Now he felt lost and unsure of himself; perhaps he should go somewhere busy and detonate his package tonight before they found him.

He drove into the town centre and parked in the Union Walk car park near the county hospital, his target for the following day. A hospital was busy all the time, it would cause a huge impact tonight; he didn't think he could spend the night in the car waiting. What if one of the others gave him up? What if that police officer had passed on his number plate and they found him before he had accomplished anything? He had already failed to blow up the house and they would find evidence of the bomb making. He opened the car door with determination to get the rucksack and go to the hospital. Suddenly, three police cars swooped into the car park with flashing lights and sirens blaring. He ran to the boot but was thrown to the ground as someone dived towards him, grabbed his ankles and pulled him down.

Countdown

30

Wednesday, July 6th, 2005
Company Villa, Baghdad

Rhett got back to the villa with Marcus and Rynold, showered, and changed into clean clothes. The gash on the side of his head had stopped bleeding, the burn on his arm stung like crazy and his bruised and bloody cheek throbbed, but he paid no attention to the pain.

Walid was still there, and he went in to see him in the office they had given him at the side of the villa. Walid stood up from behind the desk and came towards him looking ashen and tired.

'I am so sorry, Rhett. I...' he began and faltered, lowering his eyes to the floor.

'Sit down,' said Rhett indicating the two armchairs next to a coffee table in the corner.

The two men sat down, and Rhett waited for Walid to start talking again.

'The night of the birthday party, I knew that Farouq was covering for Tariq. All that business about shopping near the hotel, I knew it was nonsense. He told me about his group, Brothers of Truth and he told me that you are the killer of my nephew, Ali. He looked up at Rhett and Rhett held his gaze; he shook his head but said nothing.

'Farouq is much younger than I, he was always a bit wild, he liked to party, and he was ambitious. Our mother used to spoil him, and he had little respect for me or our older brother, Yusef. They were opposites; Farouq saw Saddam Hussein as a great father figure, particularly after our own father was killed in the war against Iran. He became friendly with Saddam's son, Uday, despite knowing that he was a brutal and dangerous man. Yusef was a professor, a scholar and he didn't agree with the oppressive nature of the regime. He didn't openly oppose Saddam, but he tried to persuade Farouq that he was on the wrong path. We didn't know how strong Farouq's love for Saddam was or how ambitious he was to do well in the regime. Now, I think it was maybe Farouq who told Uday about Yusef's lovely daughters.'

Walid shifted uncomfortably in his seat before continuing, 'I was always in the middle, I joined the Ba'ath party to keep out of trouble and I did well in the army but Farouq, he did even better. He is a shrewd and tactical thinker; he likes to play games with people and create red herrings to draw attention away from the main attack. And he is cruel.'

He sighed, 'It is hard for me to say these things about my own brother, and I think I pretended not to know what he is really like. He behaved as though he was pleased when Saddam was overthrown but I know he would have been devastated and worried about his connections with Uday. The Americans raided his home and there was some scuffle in the house, shots were fired, and Jamil, his little boy was severely injured. He became angry; his rage kept hidden, but he got involved with some people at his mosque. I didn't want to know what was going on, but I heard rumours that they were linked to Al Qaeda.'

'What was he planning, Walid? This isn't all about revenge on me.'

'I-I don't know. He used the murder of Ali to get Tariq and Salma on his side, but I didn't know anything until a few days ago. I tried to talk sense into him, but he was crazy with excitement about the plans they had in place – revenge on you and sending a powerful message to the West. He said that Reem and Sawsan were difficult to persuade at first because they had been brain-washed by the West but once he made them understand what was happening in Iraq and that you had killed Ali, they had apparently seen the light. He said that the most powerful Angels of Death were ready. I have been trying to think what else and suddenly I remembered overhearing him on the phone months ago now, sometime last year. He said the name of your old boss, Hugh Wormsley. This is the man who told him that you killed Ali. I heard him say that the deal was back on for the suitcase and that the money was ready. I am sure that he mentioned millions of dollars, but I thought at the time that I had misheard. I went into the room and Farouq started talking about the weather and finished the call. I made a joke about the price of suitcases going up and he laughed and said it was in Turkish Lira. I didn't think much about it at the time. Farouq was always making some business deals, trying to make more money than he got for driving an ambulance. But I am sure now that he definitely said dollars not lira. What does it mean?'

'I don't know,' said Rhett. 'But I don't think he was talking about Louis Vuitton luggage.' He looked over at Walid's drawn, sad face and said, 'Farouq is dead, Walid.'

Walid drew in a sharp intake of breath and nodded, 'I thought so. Thank God my poor mother is not here for even more of this pain.' He ran a hand over his face and asked, 'What about Tariq? My wife called to say he has not come home, and his oud and some clothes are missing.'

Rhett stared at him and said, 'I don't know about Tariq. He wasn't with Farouq.'

Walid nodded and looked relieved.

31

Thursday, July 7th, 2005
Flight to UK

It was in the early hours of the morning, on the 7th of July when Rhett climbed on board the luxurious Gulfstream 550 with Michele, Gordon and Malcolm. Michele had managed to persuade the CEO of Whiteriver, Chuck Elmsworth to allow them to use his private jet for a matter of National Security. Rhett had insisted that Malcolm came too; he needed to get out of Iraq and back to his family and he might be able to help them with more information. Gordon had decided that it was in Malcolm's best interest if he travelled with him, adding that he would be able to explain the situation to the company face to face. There was no way he wanted to stay in Iraq.

'Woah! This is posh,' Gordon exclaimed when they got on board, 'I could get used to this.' He was even more impressed when an attractive air steward brought him a glass of champagne.

Sitting down opposite Michele in a sumptuous, cream leather chair, Rhett buckled up and after refusing a glass of champagne, he looked over the table at Michele and their eyes locked. It was the first eye contact they had had since he returned to the villa and debriefed everybody. Walid had been devastated and embarrassed; he told Rhett what he knew, and Rhett knew that he was telling him the truth; he had been used just as Rhett had, but he had said some interesting things about Farouq's mode of operation.

He stared at Michele recognising the undeniable attraction between them but right now all he could think about was Lorraine and the baby. *'Why hadn't she told him? Would she want to see him?'*

Michele interrupted his thoughts by saying, 'I think we should consolidate what we know and see if we can get a clearer picture of what Farouq was involved in.'

Rhett and the other two men agreed, and Michele opened up a laptop on the table between them. She gave a little cough and shifted in her seat, 'MI5 and MI6 have been working together to see how Farouq links to the UK and have come up with nothing new. We know that he was working with his nieces, Salma and Sawsan, his sister-in-law, Reem and the two men based in Hereford; security forces are on high alert in the area. The video from the farmhouse confirms the identities of Salma, Sawsan and Reem but the conversation reveals nothing of value. We believe that they have planned one or more attacks on Hereford, hence his reference to the bull's eye which Rhett got him to admit to. We don't think they would attack SAS sites directly; we think the plan is to hurt families and friends living in the area. Four of the suspects from the house are in custody, but they are not known to have any previous links with terrorist activity. There is no sign of Salma, so we are watching hospitals and shopping malls. One of the men arrested, Sultan was found with a rucksack packed with home-made explosives near to a hospital in Hereford and he has admitted that that was his target but doesn't know what everyone else had to do.

The explosives were identical to those retrieved from the other suspects. We know that Salma left in the car with Sultan; the police moved them on thinking they were a young couple making out in a quiet lane. Unfortunately, he didn't pass on the number of the car as relevant until later and Sultan denies knowing where she has gone. He is still being questioned to find out when she got out of the car. The train station in Hereford is not far from where they picked up Sultan, so she could have gone there, but there were no sightings of her getting on a train or buying a ticket. We have issued her picture to all the authorities, and it will be on the news, but at the moment we don't know if she's still in Hereford or on her way to a target somewhere else in the country.' She turned her laptop to reveal a portrait photo of Salma with her raven hair and beautiful face.

Rhett stared at the picture, committing the facial features to memory and filling with rage towards this duplicitous woman.

'I hear that they rescued Lorraine, why didn't they catch all of her captors then?' asked Malcolm.

'They knew we were coming and left the house. The house was rigged with booby traps, but they didn't detonate; bomb squad are working on making the area safe before forensics can go in and see what evidence they have left behind them. Lorraine, the...' She paused and took a deep breath before continuing, keeping her eyes on the computer screen, 'The woman who was held captive by the group was in a state of shock after her ordeal. It appears that she managed to escape before the captors left the house and sustained some injuries to her hands, face and body. After she was rescued, she was given a sedative and she hasn't come round yet.'

She looked up at Rhett who nodded for her to go on. His insides churned with swirling emotions; he ached to get to Lorraine and to hold her in his arms, but he was also suffused with guilt knowing that he had caused her suffering.

Michele went on, 'We are not sure if that is why they left in a hurry or if they knew that we were on to them. Lorraine is at the SAS medical unit for her safety, her parents are with her, and Paul Davies, Head of Counter Terrorism and MI5 is on his way there to speak to her when she comes round to see if she can provide us with any more information.'

'What was their plan?' asked Rhett, thinking out loud.

'We don't know yet,' admitted Michele, 'apart from obviously planning to let off a number of bombs somewhere in Hereford. We have managed to avert four of those explosions.'

'What kind of bombs?' asked Malcolm.

'Initial analysis suggests homemade IEDs activated by cell phones.'

'It doesn't make sense,' said Gordon, sipping his second glass of champagne.

They all looked at him expectantly.

'When Rhett was with Farouq, he was talking about plays within plays and sideshows. He was also making some high-powered deal with this Hugh Wormsley fellow and, forgive me if I am wrong, but I don't think Wormsley is likely to be involved in the selling of hair bleach or whatever else they use to make home-made explosives – however nasty they might be.'

Rhett agreed, 'There were definitely large amounts of money involved. Walid said he had overheard Farouq talking; he mentioned Wormsley and something about a deal for millions of dollars last year. He also told me that Farouq was a master tactician when he was in the army; he was good at creating diversions and red herrings as a cover for a major offensive. Everything Farouq said to me boasted of something huge; he mentioned how I would live to regret letting Osama bin Laden escape in Afghanistan.'

'I thought he said that his group weren't religious fanatics,' said Malcolm.

'They don't think they are fanatics. They could be linked with Al Qaeda if they share the same goal of removing the West from certain regions; the connection would explain having access to financial support,' said Michele.

'This Wormsley chap seems to be mentioned a lot in all of these dealings. Why hasn't he been arrested?' asked Malcolm.

'That is what I was hoping to find out from Rhett,' said Michele.

Gordon and Malcolm raised their eyebrows and looked at Rhett.

'We had information linking Rhett to Wormsley,' continued Michele, 'but it turned out to be a false lead. We know that Farouq and Walid have talked about Wormsley but there is no evidence to prove that he is linked to any of this. He has close friends in very high places.'

Countdown

'It seems like this Wormsley fellow has a lot to answer for,' stated Gordon.

'Yes, but it doesn't help in the current situation. Wormsley may have sold weapons, but he won't necessarily know what they are being used for,' replied Michele.

'We need to find Salma,' said Rhett.

'Let's try and get some sleep,' said Michele, 'I suspect we are in for a long day.'

Countdown

32

Wednesday, July 6th, 2005
Train to London, UK

Salma found a seat by the window in a quiet carriage and placed the suitcase carefully on the seat beside her. She stared out of the window watching the green and yellow fields flashing by bathed in a golden light as the sun began to set slowly and beautifully. She knew that it was the last sunset that she would see.

She breathed deeply and cursed Lorraine for upsetting their plans, but then remembered Sawsan saying that their location had been discovered. Who had found out where they were? It can't have been Lorraine; she definitely didn't have a clue what was going on and even though she escaped, she wouldn't have been able to contact anyone. She knew that she had played Lorraine well and that Lorraine considered her to be her best friend. All those months of listening to her talk about her darling Rhett and how much she loved him, going to watch vapid films and dreadful plays, pretending to share the same interests; it would all be worthwhile now.

She smiled to herself; she would have revenge on all those girls in school who had bullied her and made her life miserable as a young, naïve girl coming from Iraq. She would have revenge on the murderer of her beloved brother, Ali. Her mum and Sawsan had never understood before; they loved their new lives, but Ali's death had hurt them, and they finally understood that it was the culture of the people in this land that had led to his death. She thought about her father and felt a deep rage. He had made them come here, he had torn her away from her school and her friends, for what? To keep them safe was all her mother ever told them, but Farouq had told her that her father had brought the danger upon them by going against their honoured leader, Saddam Hussein; he was the only one who had told her the truth. Only Farouq and Tariq understood her terrible sense of loss and feeling of disconnection and Uncle Farouq had made sense of it all and given them both something in which to believe. She desperately wanted to call Uncle Farouq but knew that it was too dangerous now. He had told her that there were others involved and supporting her, but that she was the most important one. She wouldn't let him down.

33

Thursday, July 7th, 2005
Medical Centre, Hereford, UK

Lorraine woke up in a strange room with an odd glow penetrating her eyelids and her hands feeling heavy and bound. Her eyes flew open, and she sat up screaming.

A gentle hand touched her shoulder, and she heard a soothing voice that she recognised. 'It's okay, darling, you are safe, you are in hospital, I'm here and your mother is here,' said her father.

She lay back against the pillows taking in his kind, worried face and as her mind connected with what she was seeing and where she was Lorraine immediately felt for the bump in her stomach, saw her heavily bandaged hands and arms, and looked at him anxiously.

Her father, Keith smiled and said, 'The baby is doing fine.' She broke down in tears and hugged him, despite the pain in her arms. Finally, she pulled away and said, 'Did they get them? Did they stop them? Oh my God, Dad. Did they get Salma?'

'You should rest,' he said. 'There are people who want to ask you questions when you wake up. Your mum will be back soon, she just went to get some coffee.'

'I am awake. I need to speak to them now, Dad, there is something terrible planned.'

Countdown

A man in a suit came up behind Keith, and Lorraine stared at him in alarm; he didn't look like a doctor. Keith turned around and said, 'Can't this wait? She's only just opened her eyes.'

'Hello, Lorraine, my name is Paul Davies, MI5. You've been through a lot, but we really need to ask you some questions if that's okay.'

Davies was a short man with a broad, square face, close-cropped fair hair, a strong nose and narrow, intelligent eyes behind large, black framed glasses. His resting face presented a calm, benevolent expression which endeared people to him and made them feel that they could trust him.

Behind him, Lorraine's mother Gillian appeared; she put the steaming hot cups of coffee down, rushed to the bedside and held Lorraine tight, with tears streaming down her cheeks. Lorraine winced at the pain in her shoulder and said, 'I'm alright, Mum. I really need to talk to this man. I want to say it all, to get it out of me.'

Gillian brushed at her eyes with her hands and stepped back, 'Yes, yes, of course. We'll be just here.' She took Keith's hand and pulled him back to the far side of the hospital room.

Davies took the chair at the side of the bed and told Lorraine to start from the beginning and to go through whatever she could remember down to the slightest detail.

Lorraine breathed in and forced herself to remember. 'The house had an unusual smell, it was musty as if it were an old house that hadn't been lived in, but there was also a distinctive smell of bleach,' she began. 'I just thought they must have been cleaning.' She paused and looked up at Davies. 'Did they blow it up?' she asked suddenly.

'No, they didn't blow it up,' said Paul. 'How did you know about that?'

'When I was in the garden, I heard Salma's sister, Sawsan. She said that she would give Sultan the order to detonate.'

'Okay, let's go back to the beginning.'

'I looked out of the kitchen window and saw that the garden was really overgrown and that the fence was falling down and broken, which I thought was a shame. I feel stupid now, but I think I felt sorry for them not being able to afford to keep it nice. It didn't occur to me that there was anything wrong. They gave me some tea which was extremely sweet, and I began to feel very warm and sleepy. I think I apologised, with the pregnancy I have had odd moments of overwhelming tiredness, and I remember Salma telling me to have a rest. I vaguely heard them talking about having a good dinner after they had got the video ready and something about the big day, tomorrow. I was wondering what video we were going to watch and then I must have gone to sleep. They were talking about the video they were going to make of… of me.' A film of tears covered her eyes.

'They definitely said 'tomorrow'?' asked Davies.

'Yes, I'm sure. What day is it now? How long have I been out of it? Is it too late?' said Lorraine getting upset.

Gillian moved forward but Keith held her back as Davies calmed Lorraine down and reassured her that it was not too late if she could help them with as much information as possible, and that everything she was saying was helpful.

Lorraine gulped and fought back the tears as she continued, 'I came round, and I was tied to a chair and gagged.' A tear slipped out of one eye and rolled down her cheek.

'Oh, for goodness' sake!' cried her mother. 'Can't you see what she's been through?'

'I'm okay, Mum,' Lorraine said. 'Dad, why don't you take Mum for a walk, you don't need to hear everything.'

Keith nodded and led Gillian sobbing from the room. Paul Davies turned back to Lorraine and told her that she was an amazing woman, that she was helping so much.

Lorraine continued to describe how the men had come in and set up the camera, 'One man stood behind me and the other stepped forward and gave a little speech. He seemed to need to tell me how important he was, and I think it wasn't part of the plan because the other man shouted at him, and he stopped abruptly and went back to the camera.'

'What did he tell you?' asked the soothing, hypnotic voice of Paul.

Countdown

'Um, something about making the Twin Towers look insignificant and the IRA attack on this site would seem like an indoor firework in comparison.' She paused, 'Oh God, I'm sorry. I was so confused, and I was worrying about Salma. I didn't know who they were, and I thought they must have taken Salma as well.'

'Everything is important, Lorraine. Just say it as you remember,' said Davies.

'I'm not sure, it sounds a bit ridiculous now, but I think he said something like there will be more bones than a little Roman girl to find,' she said, as more tears began to stream down her face. She asked for some water and Davies held a cup to her lips before she continued with a description of her escape and getting back into the garden of the house.

'When I was in the garden, I heard them talking about detonating the house and the woman called Sawsan seemed to be in charge. I think she gave Salma a train ticket to London and said that her suitcase was in the hall.'

'Are you sure that she said suitcase?' asked Davies.

'Yes,' replied Lorraine, 'because then she told Reem to get the rucksacks ready and I remember thinking that it was odd that Salma had a case. She gave more instructions about getting Sultan and Aziz, so I guess they were the men who took the video. She said that at ten o'clock tomorrow they would show the world. I heard a car leaving and suddenly realised that they were going to blow up the house when the police arrived and that I needed to warn them. I remember a kind soldier in the garden and then nothing. I'm so sorry, I shouldn't have fainted,' she said, looking distraught. 'I tried to remember everything, I knew it would be important, but oh God!'

She broke down sobbing as she remembered the terror she had felt in front of the camera, the gun pressed into her skull.

Paul Davies signalled for a nurse to come over and said, 'You have helped so much Lorraine.' The nurse plunged a needle into her arm, and she relaxed into a deep sleep.

34

Thursday, July 7th, 2005
Flight to London

Rhett moved to a single seat at the back of the plane and, pressing a switch, it unfolded under him into a flat bed. Thoughts crammed into his head, running around and demanding attention, but he knew that he would need to have his wits about him when they got to the UK. He turned his brain off, closed his eyes and allowed himself to be engulfed by emptiness.

It felt as though he had been asleep for minutes when Michele tapped him gently on the shoulder. He sprang up forgetting he had a seat belt on and fell back cursing as he undid it and looked at her questioningly.

'We're coming into land, and we have some news. Lorraine woke up and she has given us valuable information,' said Michele.

He got up and followed her back down the aisle to where her computer and phone were lying on the table. He was sure that she had not been to sleep at all. She talked as she walked, 'Lorraine overheard the women talking and one said that Salma had a ticket to London and that she had a suitcase to take with her.'

They looked at one another and Rhett said what they were both thinking, 'Hereford is just a side show. We have had our eyes focused on activities in Hereford and the big deal is going to be in London. But where?'

'Apparently, the guy who was filming her told Lorraine that what they had planned would be nothing compared to the attack on the Twin Towers and that he'd said something about the same site as an IRA attack.'

'That leaves thousands of possibilities!' exclaimed Rhett.

They sat down in front of the laptop and were soon joined by the bleary-eyed Malcolm and Gordon who also looked as if sleep had avoided them. The air steward brought them water, coffee and croissants and asked them if they wanted a full breakfast. Only Gordon said that he did.

'Even if we focus just on London, we are still talking hundreds of places. Was there anything else?' asked Rhett.

Michele looked at her screen, 'She also said something which Davies couldn't make sense of and thought it was something she had misheard.'

'What was it?' asked Rhett.

'Something about more bones than a little Roman girl.'

They all looked at each other with blank faces. Rhett stared out of the small window of the aircraft and watched as streaks of orange and pink light spread across the indigo skyline. He allowed the information to circle and settle in his brain and after a while he turned back to the others and said, 'We know that Farouq was angry about the men behind the politicians, the money men. How many attacks were on financial institutions in London?'

Michele began to type in a search, but Malcolm spoke, 'There was a bomb outside the Stock Exchange in the early nineties,'

'And then there was the huge one at the Baltic Exchange,' added Gordon.

'That's right,' agreed Malcolm, 'the biggest bomb in Britain since the Second World War,'

'What's there now?' asked Rhett.

Countdown

Malcolm and Gordon both shrugged their shoulders and Michele put in another search. She gasped when the result came up on the screen. 'St Mary Axe,' she said.

'The Baltic Exchange was demolished, and it became the site for a new skyscraper which opened last year; it has been given a nickname and is commonly known as The Gherkin, right in the middle of London's financial centre.'

Malcolm looked up with excitement in his eyes, 'That's where they found the remains of a young girl dating back to around 400BC – when the Romans were in London!'

'That's got to be it,' said Rhett. 'Now we know what Farouq meant when he said that it would definitely leave a sour taste in the mouths of Westerners.'

'The whole area is smothered in CCTV cameras, we'll easily find her,' said Michele, typing a message to her boss. 'Since the Baltic Exchange bombing the whole area has been reinforced with bollards and protection from hostile vehicles. It is known as the Ring of Steel,' continued Michele, reading information on the screen.

'But it still isn't adding up. How can she be carrying anything more than the others? What if it isn't Salma who is going there?' asked Malcolm. 'What if she's another red herring?'

They were all still baffled and frustrated when the air steward told them that the plane was preparing for landing at the City of London airport.

***

While Rhett was still sleeping on board the jet, four young men met at Luton station car park, took rucksacks out of the boots of their cars, and put them on before going into the station. As the luxury aircraft was coming down to land, the men were travelling on board a train to London King's cross station. As the wheels on the Gulfstream screeched on the tarmac the four men got off the train and joined hundreds of commuters heading for the Underground. Before heading to separate trains, the four of them hugged and went in different directions.

169

Countdown

Rhett made his way down the steps of the plane following Michele, Gordon and Malcolm to the Range Rover Sport where the driver was waiting to take them straight to Hereford.

Countdown

35

8.47am Thursday, July 7th, 2005
Passengers on the London Underground from King's Cross Station

Mariam wished she'd worn cooler clothes as she ran to catch the tube on the Circle line heading east that was waiting on the platform ready to close its doors, or to be more precise that she'd left home a little earlier so that she wasn't rushing to get to her interview. She just managed to step across the gap and into the packed carriage as the doors swished shut. She breathed in with relief and stared up at the map of the tube line checking the number of stops she had until her destination.

The carriage was packed full of commuters young and old, mostly dressed in smart office suits or trendy, smart-casual outfits. She looked down at her plain, black trousers and simple, long-sleeved top worn under her new blue jacket that she'd picked up from a charity shop and felt trickles of sweat run down her back and bead on her forehead. She hoped she'd have time to nip into a toilet and redo her make-up before she got there.

On the Circle line west-bound train, Jamal smiled at the woman next to him; she gave him a thin smile in response and turned her head away. He always smiled at people, he thought that it was the best way to start his day. Some found him odd, but others smiled back, and he knew that he had brightened their lives a little. Everyone always looked so serious in the morning, going through the motions of getting where they needed to be; not paying attention to where they were or with whom they were sharing this cramped and intimate space. A gap in their lives that they just wanted to be over so that they could get to wherever it was that they were going. Jamal thought that this was such a waste as he looked around the carriage and played his usual game of deciding who people were, what they did for a living and what their lives beyond the Underground were like. The man in a smart suit, sitting with his legs crossed and reading a book had probably been taking the same route for years and knew exactly how many pages he could read before reaching his stop; a steady job which he quite enjoyed but wasn't passionate about, a wife he loved but took for granted, who also worked and organised his clothes, his meals, his social life, and the kids. An intense looking man with the same dark complexion as his own was cuddling a rucksack as if it contained his life savings.

On the Piccadilly line, Mohammed squeezed into the packed carriage and grabbed hold of the pole next to him to keep his balance as the train jerked into motion. He shifted slightly and his rucksack bumped against the man next to him. He moved back, apologising and pressed himself against the partition. The man, Harris, nodded in acknowledgement as the train moved out of the station and into the dark tunnel and they both went into their own thoughts. Mohammed thought about his sister at home with their dying mother and prayed for them. If he could do well here in London, they might be able to pay for better treatment, even find a cure. He knew that God worked in mysterious ways.

Harris looked around the carriage. On the seats further down, a young man with a rucksack that caused him to lean slightly forward seemed to be mouthing prayers and he sent him kind thoughts. Next to him, an Asian girl looked as if she should be in school but was probably about thirty; it was so difficult to guess the ages of all the different nationalities. Her eyes were gazing unseeing at the adverts for insurance companies, helplines, and charities above the heads of the passengers facing her. Harris' mind drifted to the man he had met the night before

Countdown

and his heart warmed; there may even have been a little smile on his usually pan face.

***

Within seconds of each other, on their different trains, Mariam, Jamal, Harris, and Mohammed saw a brilliant flash of white light and before they could even begin to comprehend it, a massive boom shattered their ear drums.

Mariam was blown across the carriage and both her legs were torn away from her body. She came round to a world of smoke and screams and felt someone tying something tight around the top of her thighs and she didn't understand why. She looked down and couldn't make sense of the fact that her legs weren't there anymore; her final thought was that she was going to be late as she realised that she was listening to her own screams.

Mohammed was thrown across the gangway and lay unconscious for a while. When he came to, he couldn't make out where he was and struggled out from underneath the body of a man. He saw that it was the man who he had nudged with his backpack, and he felt his neck for a pulse but couldn't find one. Harris lay there with his eyes closed, his face and head covered in blood. With intense shock Mohammed realised that the man was dead and as he began to look around, he saw that there were bodies and body parts all around the smoke-filled carriage, and he wondered if he had woken up in Hell. Through his ringing ears he began to hear screams and shouts for help and looked down at an Asian woman whose arm had been ripped off above the elbow. He pulled off his belt and tied it around the top of the woman's arm talking to her gently and telling her that help was on its way. He still had his rucksack on his back, and he scrabbled to open it and take out his sports towel which he tore into strips using his teeth and hands with a strength he didn't know that he had. He moved through the carriage handing out strips to other people who were unhurt and trying to help the many injured people.

Jamal was picked up and thrown like a discarded apple core; the force of the blast drove the pound coin in his pocket through his flesh and into his hip bone, his spleen shattered, and one leg was ripped apart as the side of the carriage tore open and he blew through the gaping hole and landed on the tracks below. He could hear people wailing and praying inside the carriage above him and he thought about the number of lives that had just been ruined, including his own. He thought about his wife and two children, trying to remember if he had told them that he loved them recently. His life began to flash in front of him and he was sure that he was going to die, when strong arms lifted him up and told him that he was going to be fine.

Mariam opened her eyes again and lay still; she could hear people yelling and crying for help all around her and although she wanted to help, she couldn't get to them. This was Britain, things like this didn't happen in Britain. Her mind flashed back to memories of her family screaming and shouting as they were slaughtered in Nicaragua; memories she thought she had buried and put behind her when she moved to the free world.

**

The fourth man with a rucksack on his back walked out of King's cross station and headed for a bus stop.

Countdown

36

Thursday, July 7th, 2005
City of London Airport

Rhett was following the others across the tarmac towards the Range Rover Sport waiting to take them to Hereford when Michele's phone rang. She put the phone to her ear and listened. Suddenly, she stopped in her tracks and turned to Rhett, her face pale with horror.

'Are you sure? Where is this from?' she paused, listening again. 'Send me through all the details,' she said and closed the phone.

She looked at Rhett and said, 'They have received information telling them that the bomb Salma is carrying is probably a nuclear device.'

Rhett looked at her with complete disbelief, 'How the hell is that even viable?'

'The intel is solid. An anonymous person gave the information to the Home Office. They have tracked some arms deals made in the last year and Farouq's name came up in relation to the trail of the purchase of a device known as a suitcase bomb.'

Malcolm stopped Rhett from swearing some more when he turned around and said, 'Did you say suitcase bomb?'

'Yes,' replied Michele, 'Have you heard of them?'

'Goodness, yes, many years ago. I worked for the Ministry of Defence when I left university and we looked at all kinds of weaponry. During the Cold War when everyone was living in fear of nuclear bombs and the US were racing to get ahead of Russia in arms development, they created a portable bomb small enough to fit in a rucksack or a suitcase – hence the name. Officially they are known as SADM – Special Atomic Demolition Munitions. It came out a few years ago that the Russians were making their own even smaller and lighter version well into the 1980s and that they couldn't account for a large number of their stock.'

'You mean they lost some?' said Rhett.

'The Russian government denied the claims but the American version definitely exists and so it is entirely likely that the Russians had one of their own,' said Malcolm. 'The American SADM weighed around twenty-three kilos, was ten or eleven inches in diameter and about fifteen inches long,' he added.

'How the fuck do you know all that?' asked Rhett.

'Oh well, I studied physics and chemistry as well as engineering and it was just a topic that interested me,' said Malcolm modestly.

'So, the Russian one could be lighter and smaller and fit into a hand luggage style suitcase, and…'

'And be easily pulled on a wheelie bag by a young woman,' said Rhett finishing the sentence for Michele.

'What the hell,' said Gordon.

Michele's phone rang again, and she put her boss from MI6, Leyton Lewis on speaker.

'What are we talking about here?' asked Rhett, 'What are the capabilities of such a weapon?'

'We're talking about a device with the capability of one kiloton of explosive, that is the equivalent of one thousand tons of TNT; the Baltic Exchange bomb that you discussed was one ton of TNT. It would cause massive destruction in an inner-city area, causing many buildings in possibly a half mile range to collapse with the people inside them and then there would be huge radioactive contamination. Hold on,' said Leyton.

They heard him swear under his breath and come back on the line, 'There have just been three separate explosions on the

Countdown

Underground. I'll get back to you with more information, but first reports do not indicate anything on a nuclear scale, thank Christ! We still think that ten o'clock is when Salma's bomb will be detonated. It could already be set on a timer.'

'Did you get our thoughts on The Gherkin as the target?' asked Michele.

'MI5 are convinced that the terrorists are more likely to target parliament. All the emergency services have been diverted to the tube station explosions away from Westminster. We haven't got time to evacuate the whole area without knowing exactly where the bomb will go off, but we have started getting the Houses of Parliament clear. Luckily, the Prime Minister is out of the country, we have just won the bid for the 2012 Olympics to be held in London.'

'But everything Lorraine told us pointed to The Gherkin,' said Michele.

'Unfortunately, I think we are clutching at straws. Three other bombs have gone off and we thought we had arrested all the people in the Hereford house apart from Salma. We don't know what intel to trust at the moment. We're working with MI5, and we've got everybody possible scanning CCTV to find her, but she could be anywhere. She might not even have the case anymore!'

'What the hell!' said Gordon. 'Am I in London or Baghdad?' Rhett looked at his wrist and realised that Farouq had taken his watch along with his clothes the night before.

'What time is it?' he asked.

'Just before nine,' said Malcolm.

'Get a team to support me, Michele. I am going to The Gherkin.'

'Looks like we are your team,' said Michele.

'There could be a nuclear explosion, you need to get Malcolm and Gordon away from the city.'

'I'm staying with you,' said Malcolm.

'Oh God,' muttered Gordon, closing his eyes. 'Let's get moving, we don't have much time if there's a ten o'clock deadline.'

Countdown

They rushed to the Range Rover, Rhett jumped into the passenger seat and told the driver that they needed to get to St Mary Axe as quickly as possible. The driver looked at Rhett and said, 'Is it true?'

'Is what true?'

'London's under attack?'

'It seems that way, mate. You okay to drive us into the city?'

'I'm ex-army, served in the Falklands, didn't I? Yes, I'll be proud to drive, I'm Phil, by the way.'

'Good to meet you, Phil,' said Rhett. 'Let's go.'

Phil turned on his headlights despite the morning sun and headed out of the airport and into the heavy traffic pouring into the city. He turned out to be a fearless and wild driver and cut in and out of lanes beeping his horn, flashing his lights and bullying his way past the other vehicles.

On the way, Rhett and Michele made a plan that once they got close, they would both get out and approach The Gherkin from different directions, keeping an eye out for Salma. They put on wires and Gordon was to track them and call for back up if they found her. Malcolm was to find out how to disarm the device in case nobody could get there in time.

Phil knew London like the back of his hand and went in and out of smaller roads and side streets until they got near to Aldgate East station, but it was still slow going and suddenly the traffic snarled to a complete stop. They could hear ambulances, police cars and fire engines screaming and wailing ahead of them and realised that they were blocked by the jams created by the emergency services going to the explosions on the underground.

'We'll go the rest of the way on foot,' declared Rhett. 'It'll be quicker. Phil, drive as far away from the area as you can!'

They were less than half a mile from St Mary Axe when Rhett and Michele jumped out and began running towards the impressive skyscraper that towered above the mixture of ancient and modern buildings around it. The swirling stripes that spiralled around the outside and the myriad glass panels glistened in the sunlight but to Rhett's military eye it looked

Countdown

more like a giant bullet or a rocket than a gherkin. It was a quarter to ten when they both neared the perimeter and slowed to a casual walk as they separated and went in different directions around the building trying to make out a face in the crowds moving along the street.

37

9.00 am Thursday, July 7th, 2005
Hotel near St Mary Axe, London

Salma was lying on the bed in her room in a small anonymous hotel where travellers came and went daily. She had stripped down to her underwear and was flicking through the channels showing the first scenes from the bombings; she smiled with satisfaction. A picture came up on the screen and she saw that it was a photograph of her. She stared at the face, thinking that it wasn't a great photo and gave a little laugh as she realised how unlike that image she was in her disguise. She glanced at the time on the corner of the screen and got up to go to the bathroom to wash herself.

Feeling clean and fresh she strapped on her false tummy and put on the same frumpy dress and wig. Piling on the pale foundation and inserting her grey contact lenses, gone was the stylish, middle eastern beauty portrayed on the television. She stroked the enormous belly that protruded under the soft cotton material and knew she would never know what it felt like to have a child of her own. She was glad; this was no world in which to bring up a child. She thought about Lorraine and cursed her once again for escaping; she had totally underestimated her and hoped that even though she had got away, she had lost her baby. She refused to admit that her rage towards Lorraine was because she liked her; the truth was that Lorraine was kind, caring and fun to be around. She had to keep

Countdown

reminding herself that Lorraine was in love with the man who had killed Ali, that she was the enemy. When she found out that her precious Rhett was dead, she would be devastated and that made Salma smile; Lorraine would suffer more by staying alive.

Uncle Farouq would be so proud of her; her people would remember her as a martyr who had freed them from the shackles of the West.

The television reporter burbled on about the carnage caused by the three bombs and Salma wondered what had happened to the fourth bomber. Sawsan thought she was in charge, but Farouq had only told Salma about the other four bombs. Should she wait until the fourth bomb went off? That had been her instruction, but she had also been told to set the timer for ten o'clock. She decided to set the timer and then casually made her way out of the hotel and into the street only a few minutes' walk away from her final destination. Even if she didn't reach the site they had chosen, the results would be just as catastrophic, but she had plenty of time to get into position.

***

Having been once round the building, Rhett and Michele passed on the street without making eye contact when Malcolm announced that there had been another bomb on a bus in Tavistock Square and their hearts sank. It seemed clear that there was more to this whole plan than Farouq had shared. Were they even close to the truth in trying to stop Salma?

'Get us some support in here, Malcolm. I don't care how you do it.'

Michele continued forward to make another round of the building, but Rhett stopped and stepped onto the walkway in front of the main entrance and perched on the surrounding wall pretending to do up his shoelaces. There were still a lot of people walking past or milling about, but most had gone into their offices to start work and he had just seen someone with a wheelie case coming up the narrow street behind Michele. The dark blonde hair and the large stomach didn't fit the description of Salma, but it was something else that had caught his trained eye. Every so often the woman glanced over her shoulder and her eyes flitted from side to side as if she were making sure that nobody was following her. She was also walking with ease; it wasn't the gait of a woman who was in the late stages of pregnancy.

'Eyes on Salma, four o'clock' he said quietly. 'Malcolm, have we got support?'

'On its way,' replied Malcolm. 'SCO19 and bomb disposal one minute out.'

Rhett didn't know what his plan was, but he decided to walk towards Salma and confront her. If he could get into the suitcase, maybe there was a way to diffuse it. She got closer to the open area outside the magnificent building, and he stood up, but a flurry of movement caught his eye and suddenly four men appeared from a doorway and surrounded her. They pulled out machetes from under their light jackets which they held in the air threatening anyone near them and slashing out. People started running in terror, screaming, and pushing to get away from the men who strode together with Salma in the middle. Even Salma looked startled but then she smiled with confidence as they moved down the narrow street, closer to The Gherkin.

With everyone running, they didn't see Rhett bent low and dodging, using people heading towards him as a cover. He got as close as he could and rolled across the tarmac into the legs of the man on his nearest side and bowled him over. Rhett then leapt to his feet, snatched the knife out of the man's hands and plunged the glinting metal into his side. The lead man turned and lunged at him, but Rhett dodged out of the way of the long, steel edge and swung the knife in his own hand at the body of the oncoming third man who fell to the floor clutching his bleeding stomach and dropping his knife which bounced and clattered across the ground. Rhett spun round to face the two remaining men with their curved weapons at the ready and saw that Salma was hurrying towards the entrance to The Gherkin with the case. Nobody paid her any attention in the general panic of rushing, panic-stricken people.

Suddenly Michele sprang out of nowhere, scooped up the fallen knife and smashed it into the back of one of the men, who fell forward with a grunt. Rhett took advantage of the distraction and thrust his weapon at the last man, but he parried, and their knives clashed sending sparks into the air.

'Get Salma!' yelled Rhett as the man drove his knife forward and Rhett just managed to dodge severe injury as the blade cut through his shirt and slashed his bicep. He jumped back as the man let out a guttural scream and rushed towards him swinging his knife wildly. Rhett moved his weapon into his left hand and as his attacker lunged and brought his right arm across his body, Rhett brought his left arm down with immense force and severed the man's hand at the wrist. Blood spurted from the cut arteries as the man fell to the ground clutching at his arm with his other hand and screaming.

Michele threw the knife down and ran after Salma who was struggling to move quickly with the case and the cumbersome padding on her stomach. She saw her getting closer to the glass doors where people were pushing and shoving to get in and away from the knifemen; the doorman was unable to stop them, and Michele raced to get alongside Salma.

Shocked faces pressed against the windows watching the events outside with phones raised calling friends or taking poor quality photos as a slim, blonde woman suddenly dived at a pregnant woman who was trying to get away from the terrorists.

Michele hurled her body across the space dividing them and collided sidelong with Salma, knocking her hands off the case which rolled and span on its wheels across the shiny plaza. Michele and Salma sprawled across the floor and then scrambled to their feet. They stood facing one another, breathing heavily with their hands up ready to fight.

A rough voice behind Michele said, 'Oy, leave the poor woman alone!' And she felt a hand restraining her.

Michele pulled away from the man and charged at Salma, ripped at her dress, and tore it away from her body to reveal the foam contraption strapped to her front. She heard gasps of shock ripple around and then Salma screeched and leapt forward. She raked her fingernails down the sides of Michele's face, grabbed at Michele's hair and dragged her head down. Michele punched upwards with both her fists and knocked Salma's hands away, then with a crunching right hook she caught Salma full on the jaw and teeth and blood spurted out of her mouth. She flew backwards and landed on the hard ground with a loud smack as her wig slid off and her skull connected with the solid surface of the paving slabs.

Two vans screamed into the adjacent road and Specialist Operations armed police filed out of the doors as Rhett grabbed the rolling suitcase and carried it to the back of one of the vehicles. The bomb disposal team was still en route.

There was no point in telling people to take cover or to warn them about the bomb. If it went off, they were all done for. He unzipped the case and brought out a black metal box which he opened to reveal a canister not much bigger than an old thermos flask, and just as archaic looking, resting in a cushioned nest within a hard plastic casing. On the casing was a basic timer revealing forty seconds and counting down. A simple knob had been turned to the 'on' position. Above that was a plastic arm that had been removed from a safety catch.

Malcolm's voice came into his ear instructing him to move the arm back into the safety holder before turning the switch to off. With sweat gleaming on his skin, he clicked the safety arm into place as the clock continued to count down and then he turned the knob until it pointed at the word 'off', but nothing happened. The counter continued on its fatal path down towards zero.

'It's still counting down! What do I do?' he asked swearing under his breath.

'Remove the outer casing,' instructed Malcolm breathing hard.

Rhett looked around and grabbed the machete he had flung to the ground nearby. Using the tip, he forced the casing open and ripped it off to reveal three wires leading from the timer into the bomb.

'We've got red, blue and green,' Rhett said keeping his voice calm as sweat dripped into his eyes.

'I-I don't know,' said Malcolm. 'Hang on.'

Countdown

The timer counted down from five seconds to four.

'Cut the blue one!' cried Malcolm.

Rhett pulled the blue wire away from the others and sliced the knife through it. He held his breath as he watched the timer click to two seconds and then stop.

38

10.00am Thursday, July 7th, 2005
London, UK

Rhett felt a hand rest lightly on his back, he looked round to see Michele with streaks of blood on her cheeks and pulled her into an embrace as the bomb squad arrived and removed the case and its contents.

With immaculate efficiency the police cleared the area, Salma and her goons were arrested and whisked away for medical treatment and questioning, the suitcase bomb had been removed and armed police stood guard in the cordoned off area around The Gherkin. It was all over in a matter of minutes and the news of a skirmish between rival gangs near the London landmark building faded into insignificance beside the atrocities and devastation caused by the four bomb strikes in other areas of London. Nobody would ever know about the deadly and potentially fatal threat that had just been averted.

Michele pulled away from Rhett and they looked at each other. Michele saw the blood spatters adorning his chest and face and touched his upper arm gently with her fingers. He glanced down to where blood flowed through the torn material and dripped to the ground.

'Damn! I just bought this shirt,' he said.

'You need to get that arm looked at; I hear there's a good hospital in Hereford,' said Michele with a kind smile.

Countdown

They heard a voice shouting Rhett's name and they looked over to where Gordon and Malcolm were being stopped by a police officer. Michele signalled to the officer to let them pass and they ran down the street to join them.

'I thought I told you to get as far away from here as possible,' said Rhett.

'We had every faith in you,' said Malcolm. 'Phil's in the car around the corner waiting to take you to Hereford.'

Michele took Malcolm and Gordon to the SIS building at Vauxhall Cross to debrief with Leyton Lewis and Paul Davies, who was back in London. Rhett allowed a medic to quickly bandage his arm and promised the man that he was on his way to hospital to get it looked at properly, then he ran to Phil's car, and they set off through the crowded streets of central London. Rhett watched the people they passed; tourists standing on street corners studying *A to Z* map books and looking confused, others with cameras were taking shots of the many historic and modern wonders of the beautiful city. Londoners went about their daily business with dour, stressed faces, drivers hooted their horns and looked frustrated and angry. None of them were aware how close they had been to complete obliteration or radiation sickness. They might have had lucky escapes from the bomb blasts on the bus and the Tube and be filled with fear when they heard about them, but they would never know the enormity of what could have happened.

As Phil tore down the motorway, Rhett tried to sleep but adrenaline was racing around his body, and he was still on intense alert; his body was pumped up and high from fighting and he hoped that they hadn't missed anything, that there weren't any more surprises. He began to think about Lorraine and what could have happened if she hadn't escaped, and as the car drew into the hospital grounds, he realised that although he was desperate to see her, he was also terrified.

He knew fear, of course, but it was an energy he could normally channel into the task ahead; he had all the tools and usually a team with him or behind him providing intel or issuing orders. Going into battle or confronting dangerous situations didn't faze him; he knew what he had to do, and he would do it to the best of his ability whatever the consequences. However, he hadn't had any training for going to see the love of his life who he had been trying to forget about for the last six months; the woman who had broken all contact with him and who was now lying in a hospital bed because of him. The woman who was carrying his child. There was no strategy or action plan.

He ran down the corridor towards the ward that she was on, receiving strange looks from the people he passed. He reached the reception desk and asked for her room. An efficient looking, attractive nurse glanced up from her desk and did a double take when she saw the good-looking man with mussed up hair, a bruised and cut face, a blood-stained shirt and on his arm a bandage seeping bright red blood. She sat a little more upright and self-consciously tucked a stray hair behind her ear as she smiled at him.

'Do you want me to look at that?' she offered, seeing the blood beginning to run down his arm from the wound.
Confused he looked at his arm, which he had completely forgotten about, and then back at her with frustration, 'I just want to see Lorraine Carter, please.'

Disappointed that she hadn't gained his attention, she bristled and told him that visiting hours were later, only immediate family was allowed to see her. Rhett realised his mistake and instead of reaching across the desk and shaking her, which was what he felt like doing, he smiled at her and looked into her eyes.

'I bet you have to deal with all sorts in here,' he said. 'I know you hate jerks like me coming in out of visiting hours and thinking they can mess up your rules.'

She smiled at him, 'You bet,' she said. 'Lorraine is under sedation at the moment. The nurse I took over from said that people have been coming and going all night to see her. There is a police guard by her door and her parents only left an hour ago, but she's only got a few cuts and bruises. Is she someone special?'

Countdown

Rhett gulped. 'She is very special,' he said. He looked at her name badge and leant in towards her and said, 'I am the father of her baby, is there any chance you can make an exception to the rules and let me see her, Helen?'

He saw her visibly soften under his gaze, but she said, 'I really shouldn't if you are not her husband.'

Suddenly, Rhett heard someone saying his name and turned to see Lorraine's father coming down the corridor. A tall, handsome man with a full head of light brown hair looking clean shaven but tired and anxious, he strode towards Rhett.

'Rhett, thank God you are here.' He put his arm out to shake Rhett's hand and saw the bandaged, bleeding arm and the stains on his shirt.

'Jesus! What the hell is going on? Nobody will tell us anything. Lorraine was kidnapped but managed to get away. That is all they have said, but then there is all this stuff about suspected terrorists being arrested here and I have just heard about the terrible London bombings on the news. I can't help thinking that they are giving Lorraine a lot of attention for the victim of a random attack which she managed to get away from.' He was close to tears. 'She has been waking up screaming, Rhett. A man in a smart suit came to talk to her and then they sedated her. I took Gillian back to the hotel to get some rest, but I couldn't stay away. I just showered, changed and came back in case she wakes up.'

Rhett put his good arm around the older man's shoulder and said, 'She's going to be alright, Keith. This lovely nurse has told me that she has only got a few scratches and she is in a bit of shock, but she's strong. She will be fine. Let's go and see her, shall we?' He looked at the nurse for confirmation and she nodded reluctantly.

Keith heaved a great sigh as he led the way to Lorraine's private room and told the policeman on duty that it was okay for Rhett to go in to see her. Lorraine was still sleeping so he told Rhett that he would go to get coffee.

'You look like you could do with some,' said Keith. 'I won't ask what you've been doing.'

Countdown

Rhett opened the door and stepped into the brightly lit room with sunlight and a pale blue sky beyond the window. He looked at Lorraine lying on her back with her eyes closed; tubes led from under her bandages up to various machines and drips and the steady beeping of the heart monitor filled the room. He moved to the side of the bed with a knot forming in his stomach; her hands and arms swathed in bandages lay on top of the sheets and her beautiful face, not bandaged, was ravaged with bruises and criss-crosses of irregular red lines, shiny under healing ointment.

He sat down in the chair by her side and reached his hand slowly across her body to rest it gently on the curved mound of her stomach and felt a movement, a rippling of the skin under his touch and a small jab. His heart felt as if it had somersaulted inside his chest, and he was overwhelmed by emotions he had never experienced.

'Rhett?'

He heard someone whisper his name and looked up with his thick, black lashes glistening with tears and saw Lorraine looking at him with teardrops brimming and then spilling over the edges of her eyes.

He wanted to crush her with a hug but daren't hurt her damaged body, so he sat still, and stared at her.
She looked at him not believing her eyes, 'Is it really you?' she asked.

'Yes, it's really me,' he said brushing his eyes with his fingertips and smiling at her.

'If I'd known you were coming, I would have dressed up,' she said smiling back. She saw his hand still on her stomach and stared at him with worry in her eyes.

He heard another voice, this time in his ear, 'Tell her you love her, for God's sake,' came the rough voice of Gordon and he realised that he still had the piece in his ear. He grinned and Lorraine frowned at him. Suddenly, he knew exactly what to do.

'I am so sorry Lorraine, for everything. I love you so much. Will you marry me?' he asked.

He heard cheering in his ear. They were all bloody listening.

Countdown

Lorraine closed her eyes. She still wasn't sure that she wasn't dreaming or hallucinating. When she opened them again, she realised with a leap of her heart that he was still there. He was really there, and he had just asked her to marry him.

He picked up her hand and held it in both of his as gently as if it were a tiny, injured bird.

'Yes,' she said simply as more tears streamed down her cheeks.

'Don't cry,' he said. 'I'll get you a ring as soon as I can see a finger to put it on.'

39

2.00 am Thursday, July 7th, 2005
Iraq/Jordan border

Tariq and Zayed made it to the border crossing in the early hours of the morning, while Rhett was on his way to the UK in a Superjet. At the border they had no trouble getting through, the guards opened the case and admired the beautifully crafted instrument laying in its nest and congratulated Tariq on his choice of instrument, saying that most young men preferred to learn the guitar and how proud he should be of learning this ancient, traditional form of music.

Zayed drove to a small hotel, they checked in and took their bags up to the room. Once inside, Zayed opened the holdall and removed two American passports in their new names of David Feldman and Daniel Ruben. There were stamps showing that they had travelled from the United States to Israel and then into Jordan three weeks earlier. Tariq looked at his handsome, all-American face in the passport photo with his new name David Feldman and smiled at Zayed. Zayed went out to buy them some food and Tariq opened the case, looked at his beloved oud and plucked the strings. They sounded dull and flat without the hollow base to provide resonance for the notes. He checked the simple catch on the rim of the bowl and the front of the instrument popped open. He pulled the new lid up to reveal another layer of black wood and lifted that out to reveal the simple cannister that resembled a flask held safe and still in a

Countdown

nest of foam within a hard plastic case displaying a few simple knobs.

Zayed returned with simple mutton shawarmas, and they ate, drank water and got some sleep before the next three hundred kilometres to Amman airport. At the airport they found out that a series of bombs had gone off in London and smiled at each other triumphantly.

They checked in early for their flight to New York along with many young musicians from different schools who had been touring the Middle East. The precious oud was placed in the hold with fragile stickers on the case and special requests for gentle handling.

Countdown

40

Thursday, July 7th, 2005
Hereford, UK

Rhett was finally persuaded to get his arm checked out and went with Nurse Helen to get stitches in the deep wound. He sat on the edge of a hospital bed in the main ward with blue curtains on either side of him. Hospital staff wandered past with clipboards and trolleys, and he could see a few beds further down the ward where patients were sitting up reading or lying back dozing with their wan faces on thin pillows. Helen cleaned the wound and injected an anaesthetic into his arm before preparing the suture. He felt light with love and the fading pain, but his mind was still whirring. There was something missing from the whole picture, other things that Farouq and Walid had said.

Helen inserted the needle into his numb arm and began tying the ripped skin together with neat, practised stitches. She chatted away but Rhett was barely listening. A trolley trundled past bearing a young man with thick, black hair, deep in sleep after an operation of some kind with a nurse at the front, holding a drip steady.

Helen was just pulling the needle through his skin for the final stitch. 'There's a brave soldier' she said smiling, 'You'll need…'

She didn't get a chance to finish as Rhett leapt off the bed and ran out of the ward into the corridor, saying, 'Tariq!' He left Helen standing there holding a pair of scissors in the air.

Countdown

'Gordon? Michele? Are any of you there?' he said as he made his way down the busy corridor with people staring at him as if he was a raving lunatic talking to himself with a needle and thread dangling from his arm.

He made his way outside and ran towards the parking lot until he was on his own. There was no response from his team; they'd finally decided to give him some privacy. He dug into his pocket and pulled out his cell phone which was his local phone in Iraq. He tried dialling Michele's number but received a chattering message in Arabic telling him that the number was unobtainable. He looked wildly around, saw an old lady with white, elegantly styled, short hair and a kind, crinkled face walking towards him, and he ran up to her. She backed away holding her handbag in front her as a defence, frightened by the wild looking man racing towards her. Noting her reaction, Rhett stopped and smiled at her holding his palms forwards.

'Sorry, I didn't mean to frighten you. Have you got a phone that I can borrow to make a quick call to – to my wife,' he improvised.

She stood still and looked at him, 'I'm sorry, young man, I don't carry one of those new phone thingummyjigs. I don't think they'll ever catch on, do you? There's a phone box over there, though,' she said.

Rhett followed her pointing finger, thanked her, and raced to the phone box which only accepted coins. Not having any money on him, he called the operator and went through the rigmarole of being put on hold, switched from one call to another as he tried to get put through to Michele at Vauxhall Cross. His mind raced, was he being paranoid? He had made a vague connection between Walid saying that Tariq and his oud had gone missing. Farouq had said that Tariq was the one who was going to kill him, so he presumed he must have been somewhere in the villa.

'Rhett?' came the familiar voice of Michele sounding concerned.

'Get me back on comms,' said Rhett and hung up.

Countdown

He walked away from the phone box and paced up and down waiting.

'I'm here,' said Michele in his ear and he walked back to the phone box and enclosed himself in the soundproof space. He didn't want anyone overhearing his conversation. He picked up the handset and held it to up his ear so that it looked as if he was talking on it to anyone passing.

'Was Tariq found at the villa?' he said to Michele without preamble.

'I'll have to check,' replied Michele. 'We should have the names of everyone killed or taken prisoner. Why?'

'Walid said that Tariq had not been home and that some clothes and his oud were missing.'

'His oud?' asked Michele, confused.

'Farouq said that Tariq was the one who was going to kill me but that he had another mission after that. He said that Washington would hear Arabic music ringing in their ears. The oud is carried in a large case; I think that Tariq got away from the villa and is on his way to the airport. I think he has another bomb – another suitcase bomb and he's on his way to America.'

'He'd never get it past customs,' said Michele, trying to calm him down. 'There are no direct commercial flights from Baghdad to the USA,' she said tapping on her computer keyboard. 'There's a flight from Amman in Jordan to New York later tonight. Could he have got over the border?'

He could hear her talking to someone. 'I'm getting the passenger list for that flight.'

Rhett waited, his neck tingling; always a sign that his gut feeling was right.

'I've got the list,' said Michele. There is no Tariq but hang on, there are a number of group bookings for students.'

There was a long silence and then he heard her whisper, 'Shiiit. There are a number of group bookings from American music schools. They have just finished a tour of playing and meeting with other students of the same discipline in Israel and Jordan; there was a focus on students who have studied Middle Eastern instruments.

Countdown

She paused, 'I've just been told that Tariq was not at the villa where you were held. God, Rhett. I hope you are wrong. Speak later.'

'I'm coming to London,' said Rhett.

'There's nothing you can do here, Rhett,' she said, trying not to reveal that she would love to see him. 'Spend some time with Lorraine,' she added.

'I will,' said Rhett but there is something that I need to do.'

***

MI6 passed on the information to the American CIA and a team of Navy Seals in Jordan moved in without causing a major disruption to stop the loading of cargo on the flight scheduled for the JFK airport in New York and removed the oud case that was labelled as belonging to David Feldman, School of Classical and Ancient Music, New Jersey.

The school did not exist and the student, David Feldman along with a Daniel Ruben had not been on the incoming flight a few weeks earlier, despite their return tickets.

Zayed and Tariq sat near to the large groups of musical students wearing similar outfits of sweatpants and T-shirts and when they started to make their way to the gate, they stayed just behind the last members of one group being led by an old, music teacher with slick hair pulled back into a ponytail.

On board they relaxed into their seats and enjoyed the journey watching the in-flight entertainment, eating the Arabic style dishes served, and sleeping. They were well rested when they stepped off the plane in JFK, and excited. Not long to go now before they could fulfill their destiny and become martyrs to their cause.

At passport control their passports were stamped without question and feeling relieved at how easy it was to get into the country they made their way towards the baggage hall along with hundreds of other passengers. Their hearts were expanding with joy, and they grinned at each other with pride and confidence in the secret that they shared. Tomorrow they would show the leaders of this country and the world.

Countdown

As they wandered into the hall looking for the carousel holding the baggage for their flight, two men in dark suits came up to them and in a low voice one of them spoke, 'Welcome to the US of A. If you could just come with us, boys. We would like to ask you a few questions.'

Tariq looked at Zayed in alarm and then all around. Men, women and children milled around the hall waiting for their baggage or pulling cases off carousels and heading for the exit wrapped up in their own little worlds. There was nowhere to run. A strong hand gripped his arm just above the elbow, the other man moved to the side of Zayed and did the same to him. Slowly, they guided the two young men across the concourse and discreetly passed through a door marked private. Tariq's confidence dissolved, his heart hammered in his chest in fear, and tears of disappointment spiked the back of his eyes. Nobody would hear of Tariq or Zayed again.

Countdown

41

Thursday, July 7th, 2005
Hereford, UK

Rhett ran back up to Lorraine's ward. He found Nurse Helen and apologised for his unusual departure.

'Would you mind?' he asked looking at the needle dangling from the long, neat suture on his arm. She shook her head, tied off the final stitch and cut the thread. Then she wrapped a fresh, light, gauze bandage around his bicep.

'I expect it was important,' she said raising one eyebrow.

'Coffee's getting cold,' said Keith standing up from the bedside chair and smiling at Rhett as he reappeared in Lorraine's room.

Rhett thanked him and swigged down the offered styrofoam cup of lukewarm, bitter coffee, smiling with his eyes at Lorraine over the rim. He dropped the cup in the bin and pulled a chair to the other side of the bed, indicating for Keith to sit back down.

'How's your arm?' asked Lorraine smiling. 'Trying to make sure I didn't get all the attention?'

'Yes, couldn't have that,' he replied laughing. Picking her hand up, he caressed it with feather light strokes of his fingers.

Keith remained standing and said, 'I think you two have got some catching up to do. I'm going to go home to pick up Gillian now I know that my girl is in safe hands.' He bent over and kissed Lorraine on the forehead. 'Rest up, sweetheart and we'll see you a bit later. See you later, Rhett?'

'I'll be here,' said Rhett.

'Thanks, Dad,' said Lorraine, and Keith walked out of the room still looking worn and anxious.

'Did you mean what you said?' asked Lorraine when Keith had gone.

'About making sure you didn't get all the attention?' asked Rhett, and then he leant forward and kissed her full on the mouth with soft and gentle lips.

'Did you mean what you said, when you said, yes?' he asked with his mouth close to her cheek, his breath warm against her skin.

'Yes, I meant yes,' she replied. Closing her eyes and, ignoring the pain, she drew him in with her bandaged arms around his back to kiss him long and hard.

He sat back running his fingers down her arm and onto her stomach; he rested his hand gently on the bump looking at her with a mixture of intense love and guilt.

He began to speak, to explain what a jerk he had been, but she put a bandaged finger on his lips and said, 'We can talk it all through later, I'm so tired.' She looked into his eyes, 'I was so frightened, Rhett.'

He pulled her gently into his arms and said, 'You were amazing.'

Rhett spent the next few days sleeping in a cot that Nurse Helen set up in Lorraine's room; her body was healing well but they wanted to keep her in for observation and enforced rest for the baby's well-being as well as her own mental state. They talked about everything, cried and laughed, played cards, and walked along the corridors pulling her drip on wheels. Keith and Gillian came in every day allowing Rhett to go to his house to wash and change, and friends and fellow teachers came by with flowers and piles of cards made by the children at school wishing her well after her car accident, which was the given story.

She continued to wake from terrifying dreams sweating and calling for Rhett, and he would be there soothing and holding her; but by the time it came for her discharge they had lessened, and she was desperate to get out of the place.

Rhett was focussed on helping Lorraine get better, but his mind was still thinking and planning; for him there were still matters to be resolved. He had called Michele a few times to be updated on everything that was happening. Malcolm and Gordon had headed back up to their homes and work in Cambridge. SIS had notified the company of a watered-down version of events but obviously the bosses needed to know that they had been involved in a kidnapping. Neither of them wanted to go back to Baghdad any time soon. Both of their families had also been given a version of events and Malcolm and Gordon were told what they could and couldn't talk about and provided them with counselling.

Lorraine sat on the edge of the hospital bed in leggings and a loose T-shirt waiting for the doctor to sign her discharge papers while Rhett stood staring out of the window lost in thought and trying to work out how he could tell her that he needed to go to London for a few days. He walked back to the bed and sat down next to her; he took one of her hands gently in his and kissed the fingertips, smiling at her.

'I think I'll go to stay with my parents for a few days,' said Lorraine holding his gaze and smiling.

Rhett looked at her questioningly, and she continued, 'I know you've got something you need to do,' she said. 'Go, get it done and come back to me.'

42

Thursday, July 14th, 2005
Kew, London

Rhett walked into the small, greasy spoon café near Kew Bridge; he had just been to see his boss Jim Brooks at the Aztec Security office near Waterloo who had been sent a full report on the kidnapping and rescue of the client by Marcus. Rhett had filled him in on the rest of the story. On his journey across London, he had been aware of someone who he thought might be following him, but when he emerged from the station, the man walked the other way without looking at him and he decided he was being paranoid. He walked up to the counter and ordered a full English breakfast and a cup of tea from the owner, a large man in his forties with a gut pushing his grubby apron forward over an ill-fitting T-shirt that left a gap revealing a section of hairy back above his baggy jeans.

'Milk, one sugar, no bacon, extra egg, right Rhett?' said the man.

Rhett laughed, 'You remember me, Bill?'

'Never forget a face, never forget a name,' said Bill wiping down the counter with slow, deliberate sweeps of a grey dishcloth. 'Been a while, mind.'

'Good to be back, Bill,' said Rhett before taking a seat in the corner facing the door and taking in the room. Two young, scruffy men sat at a table on the other side of the room pouring ketchup and brown sauce into their bacon sandwiches. An older man with wispy hair and neatly clipped, ridged fingernails

Countdown

hugged a mug of steaming tea and sipped as he gazed with rheumy eyes into space. He looked slightly uncomfortable and out of place wearing a smart, well-pressed, cotton shirt and an expensive looking watch.

A minute later, Michele arrived looking fresh and attractive in tight jeans and a simple vest top; her hair was tied back into a bouncy ponytail. She removed her sunglasses and walked over in her black, ballet flats to join Rhett at the table. She glanced over at the chubby man leering at her from behind the counter in his grubby apron and flashed him a huge smile.

Bill grinned and said, 'Morning, love, what are you having?'

'A coffee – milk, no sugar, and a full English, please,' replied Michele, sitting down.

'Woman after my own heart,' said Rhett and then regretted it as he saw Michele blush and pull her lips into a thin line. In a flash the emotion was gone, and she laughed.

'I am bloody starving,' she said. 'Did a ten miler earlier. Along the river, before you ask, not up and down mountains carrying a ton on my back.'

'I'm starving too,' said Rhett, 'Just walked twenty metres from the train station.'

They laughed and relaxed until Bill plonked two huge plates of hot food down in front of them and they both dug in.

Leaning back in her chair and pushing the clean plate away from her, Michele reached for the mug of coffee and looked up at Rhett.

'Jeez, you were hungry,' he said, wondering where she put it all in her tiny frame. She had set about her food with intense concentration and hadn't spoken a word while she devoured the mound of not too greasy food.

'That was perfect,' she answered, patting her flat stomach. 'How did you know about this place?'

'Found it on one of my runs when I was living in Ealing,' he said. 'Along the river,' he added with a grin.

'Ealing's not on the river!' she said, and then realised that he meant that he ran from Ealing to the river and then along it.

Countdown

Rhett suddenly looked serious and leant forward to speak in a quieter voice, 'What have you got?' he asked.

Michele turned in her chair and leant casually back against the wall so that she had a view of the room. She glanced at the two young men and watched them wipe their hands on their jeans and get up from their table. They took their mugs up to the counter and said cheers to Bill before turning and heading to the door taking a good look at Michele as they walked past.

'Cheers, lads, see you tomorrow,' called Bill as they opened the door and stepped out into the warm sunshine. 'How are you doing there, Tom? Do you wanna a top up?' he asked the old man by the window as he wandered over to wipe down the table vacated by the men.

'No, thank you,' the old man replied in a very posh voice, 'Better go and get my wife's bits and pieces.' He stood up reaching into his pocket and placed a pile of pound coins on the table. 'See you soon, I expect.'

He picked up a panama hat from the chair beside him and placed it on his head, then he wandered over to the door, doffed his hat at Michele and went out into the street.

'Blimey, hope I do see him soon, 'e's left more in tips than the cost of his breakfast,' said Bill walking back to his counter with the money and the empty cup. 'You okay, Rhett? Do you want a top up, the pair of you?'

They both said that they didn't and then Rhett asked, 'Do you know him?'

'Who?' said Bill.

'The posh guy that just left,'

'Never seen him before,' said Bill. 'Think he's a bit of a train spotter; I saw him standing on the railway bridge looking down at the station just before he came over here. Probably staying at a house on the river that he owns and fancied some proper nosh for a change from all the fancy food he normally eats. We get a few in like that.'

'But you called him Tom?'

'Tom, Dick, Harry; he looked like a Tom. I call everyone one of those when I don't want to ask them outright, and then they usually correct me. That's how I get to know their names. He just never corrected me.'

'What did you call Rhett?' asked Michele amused.

'Nah, he's young. I just asked him what his name was. It's the older, posh ones who find it a bit impertinent. Like I said, he didn't correct me. Maybe 'is name is Tom.' He laughed, revealing a neat set of dentures.

When Bill had gone back behind his counter, Michele gave Rhett a questioning look, but he just shook his head. 'Just something about him,' said Rhett feeling a tingling in the back of his neck. 'Shall we go for a walk?' Suddenly, he didn't feel as though the café was a good place to talk.

They walked to the middle of Kew Bridge and leant on the stone wall looking towards Chiswick and watching the green-brown water as it flowed onward to the sea between grey, muddy banks; gracious swans and a few ducks adorned the surface, occasionally ducking and diving for fish. Sunlight glinted on the water from a clear blue sky. Rhett waited until a young couple holding hands had walked past and then nodded at Michele to start talking.

'We've got nothing on Wormsley,' she said. 'He is pure as a new-born babe looking at his files. And that's the problem.'

What do you mean?' asked Rhett.

'He's too good to be true. Successful businessman, probably in line for a knighthood or some honour due to his contribution to British business. He has shares in the biggest weapon manufacturers amongst other interests, but it is all legitimate and above board. He's very close to the Home Secretary, Cedric Travis; they were at Cambridge together.'

Rhett sighed, 'He is definitely linked to these bombs.'

'There is something,' said Michele, and he looked down at her.

'Someone got word to the Home Secretary that the bomb was nuclear. There are records of calls from Wormsley's office just before the time when we got the intel.'

'He panicked when he realised that what he had sold was going to be used on home soil,' said Rhett.

'Exactly,' replied Michele.

'Leyton told me that Paul Davies went to see Travis and asked him straight out why Wormsley's office had called that morning and of course he came back with some bullshit about Wormsley ringing to arrange a game of golf unaware that Travis was in the middle of a national security crisis. Davies said that Travis had answered without batting an eyelid and made a joke about businessmen not having a clue about politics, but he knew that he was lying. He said that Travis will never be a good poker player because he has a tell; his face reveals nothing, but his foot starts tapping. Usually, he can hide it behind a big desk, but Davies had spotted it once before and deliberately arranged to meet at a gentleman's club with open chairs and low tables. Davies was convinced that Travis was not telling the truth and did some looking; he discovered that Wormsley was at a charity dinner with Travis the night before everything had kicked off in Hereford. He thinks that Travis must have told Wormsley about the threats in Hereford and mentioned Farouq's name,' said Michele.

'Wormsley must have freaked out wondering if one of the nuclear suitcases that he had arranged to sell to Farouq was in the country. I bet he never even considered that the bomb could be brought to the UK,' said Rhett. 'But we still don't have any proof.'

'No,' admitted Michele, 'but Leyton is now convinced, and he is livid. Even if we arrest Wormsley, he has too much money and influence to go down for anything.'

'The whole thing stinks,' said Rhett.

'Yes,' said Michele and that is why Leyton wanted me to see you. He wants to set up a Black Op without the Home Secretary's involvement. He has Paul Davies on board. Apparently, Davies has been trying to get something on Wormsley for a long time.'

She turned and faced Rhett, 'Leyton and Davies want to know if you already have a plan. You said that you went to see your boss, Jim earlier.'

'Yes, needed to check in,' said Rhett.

'Good. You have the backing of the intelligence services.'

'Jim is getting a team together, Marcus and Steve are flying in tomorrow,' said Rhett.

'But if anything goes wrong it will be deniable,' said Michele.

Rhett nodded.

43

Sunday, July 17th, 2005
Ealing, London

A few days later, on Sunday evening, a man riding a Honda CG125 with a pizza delivery box strapped to the back turned into a quiet residential street in Ealing and slowed as a white van reversed out in front of him blocking the street. He was just considering driving up onto the pavement to get past when he sensed someone behind him, and he turned to see a man dressed in black motorcycle gear with a mirrored helmet.

Steve straddled the bike directly behind the young man, put one arm around his shoulders and placed a cloth over his nose and mouth with the other hand. The pizza delivery boy panicked and struggled but he was held firm until he began to see fuzzy stars and blacked out.

Rhett and Jim slid open the side door of the van and quickly carried the man from the bike, put him inside the vehicle and tied and gagged him. Marcus replaced the pizza box on the back of the motorbike with an identical one and jumped back into the driving seat of the van. Steve shifted forward on the bike and did exactly what the driver was planning to do and mounted the pavement to get past the van and continued towards Hugh Wormsley's house with the sweeping gravel drive and bay windows. It all happened in a matter of seconds.

Marcus drove the white van slowly out of the street and into the adjacent road with large, detached houses backing onto the residences in Hugh Wormsley's road. He pulled into the drive of one of the houses that they had earlier established to be owned by a Chinese entrepreneur who rarely used it and was out of the country. The corner of its garden met with the corner of Wormsley's.

Marcus, Jim and Rhett silently made their way through the garden and waited at the junction of the high walls. In the garden directly behind Hugh's house they could smell smoke coming from a barbeque and heard chatting and laughing mixed with splashes from a swimming pool. Thick trees blocked the end walls from view.

Steve pulled up outside Wormsley's drive on the motorbike, pushed the visor up on his helmet before retrieving the pizza box and strolled casually up the drive. With his shoulders hunched and his long, lanky hair hanging down under the helmet, he looked like an awkward, young man. Before he reached the door, it was opened by a man in a dark suit, with short, blonde hair wearing a wire in his ear. His jacket flapped slightly in the breeze and Steve caught sight of the holster containing a handgun. Wormsley had stopped using Jim's company after the experience with Rhett and now had his own, armed team providing security.

Steve grinned at the man, 'Pizza for Mr. Wormsley,' he said and made to go past him into the house with the pizza, but the man stopped him.

'Where are you going?' he asked.

'Just taking the pizza into Mr. Wormsley,' said Steve. 'We always take it in to him,' he said, hoping that the man didn't have a clue who came and went with the pizzas.

'Not seen you before,' said the guy.

Steve pretended to be confused and rubbed his nose self-consciously. 'I ain't been for a while,' he said. He held out the box and said, 'I don't care. You take it. It's just that, well you know, the tips he gives are always a bit of a bonus.'

The man laughed and said, 'Yeah, I know. Go on then, in you go.'

Steve walked into the house and down the corridor to meet Wormsley coming out of his office where he took the box from him. Steve shuffled from foot to foot and Wormsley watched him curiously before saying, 'Thank you. You can go.'

Steve looked up at him and said, 'Um, that'll be nine pounds and ninety-nine pence and held out a receipt.'

Wormsley raised his eyebrows looking slightly relieved, took a fifty pound note out of his pocket and gave it to Steve. 'Keep the change,' he said.

Steve took it and said, 'Blimey, cheers. Right, thanks. See you next week, hopefully.' He grinned as if he had won the lottery and sealed the impression that he really was a gormless pizza delivery boy in Wormsley's mind. Wormsley had been a little concerned ever since his friend Rupert had spotted Rhett meeting the woman from MI6 in Kew.

He had spoken to Cedric Travis who had told him that Rhett had been involved with stopping the bomb go off in London, but that otherwise he was no longer involved with the intelligence services; he was going back to Iraq to continue working for Jim. Cedric assured him that Rhett had no idea about his connection to anything and that Rhett had a bit of a thing for the pretty MI6 agent, but Wormsley had arranged for people to follow Rhett and increased his security just to be on the safe side.

Wormsley had long ago stopped receiving messages via pizza boxes, but he still enjoyed eating one every Sunday that he was in Ealing. He still had important business to conduct from the house; the demand for weapons was ever increasing. He took the box into the lounge and placed it on the table to begin his ritual.

Steve heard the music begin and said, 'Tchaikovsky,' in a loud voice. The security man turned and said, 'What?' as Steve jabbed him hard in the temple with his elbow and caught him as he crumpled and helped him fall silently onto the carpet. Steve took the man's gun and edged towards the door leading into the front room security office. A man flicking through a porn magazine sat in front of the screens, his eyes focussed on the large breasts of a reader's wife as Steve cracked the back of his head with the butt of the pistol and the guy slumped forward with his face nuzzling into the pair of 42Gs. He dragged the other guy from the hallway into the office, bound both men together on the floor in the centre of the room and gagged them before ensuring they had a long sleep by holding a cloth of chloroform over their faces. He then began checking the security screens for more men in and around the house and typed in some instructions on the operating keyboard. Michele's voice came into his ear saying that they had got the feed. He glanced at the screen showing the lounge where he could see Wormsley taking a huge bite of pizza with his eyes closed.

At the back of the house, Rhett, Jim and Marcus heard Steve say Tchaikovsky and scaled the wall. They jumped down into Wormsley's garden, pulled on black ski masks and gloves and ran down the edge of the lawn using trees and bushes for cover until they reached the patio doors leading into the kitchen.

Jim tried the handle and silently pushed the door inwards. Michele had already told them that there was a hostile in the room. The man was standing by the counter with his back to the room making a cup of tea; his jacket lay over the back of a chair and his holster was plain to see over his work shirt. The hiss of the kettle masked any sound but the sudden breeze coming in from outside made him turn and he reached for his weapon. Jim was right behind him, and he knocked the man's arm away, grabbed the weapon out of the holster and smashed it into the back of the man's head. He passed the weapon to Rhett, tied the man up, gagged him and laid him on the kitchen floor before applying chloroform. Marcus moved past Jim into the hall with Rhett following and checked that it was clear. Steve appeared at the bottom of the staircase indicating that there was someone below in the basement and two more guys upstairs.

Steve headed down the stairs to the basement with Marcus behind him and Jim covered the hallway as Rhett knocked on the door to the lounge.

44

Sunday, July 17th, 2005
Ealing, London

Rhett had a feeling of déjà vu when he heard the volume of the music reduce and the faintly annoyed voice of Hugh Wormsley call for him to go in. Rhett opened the door and closed it behind him as he stepped into the familiar, elegantly furnished room. Wormsley looked up and a flash of fear and anger crossed his face before he regained his composure and casually took a sip of his wine to wash down the last piece of a pizza slice. His other hand went under the tabletop and pressed a button.

'Margaux 2004,' he said, replacing the glass and dabbing the corner of his mouth with the edge of his napkin. 'Not as impressive as the 2000, but powerful flavours; a slight liquorice undertone, and still an exceptionally fine wine. Please join me,' he said indicating a chair. Rhett pulled out the heavy chair, sat down opposite Hugh and placed the gun taken from the guard on the table in front of him.

'I've been expecting you, of course,' said Wormsley glancing at the gun. 'I had someone follow you that day you went to meet your fancy woman in Kew. My good friend Rupert lives nearby, and I thought you might go to your old haunt, so I got him to wait in that slimy café on Kew Bridge, just on the off chance. I knew you'd soon spot anyone following you off the train so putting him in there before you got there was worth a try. Of course, he couldn't tell me much, but meeting up with the spook

Countdown

made me think that perhaps you might not want to let bygones be bygones.

'I expect you are upset about getting the blame for Ali's, or should I say, Sid's death.' He sighed and took another sip of wine, 'Ali's death wasn't because of you; I found out that he was working for MI5, and he had to go. I couldn't tell Farouq that or it might have got very messy; it was quite handy letting you think that it was your fault. In fact, it all worked out rather better than expected. Of course, you weren't meant to know that Sid was there that night. I called him when I knew you were in the garden having your evening cigarette and underestimated your attention to duty.' He emitted a short laugh, 'I had to tell Farouq something or he was going to blame me for his nephew's death. I was concerned that you knew too much, and when you went off to Iraq you became the perfect fall guy,' he said in a casual matter of fact voice.

A huge lightness spread through Rhett as he finally allowed himself to believe that he was not responsible for Ali's death. He stared at Wormsley feeling nothing but loathing for the unscrupulous, arrogant man.

Wormsley smiled with thin, mean lips, 'Still, I hear you've been quite the hero, well done, you. I must say that I am extremely grateful for your part in saving London. And how is your little girlfriend? She must have been through quite an ordeal. I had nothing to do with any of that, by the way. Most uncivilized behaviour. I couldn't understand why Farouq didn't kill you as soon as I told him that you had murdered Ali, but he was always an excitable character, who did love to play games.'

Rhett sat silently watching him as Tchaikovsky's The Nutcracker suit op 71a played softly in the background.

Wormsley glanced at the gun on the table, cocked his head to one side and observed Rhett with a smug smirk, 'Are you planning on shooting me? I must warn you that my security system is linked directly to the Home Secretary, and I have just alerted him to an intruder; security forces will be on their way. Dear Cedric, he was such an honourable man with such ardent political views when we were at Cambridge. Unfortunately, he got into a little financial trouble and came to me for support. He wants to be the next Prime Minister, you know, and with my help he can get there. A man's ambition is so easy to manipulate; he has helped me to become a very wealthy man. Do you really want to fester in a jail somewhere as an embittered ex-soldier suffering from PTSD who went over the edge, tried to rob a rich businessman and shot him?' Wormsley licked his lips and drank some more wine.

'I'm not going to shoot you,' said Rhett. 'I want you to admit that you sold nuclear weapons to terrorists who tried to use them against citizens of London and Washington and that Cedric Travis knew about the deals with those weapons and other illegal arms sales. I want you to admit that you arranged for the murder of Ali Siddiq, and I want you to apologise to your family and to all the people you have hurt or endangered by your actions.'

'Now why on Earth would I admit to things like that?' Wormsley laughed. He wiped droplets of sweat away from his top lip. 'Are you wearing a wire? Do you think you can record me admitting to something like that? It would never stand up in court, anyway. You must know that I will have the most expensive and respected defence lawyers in the country on my side, who will say, quite truthfully, that I was coerced under duress into making a false confession.'

'I'm not wearing a wire,' said Rhett, 'and none of this is being recorded. I want you to write a letter admitting to all the things I just mentioned and anything else you want to confess to while we are at it.'

Perspiration began to bead on Wormsley's forehead, and he looked surprised as he wiped it away with his serviette. 'Where the hell was his security team?' he thought with a tremor of concern.

Rhett reached into his pocket and took out a small vial made from dark brown glass. 'How are you feeling?' he asked Wormsley.

'I must admit, I have felt better,' said Wormsley putting a hand on his abdomen. His Adam's apple bobbed under the wrinkled skin on his neck as he gulped back the bile rising in his throat.

'In this vial is the antidote for the poisoning you are just starting to experience.'

Hugh looked at him with his eyes widening in shock.

'In your delicious pizza we put a carefully measured amount of venom collected from the Funnel Web spider; one of the deadliest creatures in the world. You will start to feel a tingling in your lips and begin to perspire. This will be followed by nausea, vomiting and stomach cramps. If you don't receive the antiserum, your muscles will start to spasm uncontrollably, your heart rate will increase, your blood pressure will rise, your lungs will fill with fluid and then,' he paused, 'you will die. It is a slow and agonizing death.'

Rhett stood up and went over to the antique writing bureau at the side of the room. He opened a drawer and found sheets of paper with gold embossed letterheads and a stylish Montblanc pen, which he brought to the table just as Hugh bent over clutching his stomach and vomited on his exquisite Persian rug. Wormsley sat back upright, struggling to get his breath. 'Give me the antidote, please. I'll write the damned thing,' he panted. Rhett put the pen and paper down on the table in front of him.

'Better get writing before your muscles start twitching.'

Wormsley retched and wiped at the saliva hanging from the side of his mouth. Runnels of sweat dripped down his face and splattered onto the paper as he snatched up the pen with his other hand and began writing his confession, groaning in pain. He signed it and held out his hand for the vial unable to speak as his heart pumped uncontrollably in his chest and agonizing cramps ravaged his stomach.

'I lied,' said Rhett, picking up the letter and putting the vial back in his pocket.

Hugh frowned and stared up at him, completely bewildered.

Rhett held up the letter, 'This is for your suicide,' he explained.

Hugh let out a long, low moan. His eyes felt sore and strained in his red face and he collapsed onto the floor writhing in all consuming pain from his griping belly. He breathed in deeply as the convulsions abated, *'Where the hell was his back up team? Cedric wouldn't let him down.'* He fumbled in his pocket for his phone and rose to his knees; with shaking fingers, he jabbed at the number nine, waited for the responder's voice at the end of the phone and desperately called for an ambulance before dropping the phone and clutching his stomach once again. He looked up at Rhett who was staring down at him without reacting; he was not a stupid man and he realised immediately that the call was not going to the emergency services, it had been intercepted by Rhett's team. In his arrogance he had written the confessional letter never for a moment believing that it would come out or ever be used against him. The usual cocky smirk slid off his face as he realised what was happening and was replaced by a look of confusion. It was an unfamiliar feeling as was the sense of rising panic. For the first time in his life, he was consumed by terror, his chest felt constricted, and his breathing became shallow and rasping; he knew that nobody was coming to help him and that he faced an excruciating, drawn out death.

He had seen people suffocating on his orders, people who had got in his way or tried to cheat him and he had watched with contempt as they begged for mercy before the plastic bag was pulled over their heads and their eyes began popping out of their sockets, their mouths opening and shutting like a fish on the riverbank as they gasped futilely for air; their life source denied them. Their bodies flapped, the lips turned blue as they died in terror and pain. He was consumed by nausea and his guts went into spasms as he envisioned his own body being found sprawled across the carpet in a pool of his own vomit and excrement, his contorted face displaying the horror of his final moments and he could not bear it.

'I have money, I can give you more money than you have ever dreamed of,' he squawked. Rhett shook his head once in disgust and remained still and silent.

Hugh's cold, calculating mind raced in desperation as he tried to think of something, but he had no cards left to play. He glared at Rhett with pure hatred as he realised that nothing could save him. There was only one way out. Breathing deeply, he pulled himself up to standing on the edge of the table and staggered back into his chair with sweat pouring down his face. He took the napkin and carefully wiped the sick and drool from his mouth and chin. He pulled his sweater down straight and smoothed his hair in a last attempt at dignity before reaching for the gun. Tchaikovsky's Arab Dance played softly in the background.

Rhett walked out of the room. Behind him, he heard the loud report of the weapon and the slap of gore hitting the French windows.

45

Sunday, July 17th, 2005
London

Cedric Travis was at his London home looking through some reports. He rested the papers on his portly stomach and peered down at the words through half-moon reading glasses. He pinched the top of his nose between his thumb and forefinger to maintain his concentration; it had been a difficult ten days. A sharp bleep from his mobile alerted him to a message and he sat forward in sudden alarm; the ringtone had a specific meaning and he leapt up and grabbed the phone off the table. The message told him that Hugh Wormsley's home security had been breached and he immediately called the number Hugh had given to him for such an occasion. The call was intercepted by Michele's team and the voice he spoke to assured him that support was on its way. Feeling uncomfortably apprehensive, he walked over to the sideboard and poured himself a large glass of Hennessy XO.

Countdown

46

Sunday, July 17th, 2005
Ealing, London

At Wormsley's house, Marcus ran across the garden and climbed back over the wall into the garden of the Chinese man's house. There was loud music coming from the neighbours now and the level of chatter and laughter had risen proportionally to the amount of alcohol consumed. He silently sped across the lawn and went around the side of the house to where the van was parked and pulled his balaclava back on before opening the sliding side door of the van. The young man in the back was still unconscious, so Marcus untied him, took off the gag, carried him to the porch of the house and leant the young man up against the door. Marcus then pulled his ski mask off, jumped into the driving seat of the van and drove at a steady speed out of the driveway, back along the street and into the cul-de-sac with Wormsley's house in it.

He parked on the driveway and waited for Rhett and Jim to come out and jump into the back. Steve went back to the motorbike and Marcus followed Steve back round to the Chinese man's house where Steve left the bike on the driveway and got into the passenger seat of the van. The young pizza delivery boy would find the bike there when he woke up feeling dazed, very confused, but happy to be alive.

Countdown

They drove back onto the main road as Rhett called Michele and gave her the all-clear. In a black van parked near the end of Wormsley's street, Michele gave the order to go, and the driver started up and turned into the road followed by a second van. A team, led by Michele, wearing protective clothing, gloves and shoe covers entered Wormsley's house and took away the unconscious bodies of Wormsley's security team. They tidied the house, removed any signs of disturbance, and turned the security system back to normal. Michele put the confessional letter that Rhett left in the hall in an evidence bag. She then went into the lounge and placed a forged suicide note from Wormsley on the table; it was to his wife and family claiming that he had been suffering from depression for a long time and asking them to forgive him. They left Wormsley's body, removed all traces of the pizza and exited the house. Michele called Paul Davies who issued a command for police to go to Hugh Wormsley's home in Ealing following an emergency call from the premises.

The black vans turned out onto the main road and headed in the same direction as Rhett and his team as two incident response vehicles screamed past going in the opposite direction towards Wormsley's house.

47

Sunday, July 17th, 2005
London

Cedric Travis opened his front door and ushered Paul Davies into his living room with a welcoming smile. He shuffled back to his study in his leather slippers and ran a hand through his white, wispy hair as he walked across the room to the bottles of fine whisky and brandy lined up on the sideboard. He had a frown on his face as he tried to consider what link there may be to Wormsley's emergency and Davies' unannounced visit but when he reached the sideboard he turned with a pleasant smile on his ruddy face.

'Can I offer you something, Paul? Brandy, whisky? It is the weekend after all,' he said, pouring himself another brandy. What brings you here on a Sunday evening?'

'Hugh Wormsley was found dead at his Ealing home. He committed suicide,' announced Paul.

Travis felt the blood drain from his face and his insides felt weak and queasy. There was no way that Wormsley would have killed himself and why had he pressed the emergency button? He took a deep breath and turned around. 'Good God, how awful. Wouldn't have thought he was the type.' His face looked calm and impassive, but his mind was whirling.

'Good friend of yours?' asked Davies.

'Well, no, no. I knew him vaguely when I was at Cambridge and we had the occasional game of golf together, as you know.'

He took a swig of brandy and felt the hot fumes hit his gullet without the normal pleasure.

His eyes met Paul's without blinking and he presented a face of genuine concern and caring but he could not stop the twitching in his foot.

'He left a suicide note,' said Paul reaching inside his briefcase and taking out a copy of the note written by Wormsley.

Travis put on his reading glasses and took the note. He read it quickly and sank down into his armchair. 'I didn't know about the suitcase bombs. I swear. Not until he called me to say that there was a possibility on the morning of the seventh.'

'But you did know that he was dealing in illegal arms sales, and you benefitted from enabling them or looking the other way?'

'I never knew the details, but I allowed him a certain freedom,' Travis admitted in a feeble voice as his foot bounced up and down uncontrollably.

Davies took the note from him and returned it to his briefcase. 'I expect your resignation will follow later this week. I'm sure you'll come up with a good reason. I have no doubt that there are more terrorist attacks planned; attacks which you have effectively assisted.' He turned and left the house.

Travis stared straight ahead, his Jenga tower of dreams and ambitions tumbled down around him.

***

Later that week, there were more bomb attacks on the public transport system although fortunately, they did not detonate. Under pressure from the media and the public, Cedric Travis resigned and in an announcement to the press he said that the intelligence agencies had failed to identify the perpetrators and prevent the recent terrorist attacks. His wording implied that it was the intelligence services that had failed, not him and he managed to sound magnanimous in taking responsibility, thus leaving the door open for a future post back in government.

48

Sunday, July 17th, 2005
Pub in London, UK

Michele sat at the small table in the corner of the busy pub garden surrounded by Rhett, Marcus, Steve and Jim.

'What was all that about Funnel Web spider venom?' asked Michele. 'Where the hell did you source that?'

The guys all laughed, and she stared at them looking puzzled.

'The pizza was full of strong laxatives,' said Rhett. 'But if you tell someone they are going to die from a laxative overdose it doesn't usually have the desired effect. I just needed to make Wormsley think that he was going to die a slow and painful death, then the choice was his. We didn't kill him, he killed himself.'

'To a job well executed,' said Jim. 'I enjoyed working with you again, Rhett.'

'Likewise,' replied Rhett, and he raised his glass in acknowledgement to all of them.

'Now, I hate to say this, but you lot still have a contract to finish back in Baghdad,' said Jim.

The guys all nodded. Marcus and Steve were flying back the following day, but Jim had agreed to let Rhett stay for a few days sick leave, ostensibly while his arm healed, but really, so that he could spend some time with Lorraine.

Marcus raised his glass and said, 'I believe congratulations are in order for your impending doom,' he said looking at Rhett.

'I would offer to be your best man but, as you know, long speeches are not my thing.'

'Wow! I think that may have been the most I have ever heard you say in one go,' said Steve.

'To Rhett, Lorraine and the sprog,' finished Marcus and they all said cheers and downed their pints.

Michele stood up and offered to get another round in and Rhett said that he'd help her to carry the drinks. There weren't too many people jostling to get served; Michele got the order in, and they both leaned on the bar waiting for the barwoman to pour them, neither of them speaking.

Rhett caught her eye in the mirror behind the optics and smiled. She smiled back and turned to face him.

'Good luck,' she said.

'Thank you,' said Rhett. 'It was good working with you.'

'It was almost lovely,' she said, looking at him with a little regret in her eyes. Then she grinned and said, 'But after all, tomorrow is another day.'

Rhett shook his head and laughed.

Countdown

49

Early evening, July 20th, 2005
Symond's Yat, Herefordshire, UK

Rhett took Lorraine up to Symond's Yat Rock and they walked hand in hand away from the popular tourist paths to a secluded spot with stunning views across the Wye Valley. A slight breeze whipped at Lorraine's long, auburn hair and she brushed it away from her eyes; a red line streaked across the edge of her forehead but otherwise the scratches on her face had healed well.

Rhett told her that the mark on her forehead was fashionable; she could tell people she was related to Harry Potter. She had replied that now they had something in common and could spend long winter nights comparing scars.

He suddenly stopped and bending down on one knee on the grassy hilltop, he asked her once again if she would marry him. He looked up into her dark, sapphire blue eyes with a feeling of deep certainty. She laughed and said, 'Yes,' and he slipped a simple solitaire diamond engagement ring onto her finger and kissed the back of her scarred hand.

A sudden gust of wind whispered through the grass and the trees around them swayed as if they were waving and nodding. Rhett stood up and cupped her face in his hands as he leant in to kiss her; his neck tingled and for a brief moment in time at least, everything felt right. They pulled apart and smiled, exchanging a

Countdown

look of love and understanding, then Rhett put his arm around her and pulled her in close until her head was resting against his chest. For now, Rhett ignored the rage simmering below the surface that he felt for the people that had put Lorraine and his unborn child in danger, the hidden faces behind the devastating attacks in London who he silently vowed to uncover and destroy. They stood in silence gazing across the picturesque landscape. The river Wye lazily looped around the rolling hills and the green and peaceful land spread out below the cerulean sky and scudding white clouds. In front of them a peregrine falcon soared and hovered on the air watching with its immaculate eyesight for unsuspecting prey.

The falcon suddenly pulled its wings back and dived. Falling like a stone at incredible speed, like a streak of lightning it hit the pigeon before it had a chance to feint. The razor-sharp talons ripped through the body of its victim and the falcon brought the vanquished bird down to the ground below in a magnificent display of precision, strength, and power.

'They mate for life,' said Lorraine.

'Let's hope it's a long one,' said Rhett with his strong arms wrapped protectively around her.

ACKNOWLEDGEMENTS

With great thanks to Suzanne Daniels, Penny Markham, Nicola Pawley and Craig Nixon for their proof-reading skills, feedback, encouragement and support. With love.

Also great thanks to Billy Allinson for the great cover design and artwork.

Thank you to all who work tirelessly to counter terror in all its forms and in memory of those who have died or suffered as a result of terrible atrocities.

GLOSSARY OF ACRONYMS

AC 130	Lockheed Gunship
AK47	Automatic Kalashnikov rifle
AKM	Assault rifle
CEO	Chief Executive Officer
CIA	Central Intelligence Agency
FRV	Final Rendezvous
IED	Improvised Explosive Device
GMC	General Motor Company
GREEN ZONE	Safe area in Baghdad
MA	Master of Arts
MP5	Machine Pistol (Heckler & Koch)
PTSD	Post-traumatic Stress Disorder
QC	Queen's Counsel
RED ZONE	Unsafe areas in Baghdad and Iraq
RUC	Royal Ulster Constabulary
SAS	Special Air Service
SBS	Special Boat Service
SCO19	Specialist Firearms Command
SIS	Secret Intelligence Service
TNT	Trinitrotoluene explosive
USB	Universal serial bus/memory stick
VBIED	Vehicle Borne Improvised Explosive Device

Countdown

COMING SOON! October 2022

PARAS IN ACTION

Celebrating 80 years of the Parachute Regiment through the eyes of those that served

Jason Woods

OTHER TITLES

Jason Woods

Long Road to Libya

Sian M. Williams

Disconcerting Short Stories

Calling Time

Eyes of the Soul

Quicksand

Riddles of the Rainbow

Into the Blue

Printed in Great Britain
by Amazon